I0593597

TRANSYLVANIAN
KNIGHT

Like time-travel?

Check out the Turning Points series
at jodielane.com

The Siege of Masada
Transylvanian Knight
To Kill An Emperor
Renaissance Woman
Heart and Stomach of a Queen

Turning Points Short Stories:

Siege of the Heart
The Time-Traveller's Date
A Soldier's Love
A Soldier's Honour

TRANSYLVANIAN KNIGHT

JODIE LANE

Transylvanian Knight. 2nd Edition
Copyright © 2023 Jodie Lane

Special Note on the Map, which has been modified from its original but the basis for which was reprinted with permission of the University of Washington Press: Sugar, Peter F. Southeastern Europe under Ottoman Rule, 1354-1804. pp. 114, 143. © 1977.

All rights reserved. No part of this publication may be reproduced, stored in a retrieval system, or transmitted in any form or by any means electronic, mechanical, photocopying, recording, or otherwise, without prior written permission of the author.

The characters and events portrayed in this book are fictitious or are used fictitiously. Any similarity to real persons, living or dead, is purely coincidental and unintentional.

ISBN: 978-0-6487683-2-6

First published 2016 by Jodie Lane
www.jodielane.com

To Dee,
You made this book happen.

ACKNOWLEDGMENTS

Thanks go to my family and friends who demanded a sequel and extolled Masada to others. It is extremely hard work being a self-published author, so the encouragement I receive is invaluable.

To my beta readers: Carolyn, Shannon, Kate, Zane, Rebecca, Alicia, Jess, Pat—your feedback was varied and extremely encouraging, and helped make this a better story! My proof-readers: Mum, Barb and Tracey—you put the polish on the punctuation and the good looks on the grammar.

To my writing mentor, Dee, who has taught me so much, not just in cutting out adverbs and adding in prepositions but also in formatting, cover design (she did the cover for this and all my web banners) and a plethora of other writer-related skills. Not to mention her enthusiasm for my stories and hilarious but often brutal commentary as she edited. Thank you, Dee. Happy Jodie is happy.

A Map of the Three Voivodes

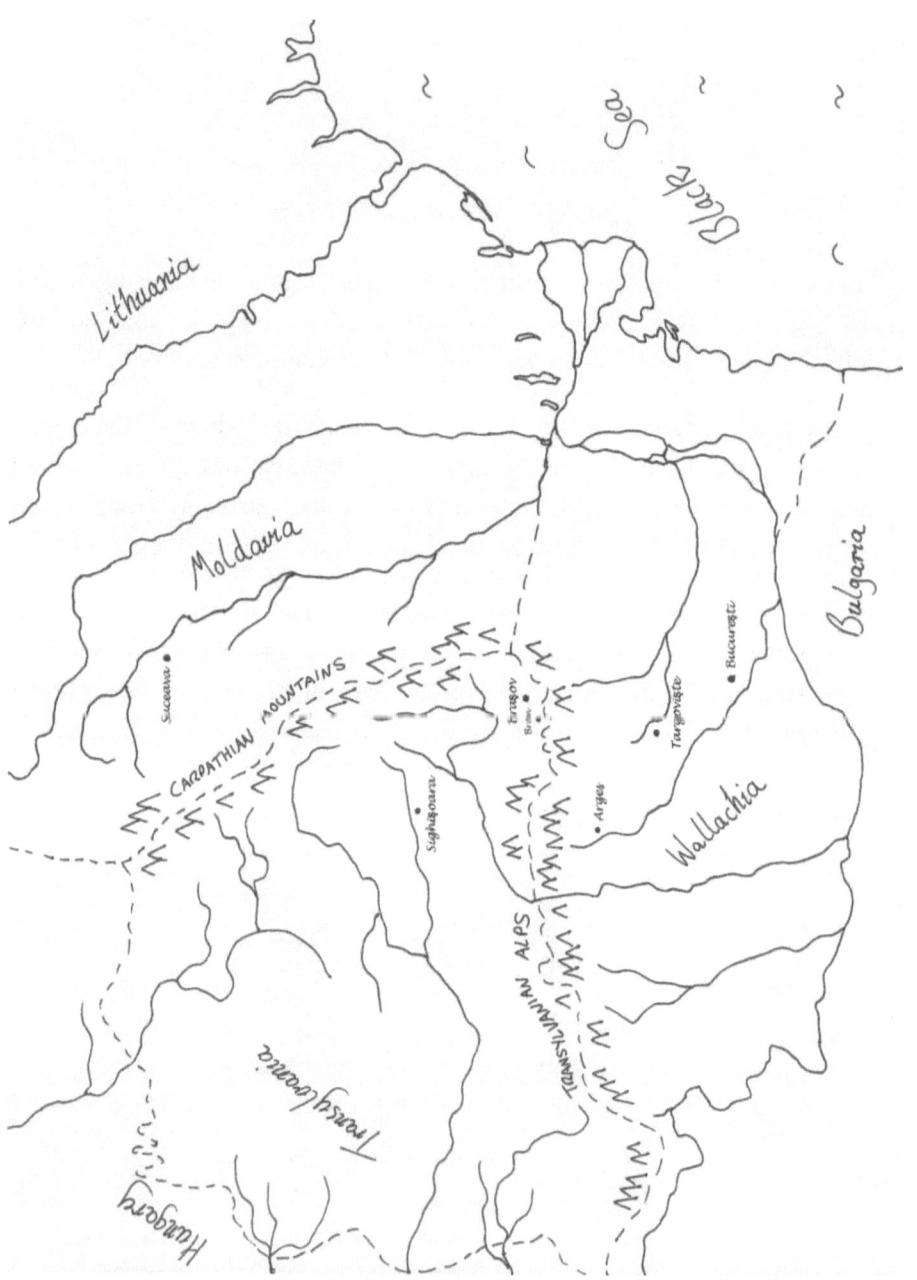

ONE

Sticky pools of blood oozed against her rough sandals. Nausea welled up in Gwyn but she was paralysed with shock, unable to turn, flee, or even shut her eyes against the scene in front of her. She retched as the smell hit her nostrils, and breathing through her mouth only tainted her tongue with a thick, coppery taste.

It was the faces that affected her the most. Bodies were everywhere, limbs askew, smeared with gore. She might have been able to pretend they weren't real, if it weren't for the faces. Despite the blood stains and bruises she could recognise the foremost ones in the pile of corpses.

Sarah. Adi. Silva. Gaius.

Gaius... Please, no!

Empty-eyed, ashen skin and slack jawed. There was no doubt they were dead, even if she couldn't see the swords, arrows and spears that pierced their flesh. Flies buzzed into open mouths, maggots crawled in congealing wounds. The bodies of other men and women from Masada slumped further back, children too, as well as soldiers from the Tenth Frentensis. Some she recognised—Eleazar, Elizabeth, Gad, the old Rabbi—but plenty she didn't. Their numbers staggered her, filling the throne room, crammed against the walls.

This is a dream, just a dream. But she'd thought it was a dream once before, when she'd gone back in time, and it had all been real...

Someone was missing. One sinister, ominous face lacked a presence in the hall of death. Gwyn had to run or he would find her, only, to her horror, the blood that had merely crept along the floor had risen to her knees and was as thick as mud. Arms pin wheeling, she fought to maintain her balance. Eyes sought the entrance to the throne room—it

1

was clear! Wading fiercely, the room seemed to tilt against her and each step made a nasty sucking sound. *Almost there...*

She strained a little too hard and lost her balance. Gwyn shrieked in panic and threw out her hands as she fell. Pushing back up to her knees she saw her arms were dripping to the elbows. Choking with terror and disgust and with tears pouring down her face, she reached the doorway. As she touched the stone frame, the blood vanished. A shadow fell on her.

"You can't escape your fate," Joshua rasped. The man who'd frightened her so much at Masada loomed over her. There was something *wrong* with his head. She gulped back vomit—half his skull was smashed in, leaving a lopsided horror that glared. His hands gripped her face and squeezed. She twisted and clawed frantically at his filthy skin, but as the pressure mounted she began to black out. The last things she heard were her own screams and his hateful voice.

"You can't escape me..."

* * *

PRESENT DAY
"Gwyn! Gwyn! *Gwyn!*"

She gasped awake and lurched up in her bed, almost braining her sister Naomi. Cold sweat clung to the back of her neck and shoulders, the clamminess driving her to pull at her t-shirt. Naomi grasped her by the upper arm.

"You had a nightmare, sis. You were yelling in your sleep."

Wide-eyed, Gwyn stared uncomprehendingly, then she let out a massive, tense breath. She looked hopelessly at her sister and their brother Justin, who was sitting up in the top bunk across the hostel room. She couldn't read his face in the dim light, but she'd wager the thirteen year old was quite alarmed.

"S-sorry guys." *It was a nightmare. A dream. Not real. Calm down.* "Thanks for waking me." She reached for her phone. It was five a.m. Dim light crept into the sky outside the window, but they didn't have to get up for breakfast for another two hours. She lay back onto the bed then sat up, turned her sweat-soaked pillow over, and tried again.

"Must have been a bad one," Naomi said, still standing at her bedside. "What was it about? Who's Guy?"

Gwyn forced a smile onto her face. "Guy? I've no idea." *I must have been yelling for Gaius.* "I can't even remember it now—don't you hate how dreams do that? Go back to sleep. I'm sorry I woke you both."

Naomi stood there a moment longer, then retreated to her bunk. Gwyn closed her eyes and feigned sleep but she could hear the twins.

"That's the third night in a row," Justin hissed. "She's getting louder."

"I know—that's why I woke her. Wish she'd tell us what the dream was. It'd probably help."

"I don't know if I want to know—sounded like she was being tortured. Did she do this before we came away?"

"No, only since we left Israel."

They both went quiet and Gwyn was left alone in her thoughts.

Great. Three nights? I don't remember waking up before tonight. I should have known it was just a dream though. She shuddered and rolled onto her side, hugging her arms around her chest, tucking her knees up. Despite it's the knowledge it wasn't real, the nightmare still coursed through her. She couldn't rid herself of the devastation she felt upon seeing her friends in the pile of the dead, and the paralysing terror thinking Joshua had come to seek his revenge for the part she had played in his death.

I can't forget about it. The pocket watch lodged in her left palm reminded her that she had experienced weeks of harrowing and difficult experiences, while mere minutes had passed for her family. She sighed and clenched her eyes shut, willing sleep upon herself. Whether it was fear of the nightmare returning or an overactive brain churning the thoughts through her head, sleep did not come.

* * *

Hours later, she tagged along behind her parents as they toured the Palace of Parliament in central Bucharest.

"Ceauşescu, like many infamous dictators, was not the tallest man." Their English speaking guide paused at the bottom of a grand staircase. "However, he was obsessed with his public image and ordered this staircase to be rebuilt three times so that each step was neither too tall nor too shallow. That way, when he used it, his height was not accentuated."

"Just like Tom Cruise standing on a box in Top Gun," Gwyn overheard her dad whisper to her mum, who giggled.

"Was this where he was shot?" Justin asked.

The guide shook her head with a smile.

"No. Nicolai and Elena fled Bucharest to Târgovişte, where they were captured, trialled and executed by firing squad. Târgovişte is also famous for being the capital of Vlad Dracula, or as you might know in English, Vlad the Impaler. You can visit the ruins of his castle there."

"Are we going there, Dad?" Justin asked excitedly.

"No." Their father ruffled his son's hair, who shied away with annoyance. "We head north for Transylvania after this."

Justin's disappointment was so obvious the guide took pity on him. "You can probably find a guide at Ghencea Cemetery to show you Ceaucescu's grave—although he was exhumed last year and moved. Or if it's Dracula you are interested in, Bran Castle near Braşov is a popular tourist attraction for Dracula fans, even though Vlad's real castle was nowhere near there." The tour group trailed after her.

Naomi dropped back to walk beside Gwyn. She frowned but didn't say anything at first, her blonde bob swaying gently with her stride. Then, in a voice that belied her thirteen years with its seriousness, she asked, "Is everything alright, sis? You've been a bit funny since Israel."

Gwyn glanced at her, sighed, and said, "I'm fine, thanks—just all this travelling tiring me out, I guess."

It was plain to see Naomi wasn't convinced. "You've been so excited about coming away for months. It was all you talked about before we left. You even talked about, you know," her voice dropped, "asking Mum and Dad about staying on when we go home."

Gwyn felt a twinge of annoyance that she'd confided in her sister about that. "You better not have blabbed,' she warned.

"Of course I haven't!" Naomi's tone was indignant. Several people in the group turned to look. Gwyn frowned and made shushing motions with her hand. Fortunately their parents were up the front, quizzing the tour guide about the logistics of the building.

Facts, facts, facts, Gwyn thought gloomily. *Always about the facts with them.* She preferred the stories about the people who had built this monstrosity—forced labour, hidden bunkers, dramatic tales from the Communist Regime.

"So?" Her sister was still buzzing like an annoying fly. "What's wrong? You can tell me." Her insistent tone was both an irritation and a temptation. *I just need to talk to someone about all this. Who knows how long it'll be before Michelle comes back for me? If she ever does.* Michelle had said several weeks. Originally Gwyn had been glad of the break, but that was before the nightmares, the daytime jitters and her lack of appetite. And it had only been three days! If she didn't get a grip she'd lose her mind. The inability to vent about what she'd been through was eating her from the inside.

Oh, God damn it. "I'll tell you later, I promise,' she muttered. Maybe her sister would think she was nuts, but if she didn't say something Naomi might tell their parents about Gwyn wanting to stay on in Europe. She had that look on her face. They didn't often argue, but the younger teenager wasn't averse to fighting dirty to get her way.

Naomi started to protest, clearly unsatisfied but Gwyn simply nudged her way politely through to the front of the tour group to join their parents, and they continued on through the Palace of Parliament.

TWO

Gwyn stared out of the window as the train drew slowly out of Gara du Nord. Bucharest was not a pretty city. Too many decades of Communist rule had left dull grey blocks of housing throughout most of the city save where the political elite had lived and worked. The ornate architecture of the city centre and tree-lined avenues in suburbs such as Primaverii were left behind as the train rattled north out of the capital through grimy industrial estates and semi-slum areas.

The Turners were heading north to Brașov, gateway to the Carpathians. The six a.m. departure time was no hardship to Gwyn, who had been woken by her alarm before her nightmare reached its horrific conclusion. Leaving the hostel also made her happy—she missed the luxurious Crowne Plaza hotel, though she struggled to sleep on a soft bed after so many weeks on the ground or a rough pallet. Now that they travelled on their own budget, not their company's, Stephen and Danielle were frugal in their accommodation choices for the family. But Gwyn still knew she was experiencing far greater comfort than anyone had at Masada, so a weird sense of guilt left her surly.

"Just got my period," she lied to her mother when quizzed about her dark mood. *That's another thing I never asked about—why did I never get my period? Why haven't I still got it now I'm back in my time. Stupid time device.* It annoyed her that the pocket watch actively deterred her curiosity about the Time Space Agent, conveniently forgetting that this feature had saved Gwyn multiple times in Ancient Judea. She was jotting down a list of questions to put to Michelle the next time she saw her, determined not to be put off by the device again.

"Gwyn, can you come with me to the toilet?" Naomi asked, rousing Gwyn from her self-absorbed sulk. The five of them took up the entire train compartment, with backpacks and their parents' suitcases balanced precariously above on the luggage racks, and day packs stashed on the sixth seat. Any other traveller looking for a seat took once glance at the crowded compartment and moved on. Fortunately the train was not particularly busy—Gwyn had already considered retreating to another compartment, but her sister had pre-empted her.

Her mother glanced up and nodded, "Yes please, Gwyn. I'd prefer it that no one wanders off alone, even on the train."

Sighing, Gwyn shoved her half-drawn earphones away and pulled at the compartment door. It stuck, old brown fittings jamming in the runners. She pulled harder, jerking it open, muttering under her breath. *Piece of shite.* The train was old; worn carpet and faded paint flaking off the walls, and a faint musty smell that permeated both corridor and compartment did nothing to improve her mood. Naomi rolled her eyes as she stepped over her father's legs and led the way down to the back end of the carriage. The hydraulics of the doors hissed and clunked as the sisters crossed the coupling into the carriage with the ladies toilet. They were perturbed to see the external door on the side of the train was open—some mechanism appeared to have failed, though the click-hiss made it sound like it was trying to close.

"Go on." Gwyn ushered her sister into the loo and stood guard outside. *I suppose I'll get in trouble if I scoot off.* The landscape rushed by; Bucharest's outer suburbs gave way to countryside and the first hints of autumn colouring in the leaves.

Lost in her thoughts, Gwyn leant against the rattling corridor wall while she waited for Naomi. The train's brakes whined as it entered a curve then a violent lurch shook the whole carriage. Before she had time to react, Gwyn was launched out of the open door!

Her arm shot out and fingers wrapped around the edge of the door frame, anchoring her just enough to turn her straight fall into an arc. Her body slammed onto the outside of the train with one foot hooked inside the carriage. She struggled to drag herself back in, but the continued rattling along the tracks and the tilt of the carriage around the curve meant that it was all she could do to hold on as the wind buffeted her violently, screaming death in her ears.

She couldn't hold on for much longer. Fingertips burned from holding her weight. Each little bump from the train edged her further out the carriage door. *Help!* She felt the panic rise like bile in her throat, and with a last desperate attempt she used a microsecond of weightlessness that came from the train's motion and hoicked herself back—

Just as a hand grabbed her forearm and jerked her inwards. Tumbling onto Naomi in a heap, her sister grabbed her in a hug and they rolled against the toilet door. Gasping and shuddering, it was all Gwyn could do to catch her breath in the sudden quiet. The funky odour and hard metal door of the bathroom was a welcome assault after the whistling, fresh air that a moment ago had spelt her fate as a gory smear on the train tracks of Romania.

"Are you okay?" Naomi stared, panting and wide-eyed.

Gwyn managed to nod, then shook her head and trembled as the realisation of what had just happened hit her.

"Come on," her sister urged her into a crawl and they moved down the corridor, pulling themselves into an empty compartment. The insulated walls deadened the sound from outside, especially once Naomi hauled the door shut.

Gwyn dragged herself onto the seat, head in her hands, elbows on her knees. *It's okay, you're alright. You're alive.* Her breathing calmed as her little sister put an arm around her shoulders and spoke Gwyn's thoughts out loud.

"You're okay, it's alright. Sheesh, that was close. What happened? I'd just finished washing my hands when the train lurched and I looked out and all I could see was your foot and I thought you'd died and I was so scared!" Her words tumbled out.

"You were scared?' Gwyn almost laughed. "I was fu—, freaking terrified!"

"Freaking?"

This time she did laugh. 'Fucking terrified." Naomi joined her with nervous laughter, until both girls were in hysterics, shaken and relieved at the close call.

Finally they calmed down. "Mum and Dad will wonder where we

are," Gwyn said, making to rise.

"No they won't, you weren't listening when we left; they were discussing pollution in the Danube. Justin was playing games on his phone. None of them will notice if we're gone for a while.'

Gwyn had to concede the point, taking another relieved breath. Her sister fixed her with a pointed look.

"Now, will you tell me what's the deal with you? You've been super weird since Israel."

Guess I can't wiggle out of it. She'll think I'm nuts, but it'll be worth it to get it off my chest.

"When did you get so grown up?" she smiled lopsidedly at her younger sister. Taking a deep breath, Gwyn looked up and froze.

Michelle was standing outside the compartment door.

THREE

PRESENT DAY

"What is it?" Naomi turned to look but Michelle had moved on. Gwyn opened and closed her mouth, then said, "I have to go to the toilet. Can you wait in here?"

Dismay fluttered across the younger girl's face. "Can't you wait?"

"I *really* have to go. I'm lucky I didn't wet myself when I was almost thrown out the train!" She grasped the door handle, ordering her sister, "Stay here. Don't let anyone else in."

"I don't think so," Naomi retorted. "I'll stand in the corridor, just not near that door."

"Fine." *Probably better. Mum and Dad would kill me if anything happened to her. At least in the corridor I can hear her.*

She stationed Naomi a little way along before heading for the door of the toilet, which faced the front of the train. Michelle stood in the little space, unseen from the corridor; apparently unconcerned by the faulty outer door that still hissed and jammed as the wind rushed past and the landscape blurred. She raised her eyebrows and nodded to the toilet. Glaring, Gwyn kept a careful hand on the rail until they were safely inside and the door was closed and locked. She wrinkled her nose at the stagnant air. The fixtures in here were as old and crappy as the rest of the train: cracked mirror, graffiti on the walls, loose fittings on the taps in the tiny sink. She tried to keep her balance without touching anything and failed, scowling as Michelle put out a hand to steady her.

"You are not an easy woman to find," were Michelle's first words. "I didn't expect you to move countries so soon. Owen had a hell of a time tracking you."

"We're on holidays," Gwyn snapped. "Mum and Dad have finished their work in Israel. Besides, I thought you were going to give me a few weeks?" Despite her relief at seeing Michelle, her edginess from the past few days bubbled up like an angry fountain.

Sure, she's proof that I'm not mad, but none of this would have happened if it weren't for her. Michelle casualness rankled. *She could have asked how I am.*

Those dark eyebrows merely raised again, unfazed by Gwyn's tone. Then Michelle sighed and said, "I know. There are things out of my control, and I—we—need your help."

Perhaps it was Gwyn's level of annoyance but it seemed like Michelle's chronokinetor wasn't doing its usual trick of deterring Gwyn's curiosity. She shot back, "Again? You future people seem to have a lot of problems. And that doesn't even make sense—you could have left it a day in your time and come back three weeks from now in mine. You can time travel, remember?"

Her sarcasm wasn't lost on the Agent, whose brows snapped together and nostrils flared. "It's too much to explain to a novice. I don't actually have a lot of time." She seemed unhappy about being there.

"Make some time," Gwyn said flatly. They glared at each other.

Michelle clenched her fists, released them and breathed out through her nose in a huff. "Alright, but quickly." She proceeded to reel out a mass of political information that went straight over Gwyn's head—investigations, groups against time travel, debates about the ethical use of technology, tension between different species of the Allied Planets. What she did grasp was that Michelle wasn't meant to be here and she was being monitored for aging, so every minute she spent here in the past was one she had to skip back home.

"I can't carry out any missions." Michelle finished.

Gwyn shrugged, hiding her confusion. "So wait until it's all over then do your missions. Shouldn't make a difference still because you can jump to whenever you need to. Why are your missions so important anyway?" She had spent a lot of time wondering this the past few days.

Michelle frowned, and Gwyn could see she was thinking hard, perhaps trying to find the best way to explain it to her in terms Gwyn could actually understand. She felt stupid next to this sophisticated future woman, and resented it.

Michelle finally tried, "There is a force at work. At least we think it's a force. A kind of energy wave in Time-Space Reality. It is affecting timelines, which is why we have an Agency to find historical turning points. We send Agents on missions to make sure certain timelines aren't disrupted. More than that is classified, though I don't suppose you're about to blab to Alliance media.

"A—I suppose you'd call it a culmination—no, that's not the right word." Michelle screwed up her face. "A gathering of this energy is due to happen in our not-too-distant future. Like the crest of a wave. Though this is purely an analogy—I'm just trying to help you understand. The Shanista are calling it The Shift. Once that takes place we won't be able to time travel. The wormholes we use will be closed. They are already starting to close in my time. If I wait till this political bullshit dies down it'll be too late."

Gwyn was intrigued despite her annoyance. "Why is it classified? If it's such a big deal surely you should tell people. They can't object then."

Michelle huffed. "It's not that simple. The group who objects to time travel would call us alarmist and bog down the Agency with even more litigation. It's like—like people in this time who deny climate change exists. It's selfish and short-sighted, but they refuse to see the evidence in front of their faces. They waste time and derail debate with spurious facts. We don't have time for that. The Agency has managed to operate with a low-profile and the backing of the Shanista, but they are not dictators. This publicity is not just bad, it's dangerous for the future of all our worlds. Every aspect of the Agency is now under scrutiny and must be debated in a public forum."

"Oh." *She does look frustrated. I suppose she is used to action not talk.* "Right. I think I get the gist. So what do you need me to do? You need this back so you can jump more quickly? Have you worked out how to get it out?" She waved the pocket watch embedded into her palm. It was more advanced than Michelle's.

"You haven't been listening!" Michelle snapped. Gwyn flinched and bumped against the wall, recoiling when a wad of stuck toilet paper loosened and brushed against her shoulder. She fell forwards and Michelle grabbed her arms, gripping too tightly at first, then relaxing her hold.

"Gwyn! Are you still in there?" Naomi pounded on the toilet door. Michelle whirled.

"It's my little sister," Gwyn hissed. "Calm down!" Louder she called, "Almost done. You better not be anywhere near that open door!"

"Yeah, yeah, I'm moving back. Just wanted to check on you—you've been ages!

"I won't be long!" Glaring at Michelle, she whispered. "You said you're in a hurry?"

Michelle's lips retained a tightness that told Gwyn she wasn't happy about this situation. The woman fished out a tiny crystal from a pocket on her shirt. "Hold out your hand."

"No way." Gwyn clenched her hands into fists. "What is it?"

"It's a data crystal. It's got a pre-programmed destination set in it. It's what we used to make big time-jumps so you don't have to do all the work mentally. I—we—the Agency needs you to carry out a mission. I can't do it—it would take too long. Every official timepiece is under lock and key. The Shanista won't let me go rogue with the one I have." She hesitated as though she was considering going rogue anyway, but said instead, "We wouldn't ask unless it was important."

Gwyn's eyes boggled at her. "Are you nuts? I barely survived Masada! I have no idea how to carry out missions!"

It was obvious by Michelle's grimace that she agreed. "We are desperate," she said quietly. "I've given you the barest outline of the situation in my time. I can't emphasise how important this work is. Not just for my world but yours too. If these timelines get off track your present will be affected."

Your present... The gravity of the situation sank in. As much as she didn't trust Michelle, Gwyn believed her. While the woman could be ruthless and arrogant, right now she sounded deadly serious.

Her brown eyes met Michelle's dark grey ones. "What do you need me to do? I can't go back to Israel. I'm travelling with my parents."

Michelle waved her hand dismissively. "It's here, in this country. Just not now. We found a turning point geographically accessible for you. We need you to go back to 1459 AD and convince Prince Vlad Dracula to resist the Ottoman invasion of Wallachia. Our calculations show a chance that he might waiver when the envoy comes to him—he needs to refuse their terms and continue to war against them, no matter the cost."

Gwyn was shocked. "I thought you people were more, well, peaceful in the future?"

Michelle rolled her eyes. "Look, I promise I'll explain it all better in time. It's not about war versus peace in the past—these events have already happened. We need to make sure it keeps having happened."

That makes my head hurt. "Okay, okay, but how do you expect me to just waltz up to Vlad the Impaler and say, 'Hey Vlad, don't chicken out when it comes to fighting those Turks. It's important.' He fails in the end anyway, doesn't he?"

"Yes, but he ties up the Ottomans for a critical amount of time, weakening their Empire. And I suggest you gain the confidence of someone close to him, rather than approach Vlad himself. He's not the nicest character, as your use of the cognomen suggests you know. Even that," she indicated Gwyn's chronokinetor, "won't protect you if you don't stay under the scanner. Be credible, be subtle, work through someone. Once that meeting has taken place, get out of there. Don't jump around when you are there—you don't have the skill for that and you might burn out. This," she held up the tiny crystal, "will drop you four weeks before the turning point. Should be plenty of time."

"Four weeks!"

"You were gone twice as long last time; Arenns did some tests on your blood for aging. The same tests they will do to me so I've got to get moving."

This is crazy.

"What's in it for me?" she blurted out, embarrassing herself with her selfishness. *Isn't saving the world enough motivation for you?* But she was afraid Michelle was manipulating her, using the mind-control aspect that Brrrys had told her about. *I'm not going to be a complete pushover...*

"Well?" she prompted when Michelle didn't answer. "What happens afterwards? Will I be able to use this thing to go to a time of my choice?" She held up her hand.

"It's not a toy," Michelle said quietly. "Nor do we use it for personal gain. But yes, I imagine some arrangement could be made if you want to visit your boyfriend. Though I wouldn't recommend it. A relationship across time is... impractical to say the least."

Gwyn blushed furiously but held her ground. "But I can?"

Long seconds passed. "You can," Michelle agreed. "Now you undertake this mission? Can you repeat back to me your goal?"

"Go to 1469—"

"1459."

"1459, go to then and convince Vlad the Impaler—"

"You do know that name was given by his enemies? I suggest calling him by his proper title if you don't want to cause disrespect."

"Fine, Vlad Dracula—"

"Prince."

Gwyn glared at her. "Go to 1459, convince *Prince* Vlad Dracula—*or someone close to him, preferably*," she added hastily before Michelle could interrupt again, "to reject the terms offered by the Ottoman envoy and wage war against the empire. I'll arrive four weeks before the meeting. Once he has refused the envoy I can skedaddle."

"You can *what*?"

"Skedaddle. Get out of there. That's it? The rest is up to me and the pocket watch?" She waved her hand again.

"It's called a chronokinetor. A time mover."

"That's too hard to pronounce," Gwyn muttered.

Michelle considered Gwyn for a moment, then held out the crystal, her expression inscrutable.

"Call it what you will. Either way, if you succeed at your mission, that timeline will be stable and we'll go from there."

"And... if I don't?" That possibility was suddenly all too clear in her mind.

Michelle smiled without humour. She took Gwyn's left hand and pressed the crystal into the timepiece there—it absorbed and vanished like a drop of water into a pond. "Then this time," she gestured around, "may not be the same."

That chilled Gwyn. *No pressure*, she whispered to herself.

Michelle nodded as if she'd read Gwyn's mind. "I told you we are desperate. Now one final thing. The meeting will take place at Târgoviște in Wallachia, but Vlad will be passing through Brașov the day you arrive in 1459. Find a way to attach yourself to his entourage—as a servant or something. Whether you return to your time in Wallachia or Transylvania is up to you, though I suggest it would be quicker and safer to time travel first, then take a train like this one."

"I don't know," Gwyn muttered. "I was almost thrown out of this train."

"Yes, I saw that door was open. You need to be more careful. You'd better go—your sister is waiting and I need to get off at the next stop so I can make a jump."

Wordless with indignation, Gwyn sighed and said pointedly, "I actually do need to use the facilities here." She nodded at the toilet. They had been standing in the cramped bathroom for a good ten minutes. *Naomi must think I'm sick.*

"So go ahead."

"Um." She valued her privacy.

"Oh, I forgot humans in this time are funny about hygiene activities. Here, I'll face the wall if it makes you feel better."

Gwyn tried not feel to uncomfortable, using the toilet as discreetly as possible, then washing her hands in the chipped basin. Water spurted erratically up her sleeves. *At least I know it's fine to get the pocket watch wet.*

Michelle nodded approvingly, "That's good, keep up the charge. Alright, good luck!"

She opened the door and gestured for Gwyn to edge out past her. Gwyn grasped the rail and peered around the corner to see Naomi down the corridor, bursting with impatience.

"You took forever! What were you doing in there?" the young teenager demanded.

You wouldn't believe me if I told you. She realised how naïve her desire to share her secret with her sister had been. Naomi would tell their parents, who'd take her to a psychiatrist, cutting their holiday short. And then she'd never get to stay on in Europe or travel elsewhere!

"Had my period," she said shortly. "Come on, we need to get back. We're pulling into a stop." They were, and Gwyn needed to get Naomi out of the way so Michelle could slip off the train unnoticed. She didn't want to raise even more questions from her inquisitive sibling.

"But—"

"Let's go!" Gwyn took Naomi by the arm and manoeuvred them past the open door before pulling the lever for the next carriage. The connecting doors hissed apart and they crossed the linking section even as the train slowed with a metallic screech.

Other passengers emerged from compartments with heavy suitcases, asking, "Cobori? Cobori?" Gwyn shook her head in apology as they shuffled past. She ignored Naomi's protests and took one glance back as the connecting doors hissed and clunked shut. Michelle's athletic figure darted past and exited the train as it moaned into the station.

Gwyn sighed. She was on her own again.

FOUR

2623 AD

Exhaustion wracked Michelle when she reached her own time. With Owen's home-made timepiece she could only conduct two year jumps, and while it wasn't the marathon effort she'd made when she had gone back to Masada, six centuries was a long haul. There was also a shuttle trip across Europe, but that was a brief respite in the twenty-sixth century before the final time-jumps. She needed to concentrate hard at the end to arrive half an hour after she had left to make up for the minutes she had been gone. Reaching her hotel room, she collapsed on the floor and voice-activated the bed-pod. It lowered itself to entry height and she crawled in. She ordered the lights off and the pod closed, bringing blissful silence with it.

An insistent chiming woke her several hours later and her eyes sprang open. Working her mouth and jaw, she cleared her throat then held down the panel for the door com. "Yes?"

"Officer Hiro, Citizen, here to escort you to the Justice Department to give evidence today."

She grimaced. She would be tied up giving evidence for days while under close scrutiny, so Colsa and the other Shanista scientists had decided to use the one time traveller that the rest of the Agency knew nothing about. On the com from Earth, Michelle had argued against it.

"She's a tyro! It's a fluke she managed what she did in Judea. She has none of my experience, knowledge or training. Let me go—give me the next five assignments and I'll sort them out myself."

Colsa's hologram fluttered its wings in disagreement. "It would take you too long to keep returning to this time to check on the status of the timelines. Turning points can change quite quickly and you can't simply jump from one mission to the next in case of sudden wormhole closure."

She knew that, but it didn't stop her from trying to convince them.

"I can handle quick jumps like no one else—I'll return to the Agency centre here on Earth and check before I proceed."

"Earth is subject to Vivaldan administration—a freeze has been enacted on *all* Agency facilities, not just the one on this planet. Our official line is that you remain on Earth to recover from your kidnapping and torture. Earth is well known for its health spas and resorts. They require you to give evidence, however, and you will be monitored for aging and disappearances. We do not wish to appear uncooperative and cannot afford to be shut down. Our work is too important."

The memory of that conversation riled her and she thumped the mattress with her fist. It didn't put up the fight she wanted so she jabbed at the panel to open the sleep-pod and clambered out.

It's still a stupid, risky plan to use the girl, she thought, frowning.

"You'll have to wait until I'm clean and have eaten," she informed Officer Hiro after she opened the door. "The doctor advised me to get as much sleep as I can as part of my recovery program, so I didn't set an alarm."

The short, brown-skinned human nodded vigorously, making his purple-streaked curls shake. "May I at least come in? Beats standing around in the hall."

"Whatever." Michelle waved him towards the couch, not bothering to conceal a yawn as she went to shower. Upon her return, Hiro helped the room-service bot unload her breakfast and she indicated he could help himself to tea as she ate. He accepted with another cheerful smile and silently scanned the news-holos. The arrest of Commissioner Hera was still in the headlines, though an earthquake on the Mayash home world had bumped it to second billing. Time travel was a controversial topic, particularly on Earth, where it had been the subject of scientific theories and entertainment for centuries.

"Should you be looking at that? I thought you Justice types were supposed to be impartial?" Michelle eyed the man sideways.

Sipping his tea, the man shook his head. "I'm just on delivery duty—

I don't take part in any of the inquiry processes. So I can read whatever sensationalist news I like, and you can tell me anything you like, and it won't be counted as evidence."

Michelle gave him a bland smile. She was not so silly as to confide in anyone just now, even to a friendly security officer who appeared harmless. *At least he's not being a judgmental jerk. We'll leave that to the tribunal they've set up.*

"We'll see," she said.

* * *

Hours later, her good mood had vanished and it took all her training to maintain her composure. *I hate this kind of bureaucratic jelly wash; clarifying each detail, querying every decision made! Panel-pressing bunch of—*

"And you say you had no idea Commissioner Hera was involved in any kind of Purity Politics group?" One older human, whose mottled skin marked her as the descendant of a Martian colonist, seemed to be stuck on this point.

"That is correct," Michelle repeated to the holograms of the assorted jurors. She was in one of the hearing rooms of the Justice Department, and the com had been set up to transmit from Vivaldis to Earth. "I hardly would have put myself in her hands if I had known she was going to torture me," she pointed out.

"Hmm," the juror's hologram flickered as gamma radiation upset the connection. She tapped away at an unseen computer and Michelle clenched her jaw, breathing out through her nose. *They keep going over the same things, like they hope I'll slip up and confess to being a political extremist! I just want to do my job!*

When she was finally released from the interminable questioning she gave Officer Hiro the slip. Avoiding the small crowd of protestors at the building entrance, she snuck out an underground passage that emerged near the Berlin Centre for Tourism. It was a beautiful day; the sun was shining and Earth's famous blue sky was on show, with fluffy clouds drifting gently across it. She was annoyed she'd been stuck inside. *I suppose that's another thing time travel gives me a taste for—the outdoors. Too many people spend their time cooped up, especially the space-born.*

"Hey Michelle!"

She pretended not to hear and accelerated, mingling with the crowds that swirled towards the monorail station.

A blue flash halted her progress and several tourists bumped into her. Most apologised but one or two glared. She ignored them.

"Brrrys? What are you doing here?"

The furry blue Mayash grinned. "Holiday? Always wanted to see Earth. Not dissimilar to my world in some parts."

Michelle snorted. "Yeah, right. Colsa sent you to babysit? Do the Shanista not trust me?" She could think of no other reason that their leader would send the Time-Space Agency's best security officer. Brrrys was more than capable of taking Michelle down in a fight but it was his emotional intelligence that meant that he could talk most people into doing what he wanted.

Unabashed, his tail twitched in amusement. "I volunteered. Figured you'd prefer a friend."

Sighing, she took his arm, the fur soft under her fingers. "Let's go chat somewhere private. You're attracting attention. Plus I need to eat." While non-human Citizens were common in popular destinations like Berlin, there were enough tourists from less multi-cultural places to cause some people to gawp.

Guiding him towards a restaurant off the main platz, she said, "I hope you've got good news for me."

FIVE

PRESENT DAY

Heavy grey clouds rolled overhead when the Turners disembarked the train in Braşov that afternoon. Moustachioed taxi drivers squabbled over who would take them to the Old Town. After some negotitation, the whole family piled into an ancient Lada, squashed like sardines, backpacks jammed on their laps.

Chatter filled the taxi as the twins read out street names and Stephen tried to converse with the taxi driver. Part of Gwyn wished she had made the jump back at the station, before she had time to think too much about it. *But then I'd have all my stuff to worry about—I'd like to make sure I'm half prepared this time! Too bad Michelle didn't bring me any supplies.* She wondered how the other woman went about preparing for one of her missions. *Seems like a lot of planning ought to go into it. Or I'm expendable....* Maybe they wanted to get rid of her? Was she a liability to these future people, whose motivations she didn't understand? Was the incident on the train a blundered attempt to kill her off so someone could pry the pocket watch from her mangled body?

You're being paranoid. They reached their destination, and she was relieved to escape from the overladen taxi. It was only just in time. A persistent drizzle started as their checked into the old-fashioned hostel, one street back from Piaţa Sfatului.

"I guess we won't be wandering the cobbled streets of the Old Town this afternoon," Danielle Turner sighed.

"We could visit the Black Church?" Gwyn suggested, undeterred by the weather. She had missed rain while she had been in the desert. "It's inside, and it isn't far. We all have rain jackets."

22

"No way!" Justin tugged his twin's sleeve. "There's a games room here. Wanna get your butt kicked in Monopoly, Nau?"

"You can play Monopoly anytime!" Danielle insisted to the twins' backs. "You should come and see the church!" She looked in annoyance at her husband, who shrugged helplessly.

"They probably want a break. And you know how I feel about churches," he said.

"You can find a supermarket and organise dinner, then," Gwyn's mum told him. "Gwyn and I will go and do something cultural."

Gwyn managed to dump the entire contents of her backpack on her bunk and surreptitiously shove various items into her day pack before she and her mother set out into the light rain. She would have to improvise but at least a scarf, water bottle and some muesli bars wouldn't go amiss. Her water-proof hiking boots were ideal for the afternoon's excursion. *At least I won't have to wear crappy sandals.* She didn't fancy exacerbating the blisters and cracked heels she had acquired on her last trip into the past.

Despite the spacious Baroque interior, the external weather cast the Black Church into a gloom more suited to its Gothic origins. Gwyn dragged her mother around the museum, attempting to find as many details as possible around the time she was about to visit.

"It's called the Black Church because of a fire in 1689 that burnt down the city," Gwyn read from an information board. "The walls were stained by the soot, but the church didn't burn down. They re-did the interior in the Baroque style though."

"Didn't know you were so keen on medieval history, sweetie," Danielle commented, smiling as she reached out and smoothed Gwyn's hair—frizzy from the rain much like her own—with a gentle hand.

"1689 is hardly medieval, mum. Besides, I'm doing an Eastern European subject next semester so I want to learn everything I can while I'm here" Gwyn fibbed, running her hand over her head to try to flatten her hair further.

They finished up in the museum and entered the cathedral itself. Gwyn knew her mother wasn't religious, but could see Danielle was enthralled by the beauty of the building, though she expressed disappointment at the lack of iconography.

"It's Lutheran, mum, not Orthodox," Gwyn told her. She watched Danielle wander down the main aisle towards the altar, exclaiming softly at the stained glass. With the dull sound of the rain outside, Gwyn used her mother's distraction to slip into a side nave. It was even darker here and the stone walls chilled the air.

Here goes. She felt her stomach somersault but concentrated on reaching out with her mind to the pocket watch. She made the mental connection and identified the new information from the crystal Michelle had deposited. It was like a sign on a map. She braced herself, then...

Flick!

* * *

1459 AD

The altar boy was hiding in a side nave, hoping to sneak out and catch a glimpse of Prince Vlad. He didn't want the priest to find him so he quietly picked his nose as he waited for a clear dash to the entry. When a figure appeared beside him in a glow of blue light, he fell to his knees; a finger still up one nostril. *An angel!*

He was too awed by the light to be confused that the angel was a woman in trousers rather than a beautiful man in heavenly raiment.

The angel held her finger to her lips for silence but she needn't have bothered. He trembled and kept his eyes respectfully low, expecting a terrible voice to sound.

"Where is the Prince?" she asked. "I have a message for him."

"Th.. the prince, oh holy one?" he stammered.

"Prince Vlad Dracula," she sounded impatient. Fearing he vexed her, the words tumbled out.

"He... he meets with the guild leaders in the Casa Sfatului." The boy had been so excited when the Prince had come into the church earlier. He knew Dracula was here to discuss fortifications against the Turks with the town officials.

"Right." The angel nodded. "And the prince's family? Where do they stay?"

"I… I don't know, holy one." Confusion clamoured at the back of his mind, but it didn't occur to him to raise an alarm. He dared peek upwards and saw she looked thoughtful. The holy glow had faded, and she looked quite ordinary in the dim light. But still he answered honestly. "Perhaps in a house of one of the burghers?"

"Hmm," the angel pondered. "Very good. You may go. Tell no one of this!"

Thin shoes scuffing the flagstones, the altar boy fled.

* * *

That went better than expected, Gwyn mused. It seemed the more confident she was, the easier it was to influence people—she had felt the warm vibration of the pocket watch in her hand. *Possibly needs to be practised. Oh well, I'm about to have a lot of opportunity. Just have to watch my step—I'm sure there are plenty who'd string me up for a witch if I make a mistake.*

She wrapped her jacket around her waist and pulled the scarf out of her backpack. Being a different shape to the shawl she had worn at Masada, it took a few tries to wind it over her head and drape down her shoulders. She had deliberately changed into baggy, lightweight trousers and a grey knit jumper she had bought in Bucharest, not wanting to wear anything too bright or eye-catching. *I'll have to change into a dress to really fit in, but first I need to find out what part I should play.*

Venturing into the main part of the church, she squinted. It was even dimmer than in her own time thanks to the Gothic architecture. A priest shuffled around the altar, lighting candles. Gwyn froze. The priest didn't turn or react, and she breathed again, taking the opportunity approach the heavy cathedral doors open, pushing them open enough to slip out.

It was so different from her time! The sun blazed onto the main square, crowded with townsfolk, horses, mules, pigs, chickens and geese. A barrage of noise and smell—rotting vegetables, animal dung and unwashed citizenry—assaulted her senses. Stall holders shouted their wares; the wealthy promenaded in their finery and greeted each other with polite decorum. Their poorer counterparts were drab in appearance but made up for it in volume as they shopped, argued and socialised. Gwyn took it all in, breathless at the busyness of it all.

She took several steps from the entrance of the cathedral and drifted along the wall. A dog skulked out of her way, but returned to sniff cautiously when Gwyn squatted and held out her hand.

"Ce façi?" She greeted it quietly in the limited Romanian she had learnt. *Though,* she reflected, *this is a Saxon town, so the dog probably responds better to German or Hungarian.*

She hunkered down against the grey stone of the church wall and scratched the dog's head, scanning the square. It was easy to see the Mayor's House—the location was the same as in the future, and the guardsmen clustered around the entrance was a giveaway. Townsmen jostled each other trying to see past the guards, arguing amongst themselves. Small boys squeezed through the gaps to jeer at the soldiers before running away.

That's where I'll find Vlad. She didn't fancy trying to get in there, even if she had planned on approaching the formidable prince directly. The guards stared fiercely at any who came too close, not to mention the crowd gathered there was made up mostly of men. Somehow she needed to find more appropriate garb, locate Vlad's household and to find a way in.

"No vagrants!"

Gwyn's head snapped around and the dog fled, narrowly avoiding a kick to the ribs. Gwyn didn't react fast enough and copped the foot in her side. She went sprawling, her head knocking wall. She struggled to rise.

"Get out of here!" It was the priest. "I thought the guards had told you beggars to stay away until the Prince had gone!" Another kick caught her in the stomach and Gwyn cried out.

I'm not a beggar! she wanted to say. Instead she rolled into a ball and covered her throbbing head with her arms, dreading another blow.

"Is this how you treat your poor, Father? I would not have thought our Lord Jesus would approve of such harsh measures."

A woman's voice floated in, quiet but displeased. Gwyn chanced a look and glimpsed velvet slippers peeking out from under heavy skirts.

The priest halted his abuse and turned to face the newcomer.

"My lady Alina, the Prince would not like to see—"

"My husband would not like to *hear* of a priest beating a beggar girl right outside our Lord's house." Her tone was imperious and brooked no disagreement.

Husband? Surely not.

"My lady, forgive me." Gwyn dragged herself to her knees. "I am no beggar, just an honest maid looking for work. I came to pray." *Let's hope Vlad's wife isn't one of those people resistant to the pocket watch.* She darted a glance upwards and saw curious eyes in a small round face, black curls springing free from an ornate headscarf. The fabric of the dress was beautifully embroidered, with full white sleeves covering the lady's arms to her wrists, and an elegant red surcoat completing the outfit. An older woman, dressed in plainer clothes, stood behind.

Gwyn looked at the ground again, still dizzy. Blood dripped and she touched the side of her head. It was wet and painful. *Ugh, what is it with arriving in new times and getting head injuries?*

"You poor girl, you're bleeding!" The lady exclaimed. "Come into the church— fetch some linen and wine," she ordered the woman beside her. Looking pointedly at the priest, she remarked, "I'm sure you have to prepare for your next service, Father. The Prince will wish to pray once he has finished his meeting with the mayor."

The priest scuttled off. Rather impressed, Gwyn attempted to rise, saying, "Thank you, my lady. I'm sorry to cause a fuss. Please don't trouble yourself." Her body betrayed her and she lurched. Lady Alina caught her in outstretched arms and Gwyn tingled with embarrassment. Pretending to be helpless to try and attract attention was different to actually being unable to stand. Steadying herself, she ducked her head and protested her wellbeing but was ignored and ushered back into the gloom of the church.

More candles were lit, so it was not as dark as before. Lady Alina's companion, a grey-haired dumpling of a woman, reappeared and proffered a bowl of wine along with several pieces of cloth.

"Terrible thing to see, milady," the old woman muttered, holding the bowl. Gwyn tried not to wince as Alina pressed a wine-soaked cloth onto her split head.

"I find often men of God are not always as holy as they like to pretend." Alina's voice was mellow, her hands soft and gentle. Creamy skin framed gently curved lips that smiled kindly, and with a thud in her chest Gwyn realised how truly beautiful the noblewoman was.

She coughed and looked down. "You are too kind, my lady," Gwyn said gratefully. Her head hurt a little less, and she thought with amusement that reading fantasy and historical fiction novels did prepare you for was a more formal way of speaking. *What they don't prepare you for is persuading people to start a war...* The fact that Alina has shown such extraordinary kindness to someone she thought was a beggar, stood up to the bullying priest and took the time to tend Gwyn's injury with her own hands spoke of an empathetic woman, but one who was used to getting her own way. *I wonder if Vlad listens to her?*

She re-wrapped her scarf over her hair as Alina asked, "What will you do now, mistress...?"

"Gwyn, my lady." *Quick, what did you say? You are a maid, looking for work.* She cleared her throat.

"I intended to pray, my lady, then seek work in a reputable house. I have no family, and I do not wish to fall into bad ways." Here was the test, would her story fly? It was slightly more credible than the one she'd spun in Masada, but it would depend on the lady's natural susceptibility to the pocket watch.

"Indeed." Alina considered. "Well then, let us pray together and may the Lord grant us what we need."

That's it? Gwyn's heart sank. What had she been hoping for? That the lady would ask her advice on Vlad's dealings with the Ottoman Empire? She scoffed at herself. *Never mind that now, just keep improvising.*

"I shall pray for you and the Prince, my lady, if it pleases you," Gwyn bowed her head respectfully again. "But for you I would be ill-used indeed and most likely turned away from any decent place."

Alina smiled distantly and nodded, then knelt and bowed her head. Gwyn copied her, as did the lady's servant. *I suppose she's bored with me now,* Gwyn thought. *Maybe she's one of those nobles who takes an interest in the poor for amusement but forgets about them just as quickly.* The only nobles she had ever met were in fiction.

Still, Alina deserved her thanks for intervening. Gwyn closed her eyes (her head still ached) and sent a quick prayer to whomever might be listening. Like her parents, she wasn't religious, but she supposed it couldn't hurt. She was surprised to see Alina considering her with a thoughtful gaze when she reopened her eyes.

"I have asked for guidance and I think the Lord has placed you in my care. Old Nanny here is going deaf and her eyes struggle—she will stay with her family here in Kronstadt, so I require a new maid. My last one left under... difficult circumstances."

What on earth does that mean? but the rest of Gwyn was too excited at the opportunity.

"I would be so grateful, my lady!" she gushed. *Guess this pocket watch—chrono-thingy—is doing its thing after all!*

"Charity is our duty as Christians but you would be of use to me, and without a reference I think you will struggle to find decent work in this place. I would not like to imagine you begging, or worse." Her ominous tone indicated that she knew stealing or prostitution awaited a girl with no friends or connections to give her a job.

"Thank you, my lady," Gwyn said. Alina tipped her head with a smile and waved a hand before she rose, dispensing with the need for copious gratitude. When Gwyn got her feet, she was beckoned to follow the lady and servant. For the second time that day, she left the church.

SIX

1459 AD

Gwyn pulled on the old green dress that Alina gave her to replace her trousers and jumper. She wondered what Michelle usually wore on missions, or if the powers of the pocket watch were enough to help her blend in. Certainly Alina seemed disinterested in her background.

"Come on." It was old Nanny, peering around the change screen. "You must help her ladyship dress for dinner. I'll show you how."

Despite never having been much into clothes and fashion, Gwyn found assisting Alina into her lovely evening dress rather fun. She smoothed the green and black surcoat over cream skirts and straightened them with a satisfied smile—the cut of the dress made the short and slightly plump Alina look taller and slimmer. *Maybe I was meant to be a maid.* She laughed silently at herself.

"I do not know if my husband will be joining us," Alina confided to Gwyn, "but let us assume he will. If his meeting went well he will be in a good mood and may wish to hunt tomorrow. But if he is displeased with the merchants in this town... Well, let us serve the good wine, anyway. It may cheer him."

Gwyn was glad she wasn't expected to wait on Alina at dinner. She sat on a lower table next to old Nanny, but she flinched as the notorious Prince struck one of the servers for not being quick enough.

"Hurry up, fool!" Vlad barked. He slammed his goblet on the table for the shaking servant to fill.

If this is Vlad in a good mood, I don't ever want to be around when he is cranky.

Prince Dracula was not at all what she thought he'd be. She rather foolishly realised she expected a vampire look-alike; tall, with straight

30

black hair and a penchant for evening dress. He wore cloaks, but that was about it. His hair fell in long dark curls and a trim moustache sat under a long nose. Skin was pale, and green eyes were hard and sharp under black eyebrows. He was also in his late-twenties and not much taller than Gwyn.

He shouldn't be drinking so much if he wants to get up early for hunting. But she hid her thoughts, especially since Alina seemed not to notice Vlad's ill-manners, and his soldiers merely chuckled. It was with a sigh of relief that Gwyn was permitted to escape to help the lady prepare for bed. She brushed Alina's long black hair and did up the ties on her nightdress. Once the lady was settled in the large four-poster bed, Gwyn was dismissed.

She ventured out to the antechamber and curled up under a blanket on a rug. The outer door to the apartments opened and Vlad swept past, not even acknowledging the servants. Old Nanny fell asleep quickly and snored quietly, but Gwyn lay awake trying to shut out the sounds from the bedroom. The grunting and creaking of the bed left her embarrassed and thinking of Gaius, and even after all fell silent, it was a long time before she slept.

Once the Prince left in the cold light of dawn, Alina rang a bell. Nervously, Gwyn entered the room.

"Climb in," she advised.

Gwyn stood confused.

"Quickly!" the lady demanded. "I want to go back to sleep and the bed gets cold fast. We have a long journey tomorrow and I want to get all the rest I can."

Realising her meaning, Gwyn advanced towards the bed.

"You'd better take the dress off," Alina said with sleepy amusement. "Did you sleep in it? I suppose it was a lot chillier out there. Still, you'll be more comfortable in just your shift."

Gwyn shrugged awkwardly out of the green dress and clambered onto the four-poster bed. She slipped under the blankets and, when Alina rolled over to face away, she settled herself close but not touching.

I don't know the servant-lady protocol in this situation... Is this normal? Or just something she does? I suppose I can see why she doesn't want Nanny; that old lady snores and farts in her sleep!

"You won't warm up either of us over there," Alina muttered impatiently. She reached back to yank Gwyn's arm over her body. Gwyn wriggled closer and pressed herself against the lady's back. She lay tense for some time, then realised, by the sound of regular breathing, that Alina had fallen asleep. *At least this is more comfortable than the floor.* Finally Gwyn relaxed and drifted off herself.

The following night Vlad didn't visit his wife, instead riding out with the hunt and staying at Castle Bran, south-west of Kronstadt. Lady Alina and the rest of the household were to follow. While Gwyn was fortunate enough to be allocated a patient grey mare to ride, she was so bow-legged and sore by the end of the day her eyes welled with gratitude to be allowed to share the bed again.

"I see you aren't much of a rider," Alina said with amusement.

"No, my lady." Gwyn was learning her new role quickly. She found it mesmerising to brush Alina's lovely hair, although standing right now was agony. "My father could not afford horses." She had given the impression that her family had been free peasants, not serfs.

"Hmm. It gets easier. I'll help you." Alina opened her handwritten Bible and began to read. Gwyn kept brushing long after the knots were all gone. She knew she was extending the chore and was glad Alina couldn't see her blush. *Maybe the pocket watch is creating some sort of bond between us.*

Her muscles stiffened each night and protested every morning, but gradually the riding got easier. Proud that she was improving as a rider, Gwyn was nevertheless grateful for the advice Alina offered regarding the way she held the reins or sat in the saddle. Fortunately their pace was slow as Vlad often detoured to inspect fortified hilltops and talk to boyars, so they went from manor house to castle no faster than the pace of the baggage wagons.

Alina was not a hard mistress. Educated, pious and kind, never angry except when she saw cruelty or wanton stupidity. Only in the case of her husband did she make no criticism of his behaviour, cruel or not.

It's not that she's blind to it, Gwyn realised, *but she knows there is no point. Her serenity is what attracts him to her, especially when so many of the boyars spend time arguing with him.*

She forgot quickly that Vlad wasn't a tall man. His broad-shouldered presence filled the room and on a horse he moved so naturally he seemed an extension of the animal. On foot he was a ferocious fighter, even just sparring against his men-at-arms. Gwyn attended Lady Alina in watching these sessions sometimes as they progressed down from the Transylvanian plateau, riding south through mountain passes and valleys.

If it came to a fight, she shivered, *I'd want him on my side.* The viciousness and violence of his sparring made her wonder what he was like in the rage of battle. She decided she would prefer not to find out, but she couldn't help but watch him all the same.

Her new mistress was something else. Gwyn guessed Alina was a few years older than her but found engaging her in conversation was something of an effort at first. *It's weird to be so physically close to someone but for them to be indifferent to you. I guess that's because I'm a servant.* She wondered what had happened to the last maid.

One topic she quickly learnt to avoid was that of having children. The lady suffered bad monthly pains and Gwyn wondered if Alina had a condition that prevented her from getting pregnant.

It's certainly not for Vlad's lack of trying. The prince visited every few nights and typically left early in the morning to ride out. He was inexhaustible when it came to riding, hunting, fighting and… other things. He only ever seemed worn down by the discussions and arguments he had with his nobles. It was times like that he joined his wife and vented his frustrations at those who professed loyalty to his rule, but found excuses not to follow his decrees.

"They are a thankless, fickle, lot," he growled over roast boar and rich, red wine.

"They are fools," Alina soothed. "They don't realise how your knowledge of the Sultan will save them if it comes to war. They mistrust you because you were away so long, and have enjoyed their own power too much."

"I am losing my patience with them," he muttered. "Time to show them what a stern master I can be."

"You will choose the right time, my lord." She sounded confident. "You won't move against them too soon, not while the country is vulnerable. You will unite them and crush any opposition at the opportune moment." She leaned forward and touched his hand.

Vlad settled and Gwyn nursed a sly hope she might be able to convince the noblewoman of the importance of rejecting any terms from the Ottomans, and influence Vlad of the same.

It was with this hope she began a conversation the next night before dinner.

"Will he fight against the Turks, my lady?" she asked Alina.

Alina shot her a surprised look. "Why do you ask?"

"I'm afraid of war, my lady. Afraid of our country being invaded." *Because what young woman wouldn't be afraid of a foreign army?*

When Alina looked at her, Gwyn felt the weight of her stare. She blushed and wondered if the lady just saw a figure who hovered around with a brush or goblet or shoes, or if she remembered rescuing a girl from being kicked outside the church in Brașov. *Kronstadt—I must remember that's what it's called in this time.*

"It may well not come to war," Alina smiled reassuringly, seeming pleased that her servant was taking an interest in the political situation. "My lord lived with the Sultan for many years as a boy, she explained. "He understands how the Turk thinks, and may maintain good relations with them."

"Yes, but at what cost?"

"What do you mean, at what cost?" A perplexed note entered Alina's voice.

"Well," Gwyn ventured. Was Alina in favour of peace no matter what? She seemed more practical than that. "Perhaps the Sultan will demand payment of the tribute and not accept no for an answer." She shrugged.

Alina looked at her a moment longer, unreadable. "I have faith the Lord God will guide us."

That's a bit of a cop out. But Gwyn didn't want to persist so she changed the subject by asking the lady which dress she would wear that evening. She had never been one for dolls but found Alina a pleasure to dress and care for, especially as their conversations improved from that day onwards. Gwyn's skin tingled every time they touched, but she told herself it was the pocket watch. Her sewing became neater as she picked up tips from other servants and she surprised herself by suggesting combinations of headscarves and surcoats that accentuated the lady's good looks. This led to talks about fashion and customs in different lands and Alina shared stories of her youth in Moldavia. Gwyn enjoyed listening to these tales and Alina seemed pleased with her new maid, so the spark of friendship grew as they progressed on the road into Wallachia.

SEVEN

2623 AD

"What do you mean, they don't believe us? That's ridiculous!" Michelle was incensed.

"Shh, keep your voice down," Brrrys hushed, looking around the restaurant. "It's that anti-time travel group. Seems they've got more backing than we originally thought. Shipping magnates, people in the banking sector. Enough to drag the Agency through the courts and suspend our activities indefinitely."

"But the Shanista—"

"Are doing everything by the book. They may be our leaders in technology but their numbers are limited. They are finding it difficult to be heard." Brrrys' tail was drooped.

"I didn't realise the anti-time travel faction held so much sway." Michelle sipped her tea and made a face. It was a Nolii brew—this restaurant catered for all species—but a cheap imitation of the stuff she could get on Vivaldis and expensive to boot. *Shouldn't have wasted my credits on it,* she thought with irritation. *Earth tea is passable, after all.* "I've been out of the loop. I was so focused on my missions I've not kept up on current affairs."

The Mayash shook his head. "It surprised us all. They've been waiting in the wings, as you humans say. Hera's arrest spurred them to action."

"Hmm. So what's your remit? Keep me from going off the deep end? Or cover for me?" She grinned hopefully. Maybe the Shanista wanted her to run a few missions after all. *Maybe Brrrys has a way of extracting my timepiece from Gwyn.*

"Digging," he replied.

"I beg your pardon?"

"Digging for information. Colsa wants to know if the anti-time travel movement is linked to Purity Politics. If humans are causing a problem, it makes sense that Earth would be their base. World of origin and all that. We have to find out if there are people trying to upset the equilibrium of the Allied Planets for their own gain."

"Xenophobes." Michelle sneered.

"Correct. Your species—some members of it anyway—always want a little bit more. It's evident in your history. Makes sense that some are continuing that trend."

"Ugh." This was not the work she wanted to be doing. *At least when I go back in time I know who's who and what they want.* This was playing the political game in real time and she didn't like it one bit.

"At least we know you're not a xenophobe." He patted her hand and winked. She rolled her eyes at him.

"Come on then," she said. "Where do you propose we start?"

EIGHT

1459 AD

Bright sunshine and crisp air rolling off the mountain slopes imbued Gwyn with joy as their horses ambled along a gentle, narrow road. The autumn leaves in the woods were a riot of reds, oranges and browns. The colours, the smells, the air—it made her feel so alive and Gwyn could almost forget the strangeness of where and when she was and just enjoy the adventure. She hadn't quite lost her toughness from her time in Masada, and once her body had become accustomed to every day on horseback, the exercise left her invigorated.

A shy friendship grew between her and Alina, but some distance persisted on the lady's part. Even when she ordered Gwyn to be a human hot-water bottle, the social gap remained despite their physical closeness. Gwyn found it hard to reconcile the kind Alina with the reserved noble mistress. *I just want her to relax around me.* She peeked at Alina riding beside her. Alina saw her looking and smiled and Gwyn's stomach did a somersault.

A whooshing noise startled her out of her reverie. *That didn't sound like a bird.* And what bird was stupid enough to fly straight into a man-at-arms? Feathers seemed to have exploded on his neck...

"Ambush!" Vlad's roar sent his men scrambling for their weapons. More arrows whooshed through the air and found targets. Horses whinnied and reared. Soldiers shouted and the ringing of steel drawn from sheaths filled the air.

"Move, Gwyn!" Alina kicked her horse and slapped Gwyn's mount hard on the rump. The normally placid mare was stung into a wide-eyed gallop and Gwyn clutched her reins as they bolted back along the path, attempting to flee the attack. Vlad corralled his men into a fierce counter-attack as more arrows flew. His knights and men-at-arms hacked their way into the bandits who had been foolhardy enough to attack the Prince of Wallachia. Dying screams chased Gwyn and Alina and it seemed as though they had escaped the carnage when—

"Hah!" A man in a dirty tunic rose up from the side of the path, swinging an axe. Both horses reared. Alina was skilled enough to stay on, but Gwyn had no such chance. She tumbled off and sprawled onto her back. Winded, unable to move, she panicked as the man with the axe advanced on her. Sucking in air, she scrabbled to rise but her skirts tangled and she flailed.

She was so focussed on the man so she didn't see Alina's horse until its hooves came crashing down onto her attackers back with a sickening crunch. Spine, neck and face were pounded into the mud. The hand that held the axe released it upon impact and it landed at Gwyn's feet.

Grab it! She dragged it from the dirt and looked for Alina. The lady was still astride her horse, with the dead man lying broken in the mud between them. A younger man ran out from the trees, yelling, "Father!"

He threw a knife so fast Gwyn barely saw it leave his hand. Alina screamed as Gwyn swung the axe up like a cricket bat and chopped awkwardly at the man. His scream sounded in her ears and while the impact shook her grip, she managed to reverse the swing, hacking his back. This time the axe bit deep and tore from her hands. Losing her balance, Gwyn fell sideways and landed on the first attacker, trampled in the mud.

She shrieked in revulsion. *Get off! Oh my god, get off!*

"Stop screaming, girl!" Strong hands pulled her to her feet. She fought the grip then registered it belonged to the Prince. She stared at him, then at the young man she had killed, then looked for Alina.

"My lady," she pointed. Vlad dropped Gwyn when he saw his wife slump forward in the saddle. He caught her as she slipped off and Gwyn ran to them.

"Alina!" His voice held true alarm.

She forced a small smile. "I'm quite well, my lord, do not concern yourself—" she bit off the rest with a grimace.

"My lady!" Gwyn pressed her fingers against the wound in Alina's right arm. The small knife was lodged just below her shoulder. Her arm fell slackly and dark red blood stained through the sleeve. Vlad reached for it.

"Don't take it out!" Gwyn barked.

He stared at her.

Gwyn gestured to the wound. "It needs pressure to stop the bleeding until we can get somewhere safe. How far are we from the next castle?" She forget to address him correctly but Vlad didn't rebuke her.

"Well?" he demanded of a man-at-arms.

"Three miles, milord," the man tore cloth from his sleeve. Gwyn snatched it and wrapped it carefully around her lady's upper arm.

"Keep the wound high—it'll slow down the bleeding." The man gave her an incredulous look but Vlad merely flicked his eyes over her once and called for his horse. Alina was passed gently to the Prince, who cradled her against his chest. He was careful to drape her injured arm over his neck, even as she whimpered.

"Bring her," the Prince ordered, nodding at Gwyn. She was hoisted unceremoniously into a knight's saddle and wedged uncomfortably against the pommel. Every hoof beat jolted her as they launched into a canter.

Her bruised body was grateful that they reached the castle quickly. The horses thundered over the drawbridge and into the outer courtyard. Guards on the gate clearly saw the Prince's colours and raised the portcullis. They were rushed into a guest chamber and Alina was laid carefully on the bed.

"Have you a physician?" Vlad demanded of the servants. They stuttered that, no, the only healer was a monk who lived in the monastery several miles down the river.

"Boil water," Gwyn interrupted. "Bring wine and salt if you have any, and honey. Clean linen. Needle and thread! My lord, we need to clean the wound, stop the bleeding and stitch and bind it." She didn't even realise how boldly she was addressing him. *Need to stop any infection before it sets in.* She knelt at the bedside, gently lifting the wounded arm onto some pillows to elevate it. Alina's eyes were closed, her breathing shallow. Gwyn stroked Alina's cheek. "It's okay," she whispered. "It'll be okay." *I don't want to lose her.* Her heart jolted with the realisation.

"Do as she says," Vlad ordered curtly. He knelt beside Gwyn. "You have skill as a healer?" His voice rumbled, with threat or worry, she couldn't tell.

"A little," she replied, concentrating hard. "Not much experience though." She'd never had to deal with anything more serious than cuts or scrapes, or holding Justin's hand when he'd broken his leg. *But I can't afford to have some grubby local monk pray over her while bacteria gets a hold. I need to save her.*

The bleeding appeared to have stopped. Vlad silently passed her his belt knife so she could cut away the sleeve to expose the area.

"Where is that water?" she muttered. The knight who'd brought her exited the room and Gwyn heard him roaring at the servants. The castle steward accompanied the pots of hot water, protesting.

"Salt is extremely expensive, my lord! What use can it possibly have here?"

Vlad raised his eyebrows at Gwyn. She glanced sideways at the steward. "Salt water will kill any dirt in the wound. So will honey and wine. If we don't clean it thoroughly it may become infected and give her blood poisoning." *Though I'm not sure if combining all three remedies is the best idea. Whatever. Got to try.*

"The expense will be greater if my wife dies," Vlad informed the steward curtly.

The steward gulped. "Of course, my lord. Salt it is. And the best wine."

"It doesn't have to be the best," Gwyn told him, soaking a clean cloth in the water. "Just strong alcohol. Spirits would be better."

"Țuica?"

She'd forgotten about the plum brandy. It was a peasant's drink but the alcohol content was extreme. "Perfect," she said.

"My lady, this is going to hurt," she advised when she was ready. No response. She looked at Vlad, who nodded and gripped the small knife sticking out of his wife's arm. Alina gasped when he jerked it out swiftly and Gwyn pressed the cloth to the wound, staunching the fresh flow. Her vision and hearing had shrunk to the wound, her hands and her mistress' ragged breathing. Working quietly, she applied pressure, then cleaned the area using salt water and țuica. Grimaces were her only response, for the lady's eyes stayed closed. *It must sting though.* Smearing honey across the area, she had to brace herself to push the needle's point through the skin. Her hands started to shake, until Vlad's rested briefly on hers and squeezed gently, then released. She took a deep breath and began to stitch. *Glad I learnt to sew in Masada.*

Finally she wiped it over again, then applied more honey and wound a firm, wide bandage over it all. Exhausted, she sat back, releasing the cramps in her feet and calves.

"She needs rest and to keep her fluids up. Soups and cooled boiled water on silver spoons if possible. No wine."

"See that it's done," Vlad ordered the servants hovering anxiously near the door. He helped Gwyn to her feet. "And take care of this girl too. She killed the man who attacked my wife and is to be given whatever she needs." He strode out of the room, taking his knights and the steward with him, demanding to see the lord of the castle.

Gwyn didn't turn to watch him go. She and a maidservant from the castle worked carefully on Alina. They cut off the dress as neatly as possible in the hope it could be re-sewn later. Then they bathed pale limbs and tucked the lady into clean sheets, resting the bandaged arm on top of the covers.

Once that was done Gwyn struggled out of her own muddy dress and washed herself as best she could. The maid gave her a nightdress to wear and she collapsed onto the bed, near enough to hear Alina's quiet breathing. She lay awake for hours, listening, so tired but unable to relax her vigil. The maid returned with food and told her to sleep. Gwyn insisted on checking the bandages first, reapplying fresh honey and wrapping clean cloths over the wound. A little blood seeped through but the stitches held. She caressed Alina's still face again, then kissed her gently on the forehead. Finally she closed her eyes, praying that Alina wouldn't die.

NINE

2623 AD

"You humans love to collect things." Brrrys examined a display of medieval armour in the London Branch of the European Centre for History. He and Michelle strolled through, pretending to be tourists.

"Some humans do. Not me." *Orphans tend not to acquire much in the way of possessions. Just something else to lug to the next care facility or school.* "I'm away too much. Did you know this used to be called the British Museum?"

"What's a British?" her blue companion flicked his furry ears curiously.

Explaining the identities of different nation-states confused him. The Mayash were organised into tribes and lineages but had been colonising other planets for centuries before they joined the Allied Planets. Any political division smaller than a whole world seemed petty and ludicrous to him. Several millennia ago, tribes had gone to war against each other over resources, but, he told Michelle, to divide a species on skin or pelt colour, or even language, was bizarre.

"Our fiercest warriors were always females," he informed Michelle loftily. "They knew that to control the water or food source meant survival for their kits. We males fought if the home was attacked, but spent too much time growing food, building and mining to go out on war parties. Mind you, all that is ancient history. Any Mayash can join the armed forces now. But sometimes there is a throwback." He grinned. "You've seen Grrrel fight."

Michelle dragged him away from the exhibit and took the lift several floors down to the archives. Any Citizen could access these files by logging into a computer and searching. There were thousands of crystals' worth of data, but sifting through it would take time.

"We're looking for information on political coups in the last millennia of Earth's history." Michelle cracked her knuckles and took a seat at a computer. "Compile notes on tactics, propaganda, leader figures. Hopefully we find something we can work with—I don't fancy sifting through databanks for info on takeovers and mergers in the business world."

"And we are looking for some sort of pattern?"

"Pattern, clues, something we can superimpose over current political manoeuvrings in the hope it might indicate who and why."

Brrrys sighed even as he tapped away at the screen. He muttered notes into his computer band, worn on his tail that draped lazily over his shoulder. "This is going to take a while. Do you know how many coups your species has had in just a few hundred years? And there isn't great information on many of them."

"I know." Michelle tried not to grind her teeth. "Let's get into it."

By the end of the day their brains were stuffed with tales of betrayal, corruption and blackmail committed by politicians, would-be monarchs, ministers and military men.

They emerged from the museum as the doors were about to close for the night. Brrrys fluffed his fur against the brisk air of the London evening. Michelle had her all-weather breathable coat on—the best tech in clothing when it came to temperature regulation, and possibly the most expensive thing she owned. *Worth it, though,* she thought smugly, *means I can always pack light.*

"Your species is nasty," Brrrys commented, dragging his claws through the fur between his ears.

"Not all of us are like that," Michelle defended. Trawling through Earth's history often sickened her, but it only made her more dedicated to her work. A better future for humans, Mayash, Shanista, Rilans and Nolii alike. If history on Earth derailed, the technicians at the Agency had predicted several outcomes for humanity, ranging from terrible to devastating. This in turn would affect the composition of the Allied Planets, and its projected future. She sighed as they waited to cross the road.

"Look mummy! A giant blue cat!" A little boy near them pointed excitedly. "Can I pat it? It's got clothes on!" He tore free from his mother's hand and came belting up to them. Michelle frowned. It was very poor manners to call the Mayash "cats". *And not the kind of thing you'd expect in a cosmopolitan city such as London. Maybe out on the edge of the wasted lands, where only dirt-grubbers live.*

Brrrys ignored the slight and knelt down, smiling.

"I'm not actually a cat," he said. "I'm a Mayash. Have you never seen us on the holos?"

Struck dumb with amazement, the boy shook his head. "Can I pat you, Mr Mash?" he ventured. He waited for permission, then reached out when Brrrys extended his arm and nodded—

"Chloen! Don't touch that!" Chloen's mother gasped as she approached at a run. She snatched her son's hand away and shot a disgusted look at Michelle, storming off, dragging her errant child behind her.

Brrrys got to his feet and looked questioningly at Michelle. "Scared of space-bugs do you think? Some people have funny ideas. As if they would let a ship dock without decontaminating it."

"No..." Michelle narrowed her eyes. 'Don't touch *that*', the woman had said. *Not 'zir' or even 'that Citizen'.* It had been obvious that Brrrys was happy for the boy to touch his fur, and the mother hadn't issued an apology for the boy's manners.

"Credit for your thoughts?"

She looked at him quickly. "Let's follow them," she said quietly. "I want to see what kind of family teaches its children that non-humans are non-people."

He caught on. "Ohh... you think?"

"Just a hunch."

Ambling down the street, they passed the famous Harrods and up the road towards Hyde Park. They crossed into the park, falling back once people and vehicles weren't shielding them. They lost the mother and child for a few minutes, but as they neared the Serpentine, Brrrys caught sight of them. He slipped off onto another path to skirt ahead, leaving Michelle to tail them. She had almost caught up when they reached the far side of the park and disappeared into a gated community.

Must be well off to afford to live there. She stared as the figures blurred behind the forcefield. She whirled and stalked down the road, thinking hard.

Her colleague caught up with her a little way down. "Well?"

She brooded for a few seconds. "Let's find out who lives there, and what they do. Might be nothing."

He nodded as they descended to the metro station. "Maybe. But your instincts are usually good. Your unconscious brain did test very highly when it came to making connections and seeing patterns. I saw your report."

"Hmm."

Back at their hotel she suggested they dine in the restaurant, stating she was too tired to go back out. As they finished their meal, she asked nonchalantly, "Want company tonight?"

Brrrys' tail twitched in amusement. "We are colleagues, you know," he teased.

She grinned. "Never stopped you before."

They left the restaurant with his tail twined around her waist, ignoring looks from hotel staff and guests alike.

TEN

1459 AD

For five days Gwyn barely left Alina's side; changing the dressing, checking the stitches, spooning broth and soup into her mistress, helping her use the chamber pot, bathing her. After two days Alina insisted on feeding herself, despite being awkward with her left hand. She had lost enough blood to make her weak, but not completely helpless, though she permitted only Gwyn to attend to her.

Once Vlad was satisfied as to his wife's returning health, he concentrated his efforts on discussing the political situation with the lord of the castle and others nearby. He did not join Alina for meals or anything else, merely checked on her every evening. Gwyn soon despaired of finding an opportunity to convince him that he must fight the Ottomans. Time was creeping on, and it wouldn't be long until Alina was ready to ride. If she wasn't, Vlad would go onto Târgoviște without her and receive the Ottoman envoy as scheduled.

You've become distracted! Gwyn berated herself. The closeness shared with her mistress had grown stronger than mere care. Since almost losing Alina, Gwyn had become attuned to her every movement, every word. It left her lying awake, confused and wondering if it meant she no longer cared for Gaius. She still dreamt of him but the images were fading and she found it hard to bring his face to mind.

Am I fickle? Or is it because she's here and he isn't? She had to be careful not to blush when she dressed Alina, or helped her wash, or brushed her hair. Skin contact sent shivers down her spine, and sleeping beside the lady often sent her overactive imagination to new heights. *Or depths, possibly.* She wasn't fool enough to think that any feelings might be reciprocated, and was scrupulous in keeping her behaviour chaste. Vlad's wife had continuously demonstrated herself to be a good Christian lady, and Gwyn didn't for one second think any kind of extra-marital dalliances would be considered, especially with a woman. *Even in my time most churches are ridiculously homophobic.* So she subsided into despondence, unable to complete her mission.

"It's not her fault she's so attractive," Gwyn muttered one evening as she trekked up the servants'' stairs from the cavernous kitchen, carrying a tray of food for Alina. "I need to get a grip. She's been so nice to me and she'd be horrified if she knew what I felt."

"What you felt about what?"

She jumped but managed not to drop the tray of food. Prince Vlad was standing in the shadow of the corridor, looking ominous.

"Forgive me, my lord! I did not see you there."

"Were you speaking of my wife?" he asked. "What would horrify her to know how you felt?"

"Uh, about the Turks, my lord. They should be halted at any cost. She is such a good Christian lady she would be appalled at my blood-thirstiness."

"Hmm," he approached her slowly and looked her over. "Your blood-thirstiness saved her, that day when we were attacked. And your knowledge of healing also saved her. I think she would forgive you."

"You are too kind, my lord." Why was her heart beating so fast? *It must be nerves.* The brief camaraderie they'd shared in trying to save Alina had lasted only while he'd seen her confidence and decided it was the best chance for his wife. He'd not looked at her before. She supposed picking up an axe and killing a man, then keeping calm enough to deal with a knife wound had aroused a curiosity in him.

Perhaps it aroused something else in him too. Gwyn's eyes widened as the Prince moved to stand close. She admired his dedication to his wife, but realised with a lurch that it didn't extend to fidelity. She shimmied sideways and held up the tray between them.

"Forgive me, my lord, I must take my lady's soup to her." *Come on, I just wanted to talk politics. Why do so many dudes take polite conversation and twist it to their own agenda?*

"Of course, young...?" he smiled in a predatory fashion, and Gwyn suddenly saw the vampire resemblance that had been lacking until now. Her skin tingled.

"Gwyn, my lord." She bobbed an awkward curtsy and backed towards the door. He was there again, graceful but fast.

"Let me get that for you, Gwyn." The smile was wolfish now as he reached past her and opened the heavy wooden door. She ducked under his arm and bore the tray through the antechamber and into the next room. Alina sat by the fire, a blanket covering her lap. Vlad strode past Gwyn, kneeling next to his wife and enquiring as to how she felt. Gwyn placed the tray on the table and began to tidy the room.

"I am quite well, my lord," Alina smiled demurely. "I wish to accompany you as soon as you are ready to leave."

He patted her hand. "Then we shall press on, for I wish to prepare for the Sultan's envoy. I've wasted too much time on these treacherous boyars. They smile and bend the knee, then bicker and squabble behind my back. But I don't have the numbers to meet Mehmed in battle without them."

"You will find a clever way to avoid war and they will be grateful, my lord," Alina clasped her husband's hand, looking earnest. Gwyn struggled not to scowl. *He doesn't deserve her. She does everything to please him and support him and he would cheat on her in a heartbeat!* She fluffed the cushions on the bed a little too vigorously. This noise attracted the attention of the noble couple, who glanced over.

"Perhaps your servant girl here should advise my boyars," he commented, though his eyes flicked between Gwyn and the bed in too obvious a manner. "She thinks the Turks should be resisted at all costs. I know she can use an axe. Should we send her out against them to shame my cowardly nobles into preparing for war?"

Alina's smile didn't fade, though her eyes hardened. "You jest, my lord. I trust that soon your rule will no longer be contested or challenged."

He tensed as though stung and rose to take his leave. "Rest up, my dear. We shall leave on the morrow."

Silence reigned in the bed chamber for several minutes after he left, until Gwyn mustered the courage to ask, "Would my lady like her soup now?" She tried to convey that she had not sought the Prince's attention with a look that beseeched her mistress to understand.

Alina's manner was cool as she ate her meal and it was cleared away. Finally, as Gwyn began to brush her mistress' hair in preparation for bed, she asked, "Please forgive me, my lady, if I have offended you in any way. I did not mean to."

Her mistress stirred and raised her hand to grasp Gwyn's, halting the brush strokes. The touch sent tingles through Gwyn.

"What offense could you have committed, Gwyn?" the tone was mild, but the question loaded.

"You seem a little... reserved, my lady. I hope you know that *I* do not seek anything but your comfort and happiness." That was a lie, and guilt crept into her stomach. She didn't want to lie to Alina.

Alina relaxed, though her hand remained on Gwyn's. "I know," she replied sadly. "We all have our crosses to bear." Her eyes lost her usual distance, and Gwyn's heart leapt. Curiosity entered her mistress' gaze, and realisation seemed to click. Alina released Gwyn's hand. "You are an enigma, Gwyn. Most of the time you are just there, quiet and dull, but sometimes you bloom into sight like a bright flower. Perhaps that is what my husband saw."

"I did not mean it," Gwyn whispered. But the guilt coupled with the thrill that Vlad had noticed her, whether she had intended it or not. What was wrong with her?

"I'm sure you did not," came the sad reply. 'You are not like my last maid."

Ohh. Maybe that was the 'difficult circumstances' she mentioned when she took me on. Pregnant perhaps? Yeesh, that is certainly something I want to avoid! She sighed and suddenly felt incredibly tired. The adventure was wearing thin; Alina's unattainability, guilt over not missing Gaius more, Vlad's attention, and the lack of progress in her mission disheartened her. *Why did I think it would be easy?* The slowness of it all frustrated her, and she lifted the brush to continue with her task when Alina said, "He always gets what he wants."

Gwyn started, then forced herself to continue brushing. "Yes," she agreed tonelessly. "I imagine he does."

The fire crackled and threw shadows through the room. The shutters rattled as the wind picked up outside.

"You should say, 'of course he does, he is the Prince'," Alina reminded her.

"Uh, of course." *Dammit, where is this conversation going? Is she going to dismiss me for impertinence? Michelle would be so unimpressed.* The thought of the Time-Space Agent irritated her. *She's so ruthless she probably would jump right into bed with Vlad and convince him to do whatever she wanted.* The future woman's ability to persuade others was what had put Gwyn in this mess in the first place!

"But you also think it is unfair." A dangerous silence fell, broken only by the shifting logs in the fireplace as the flames consumed them.

Gwyn swallowed. "My lady?"

Alina whirled in the chair to face Gwyn. "It is unfair!" Her reserve was gone, her coolness evaporated. Eyes blazed and the firelight danced fierce patterns on her ivory skin. "Any woman would feel the same. I pray and smile and follow my lord wherever he goes. I turn my eyes from his sins, and seek to counsel him well, but what thanks do I get?"

Pity and anger welled in Gwyn. "He does care for you," she whispered. That was true, at least—his response after the attack made clear the regard he had for his wife.

The lady smiled bitterly. "While I am young and beautiful and obedient he cares well enough. But I cannot give him a child. My place is not secure. But it would be even less secure should these boyars overthrow him and place another on the throne, so I must work for his gain. Still, he will discard me one day, in favour of a wife who can bring him both political advantage and heirs. In the meantime, he simply takes his pleasure with me and anyone else he chooses. Perhaps my barrenness is God's punishment for my jealousy."

"No!" Gwyn dared to reach out and take Alina's hand. 'There are many reasons a woman cannot have a child, most of them are not her fault. Maybe it is him!" She thought of England's most infamous king, not yet born in this time.

Alina reached out both hands to take Gwyn's face. For one wild moment she hoped Alina would kiss her, but the lady merely stared hard and shook her head before releasing her. "It makes no difference. My days are numbered. You are a strange girl. What was I thinking to take you on as a maid? Pity? Charity? I don't remember. You are the best maid I've ever had, but he will take even that from me. It will change things. It always does."

How many times has this happened to her? "My lady," she spoke softly, urgently. 'I could take you away from here. If you really wanted to leave. You don't have to stay and wait to be disposed of."

Confusion clouded Alina's grey eyes. "You are speaking nonsense, Gwyn. Where could I go?"

Gwyn straightened and put down the hairbrush. She bit her bottom lip and tried not to think about how Alina's mouth would taste on hers. "There are... places, where a woman doesn't have to hang on the whim of her husband. Just think about it, my lady." *Because in a few weeks I'll be gone, one way or another. But maybe I can do something for her, and not just leave her like I left Adi and Gaius.*

Alina rose and the coolness was back. "It is late, and this conversation serves no purpose. I would sleep now."

Gwyn curtseyed and hid her frustration. "Of course, my lady." She berated herself for getting caught up in her feelings.

I need to focus on the mission, but I'll not sell my soul for it. They might be real people but they are dead and buried in my time, and keeping my time intact is what matters.

ELEVEN

1459 AD

The last few days of their journey took them past blue lakes and green fields. A light rain started to fall on the final morning, leaving the company damp and eager to reach their destination. Gwyn worried about Alina catching a chill and fussed over her every time they stopped. She noticed Vlad looking over with a small smile, so she stuck to her mistress like a burr. She didn't know what she'd do if he caught her alone again.

Around midday the rain let up and they entered the gates of Târgoviște. Passing through the city streets, people bowed low then make themselves scarce wherever possible. Alina saw Gwyn's puzzled look.

"They fear my husband, and rightly so," she explained. She often sought to educate Gwyn about the places and people they encountered. "Those who were involved in the assassination of his brother and father were executed. Their families were marched to Poenari to build his citadel above the River Arges. Most of them died also. He is not a ruler to be trifled with." Her words were matter of fact but her voice quivered with distaste. Gwyn bit her lip. *Don't forget they call him Vlad the Impaler. Just because you're on his good side doesn't mean you should forget that.* A shiver ran down her spine as she remembered the violence of the ambush. The temptation to use the pocket watch to jump away from this time rose up, but she pushed it back down. *Keep your nerve. Only another week.*

Their horses clip-clopped up the streets and crossed the moat to enter the outer ward of the castle. Ostlers took their mounts away to warm, dry stables. It began to drizzle again so Alina and Gwyn hastened inside and were met by a bevy of servants who had prepared the lady's apartments. Hot soup, mulled wine and warm baths were ordered. Gwyn was permitted to bathe quickly and dress in dry clothes before waiting on her mistress, thankful to have finished their journey.

The afternoon continued grey and darkened into storminess. Alina pleaded exhaustion and retired early, leaving Gwyn to explore the castle. She intended to keep a low profile, wanting to test her theory about the powers of the pocket watch. Alina's comment about blooming into sight made her think about how it worked.

Maybe it never worked in Masada because I was so scared. Maybe when I'm emotional I don't blend in as well.

She sat for a while in the quiet antechamber, gathering herself, then she ventured out into cold stone hallways. She wandered the servants' halls, ducking through the kitchens and pinching a cake fresh out of the oven when no one was looking. The cooks and other servants glanced her way but otherwise ignored her. She ate her purloined cake and courage filled her stomach. *I can do this.* She smiled.

Up a stairway and into the stable yard. She ventured around the edges. Rain fell heavily now; rivulets pouring off wooden awnings and creating muddy streams that coursed through the yard. As a cold wind gusted and sprayed her with rain, she regretted her decision.

This is stupid. Wet feet and muddy skirts were all she could expect if she stayed out here. She tried to find a shortcut back to Alina's apartments but found herself in a storeroom instead. It was occupied by five men-at-arms perched on boxes, playing dice and drinking mead. They looked up as she entered, and she could see their eyes light up as this new form of entertainment walked through the door.

She took a deep breath. *You've bluffed your way through suicidal Jews, Roman soldiers, officials from the future—you can do this.*

She tried to project dullness, looking through all the men as though they bored her. She walked casually as she made for the opposite door, and a warm tingling in her left palm gave her confidence. One of them opened his mouth to speak but stopped as she gave a polite half-smile and nod. The others looked confused and turned back to their game. As she put her hand on the door handle, he managed to say something.

"Join us, wench..." he trailed off uncertainly.

"No, thank you," she gazed at a point past his left ear and stepped through the door, closing it on the sound of them arguing over whose turn it was.

That. Was. Incredible! She suppressed her elation until she was up the stairs and away from the servants' level. As she reached the hall to Alina's rooms a wide smile burst across her face and she shook her head in disbelief, chuckling in glee.

"Ha, it really does work! I'm practically invisible!"

"You're hardly invisible, Gwyn."

Panic flooded her; she tried to regain her sense of calm but it was too late. Vlad's voice came from the doorway in front of her—he must have been on his way to see his wife, only to be told she was already asleep. He would have been disappointed, but here she was—the perfect consolation prize.

"Such a lovely smile you have, he told her as he advanced. "You should show it more often."

She didn't like the look of *his* smile—like a hunter that had sighted his quarry. Her breath came short but all she could do was back against the wall as he moved in, leaning close. He was barely taller than her but his presence dominated, and when his hand found her chin and tipped it up slowly, Gwyn stayed still, not sure if she was unwilling or unable to move. His lips found hers and she found she couldn't breathe.

His kiss started gently, and a slow burning began deep down in her body. A million thoughts clamoured in her brain, yet she couldn't focus on a single one. His moustache tickled her face but she didn't care. As the kiss deepened his hand slid down her neck, thumb pressing lightly on her windpipe. Panic welled up again—those hands were deadly, she knew. He must have taken her tension for excitement, for his mouth parted and his tongue stroked slowly, teasing his way in. Was she excited? She didn't know. She was dying to push him away now—the wetness of his tongue lapping into her mouth making her feel invaded—but knew that to fight him would be useless. Her only chance was to use the pocket watch to make him lose interest.

She acknowledged her fear and disgust and compartmentalised it, imagining herself as a ghost, a shadow, of no interest to anybody.

With a look of puzzlement, Vlad pulled away. She could see desire battle with ennui and did her best to exude dullness. The Prince straightened, and with a perplexed smile chucked her gently under the chin, murmuring, "Another time," before walking off down the hall.

Gwyn stood still, fighting the hysteria that bubbled up in her. *Too close.* Her hands shook so she bunched them into fists and crossed her arms tightly. She promised herself she would keep away from Vlad and redouble her efforts to convince Alina to advise him to go to war.

Alina... The mortification that she had kissed her mistress' husband turned her stomach and her face burned. Gwyn crept into the apartments and found the servant's pallet that had been set up in the dressing room. Stripping off her outer gown, she rolled herself into the blankets, feeling grubby. *I'm so glad Alina is asleep.* How could she face her after this? Knowing she hadn't invited Vlad's attentions didn't really help—she'd responded to them all the same. Her breath caught as she remembered the thrill and terror of his touch. She found her hands creeping across her body, pressing against her breasts and between her legs, then shame and resentment flooded her soul and she clenched them into fists again. There must be something wrong with her. She fell asleep confused and cranky as the storm battered the shutters outside.

* * *

"Gwyn! Gwyn! Wake up!"

She lurched upright with a gasp. "I'm fine, Naomi! I'm fine! It was just a dream!"

"What?" It wasn't Naomi who stood over her; it was Alina, looking rather dishevelled and alarmed. She released Gwyn's shoulder and peered at her in the light of the dim candle.

"Oh. My lady. I'm so sorry. I woke you." Staccato sentences slipped off her tongue. The air was cold, the fire in the bedroom having long since died down to glowing embers. The rain had stopped but thunder still rumbled in the distance, and the occasional flash of lightning lit the room. The two women stared at each other for a few moments, then Alina beckoned. "Come on."

Wordlessly Gwyn padded after her and they climbed into the massive, four-poster bed. For once Alina rolled to face her. Gwyn didn't know where to look. She managed to suppress her attraction to the other woman most of the time, but she was shaken from the events of the evening. She just wanted to be held and distracted from her fears, and she knew what form of distraction she'd prefer.

"What gives you bad dreams?" Alina asked quietly.

Gwyn avoided her gaze, and shrugged, trying to get herself under control. Her mistress was just being kind. She could just have easily ordered Gwyn to be quiet and left her on the cold pallet. "It was just a dream."

"You've had them before.'

"Sorry I bothered you," Gwyn whispered.

"Did your family die? Is that what gives you the nightmares?" Alina pressed.

Gwyn flicked her eyes over Alina's face, unreadable in the dark. "Friends. I didn't even know them that long. But I had to leave them in a hurry. They survived what happened, but most people didn't. It was... horrible."

"Where was this?" Alina's tone was curious.

"Israel." She saw no point in lying.

"You've been to the Holy Land?"

"Yes."

"But that's not all."

"No. There was... a man there. He hurt my friend. He would have killed her. I killed him. In my dreams, he wants revenge. He comes for me."

"I see."

The silence stretched between them. Gwyn couldn't bear it. "He deserved to die!"

"I believe you." Alina's voice was sincere.

Gwyn sighed. "I know. But now in the dream that man from the road is with him."

"He tried to kill me. His son tried to kill you. This is the way of the world. You struggle, and if you are lucky, you survive."

Gwyn was confused. "What about 'thou shalt not kill'?"

A brief flash of lightning showed a wry smile. "We can only hope God will forgive us for doing what we must in this imperfect world."

"I suppose," Gwyn replied doubtfully.

"Besides, you yourself said the Turks must be resisted at all costs. They may be Moselmans but they are people too."

"I know." The same dilemma had plagued Gwyn. "It's... complicated."

"It always is. Roll over, Gwyn. Go to sleep."

She obeyed and for the first time Alina cuddled in to her back, rather than the other way around. She was comforted, and as she listened to the thunder grow more and more distant, she drifted off to sleep.

TWELVE

1459 AD

"Mehmed's envoy will arrive in two days' time, my dear, and I am still uncertain how to deal with them," Vlad confided to his wife as he escorted her to dinner. His voice faded down the hall, but Gwyn could hear him continuing, "Perhaps the rain is a blessing; it has slowed them down and given me time to think."

It was raining again and the weather accentuated Gwyn's gloomy mood. *I'm so over this damp. I want to go outside. And my deadline is two days away and I'm not any closer to tipping the scales in favour of war. And Prince Unfaithful Bastard there keeps finding reasons to pop into his wife's apartment. I'm not buying the ' let's discuss the political situation' because he keeps giving me the* look.

She'd managed to dodge his attempts to catch her alone, concentrating on being grey, a stone, a ghost, when he was in the room seeing his wife, and pleading ill from her monthlies to avoid attending on Alina when they dined in the great hall of the castle. In fact, she'd still not had her period, not since the pocket watch first infused into her. She wasn't complaining, since it was one inconvenience she was happy to do without, but it did worry her. She intended to ask Michelle about the long-term effects of having the pocket watch in her body.

Alina noticed and supported Gwyn's evasions. The silent alliance filled Gwyn's heart and it sent thrills through her every time Alina spoke to her. *I'm not just a servant to her. She cares, she must do.* She knew the way Alina's lips would curve in a slight smile when she was amused. She knew that Alina liked barley soup and roast pigeon, and that she read the book of Ruth whenever she felt sad. Sometimes they would lie awake talking or listening to the rain at night. It tormented Gwyn, but fear of rejection held her back, not to mention her guilt over what had happened with Vlad. She didn't doubt that Alina's faith in her God and duty to her husband would put a screeching halt to any kind of sexual relationship, even if the attraction was mutual.

Still, she couldn't help but be happy every time her mistress walked in the room, and she tried not to think of when she would have to leave Alina. She missed home and her family less this time round, though the food was starting to pall.

Speaking of food, I'm hungry. She had feigned a headache to avoid going down to the hall tonight, and it had been two or so hours since the Prince and Lady Alina had left for dinner. She didn't want to venture out when she was supposed to be unwell, so she would have to wait until Alina returned and order the kitchens to send something up.

The knock at the door made her jump. *Oh good, she's back. She must have known I was starving; she normally takes a lot longer than this.*

Opening the door with a smile on her face, she froze then instinctively tried to shut it again. The Prince forced his way in.

No, no, no, no, no! The weight of the door pushed her backwards and Vlad advanced into the room.

"There's that lovely smile again," he chuckled with feline amusement, his own smile wide. "I came to see if you'd recovered from your headache." Green eyes glittered and he grabbed her wrist. Gwyn yanked and twisted, determined not to panic but desperate to flee, and if not flee, fight. She realised she had no chance of breaking loose from his iron grasp, so she stomped hard on his instep as he dragged her close.

She might as well have stomped on a rock. Her slippers did nothing against his boots, and with his hand gripping her tight she couldn't find any web between fingers or thumb to pinch. A knee to the groin was fended off easily, and her attempt to attack his eyes was thwarted when he snatched her other wrist, drawing her arms up above her head.

He clasped her against him.

"I knew you were a fighter," he whispered huskily, thrill dancing in his eyes. "I saw it that day on the road, when you killed a man." Lust thickened his voice.

Be drab, be grey, be a ghost, she thought desperately. But fear was controlling her, she couldn't calm her mind enough to project the image she wanted. *Make a jump!* she screamed inwardly. *Jump away from here and now!*

It was no use. Trying to reach the pocket watch right now was like flailing for a feather in a hurricane.

Gritting her teeth she tried to head butt him, but he merely leant backwards. She glared at him. He laughed and kissed her so hard it hurt then pulled away so she couldn't bite.

"You do have spark," he chuckled and forced her backwards towards the bed chamber. When she dropped her weight suddenly he hauled her up and threw her onto the bed face down. He hauled up her skirts and when she kicked out he pinned her neck and leant over her. His lips brushed her ear. "You've had your fun, now," his tone was mild, even reasonable. "We can have some fun together, or I can knock you senseless and take you anyway. Your decision."

"Perhaps her headache would be better cured by a tisane and some rest, my lord." Alina's voice could have cut ice.

Vlad was completely still for a breath, then straightened up and turned to smile at his wife as if he was pleased to see her and hadn't been about to rape her maid.

"My dear, I thought you were still at dinner," his voice remained pleasant. Gwyn lay there, frozen, unwilling to draw attention for even a moment.

"You said you felt unwell, my lord,' Alina was expressionless. "I thought to make a tonic for you and bring it to your apartments. I find a little mulled wine also eases any ill feeling."

"How considerate of you, my dear." He stepped towards his wife and took her hand. Gwyn took the opportunity to slide off the bed and pull down her skirts.

"I… I shall fetch the spices for the wine, my lord, my lady.' Gwyn heard her voice shake but it sounded distant. She bobbed a curtsey and blinked furiously, knowing if she let one tear out the rest would follow and she'd be unable to stop. She quickly assembled the ingredients and heated a poker in the fire. Pouring the rich red liquid into goblets, she resisted the urge to down half a glass herself.

"You are too kind," Vlad was still smiling.

Don't know how she doesn't just punch him in the face. Gwyn shot a brief look at Alina, whose face was a portrait of severity.

Gwyn took longer than she needed to grind the spices, clasping the pestle tightly. Once her hands were steady, she grasped the poker carefully and heated the wine. Then she added the spices and handed the goblet deferentially to the Prince. He took it graciously, allowing his hand to close briefly over Gwyn's fingers. She cringed and wiped her hand against her skirts. Vlad toasted his wife, who raised her mulled wine in silent reply, lifting it to her lips but not drinking.

"I'd best take my leave," he said casually, after draining the cup. "I have much to prepare before the Sultan's men arrive." He sauntered out, leaving Alina stony-faced and Gwyn humiliated.

Long moments passed after the door closed behind him. Alina put her goblet of wine down and looked hard at Gwyn.

"Did he... hurt you?" the noblewoman asked reluctantly, as if wanting to pretend the whole incident had never happened.

"No." Gwyn shook her head in reply. Weariness and teariness washed over her and she began to tremble. Whether in shock or relief or shame or something else, she didn't know. Pity leapt into Alina's eyes and she guided Gwyn to a chair by the fire, pressing her own cup into the girl's hand. Gwyn took a long swallow of the strong, sweet wine, feeling its warmth flow into her. The other woman turned Gwyn's hands over gently, seeing the fresh bruises on her wrists and the one forming on the side of her mouth where he'd kissed her. Alina's own mouth twisted in anger.

"I'm sorry," Gwyn whispered.

"No.' Alina shook her head. "I told you he always gets what he wants. He got my last maid pregnant—I had to send her back to her family with money in the hope they could use the dowry to find her a husband quickly. The one before that drowned herself from the shame.' She shrugged. "I'm sorry I cannot protect you. I won't even be able to protect myself when the time comes. If I'm lucky he'll get an annulment and I'll be able to retire into a convent. If I'm unlucky..." She left the words hanging.

My god. She thinks he'd kill her off so he can remarry!

"No." Gwyn stood. Her head spun from the wine but she jerked the feeling aside. "No. I'm not sticking around to let that happen to me. I'm going back home where at least my chances of being raped and humiliated are slightly less than they are here." *To hell with Michelle's mission. She never should have sent me. They'll just have to work out some other way of fixing this timeline.*

"Is your home so safe, that men cannot harm you there?" Alina was curious, but her tone sad.

'Not exactly," Gwyn sighed. She got up to pour a cup of water. "But safer, and you are more likely to get justice if something does happen to you. In most places. Some places. Anyway, I have to get back there." She looked up, her eyes serious. "I meant what I said, you could come with me."

She held her breath. What was she thinking? *You're going to mess up this timeline even worse if you pluck someone right out of it and take them with you to the future.*

But... wait. Alina is the one telling Vlad not to go to war. If I take her away, maybe that will make history happen right and I'll have succeeded!

The idea of saving Alina *and* completing her mission successfully was too tempting to ignore. *Maybe this was what I was supposed to do all along?* She ignored the voice that said she wanted to keep Alina for herself, squashing it with the far more noble thought that she was righting history.

Her mistress turned away and paced before the fire. She walked to the bed and unpinned her hair ornaments, throwing the jewelled pieces onto the blanket as if she wished to banish the scene she had witnessed there. Gwyn followed her and reached for the hairbrush but Alina stuck out a hand and stopped her. The fire in Gwyn's skin raced all through her body.

Grey eyes met Gwyn's. "You care for me, I think, Gwyn.'

Gwyn gulped. "Yes."

Alina considered this a moment. "And you are willing to risk my husband's wrath to try to spirit me away from here. You fought him when it would have been far easier to submit. You haven't seen his violent side. He is fearsome."

That wasn't his violent side? "I don't care,' Gwyn croaked. "You don't deserve to be treated like that. I don't deserve to be treated like that. I'm getting out of here, and I can take you with me."

A brilliant smile sprang upon the other woman's face and her eyes blazed with life. "Very well," she said. "We shall flee to my brother in Moldavia. Or die trying."

Gwyn couldn't help but grin back at her. "I hope it won't come to that."

They both laughed. 'I must be mad," Alina shook her head.

Or under the influence... Gwyn noticed the pulsating warmth of the pocket watch in her palm, and knew that she had persuaded Alina with its help, just as she had once persuaded Gaius. *It's for the greater good.*

"We will leave tomorrow," her mistress raised her chin thoughtfully. "He will be pre-occupied anticipating the Ottoman envoy. I'll insist I need to ride out for exercise, that I've been cooped up too long. We'll bribe the guards to let us venture on alone and lose them in the woods."

"Um... what if it rains?"

Alina took a deep breath. "Let us pray to God it doesn't. We'll take the mountain road to Kronstadt."

"We just have to get far enough," Gwyn said determinedly, "then I have a way to get us completely out of his reach." *Forget Moldavia, wherever that is. As soon as we're close to Braşov I'll jump us to my time and we'll be safe.*

THIRTEEN

2623 AD

Transmission received via secure com:

FT7741: REPORT: Subject appears to have expressed an interest in the activities of various members. Possibility of converting subject extremely unlikely given subject's interactions with undesirable. Preferred option is to eliminate both subject and undesirable. Seeking permission.

FP6982: Permission denied. Subject may still have knowledge of location of item. Elimination of undesirable may cause political ramifications. Draw both subject and undesirable away from major centres, then implement capture. Subject's relationship with undesirable can be used as leverage. If no result, seek further instructions.

FT7741: Received. Will send further report.

FOURTEEN

1459 AD

Vlad Dracula stared out the window, watching storm clouds roll in as the afternoon light faded. The bad weather didn't quell his good mood—he was contemplating the conquest of his wife's maid. He intended to get Gwyn out of Alina's apartments on some errand, then make sure his wife was distracted so she wouldn't come looking. This amusement kept his mind occupied and was a far more pleasurable exercise than thinking about how to deal with the envoy, which was due to arrive on the morrow. He was still uncertain what terms they might offer and what path he should take. He knew the power of the Empire—he and his brother had been taken as tributes when they were but children, and there had been nothing their father could do about it. He also knew he didn't have the means to fight the Ottomans on his own, even with the backing of the Pope. His boyars frustrated him with their bickering and insubordination and couldn't be relied upon.

But if the terms were too steep? He'd fought too long and hard for the Wallachian throne to just give it away. It was easy for the Hungarians—they didn't have the Turks on their doorstep!

Alina's right, I'll have to negotiate. He grimaced, then swigged his wine and set the goblet down with a thud. Hearing a commotion outside, he leant through the thick stone window and saw a colourful party crossing the drawbridge over the moat.

The Sultan's envoy! Damn them! They were a day early.

A knock came at the door of the chamber.

"Enter!' he barked.

"My lord Prince." One of his most trusted knights strode in and knelt, leather greaves creaking, gloved hand resting on the pommel of his longsword so it did not scrape the flagstones.

Vlad grunted, "Get up. What is it, Nicolai?"

The tall knight rubbed his fingers through his dark brown beard. "The Turks have arrived, my lord. They are early."

"I can see that." Vlad was acerbic. "See that they are housed appropriately. I'll meet them on the morrow, as planned. It's rude of them not to send word ahead. Thinking to catch me on the back foot, no doubt."

"My lord," Nicolai bowed again and made to leave.

"Nikki," Vlad had known this man from childhood and was one of the few who could use the pet name with impunity. "When yo"ve done that, tell my wife her maidservant is required for her healing skills here in the northern tower. Send the steward to my wife at the same time to go over the details of the food we shall serve the envoy."

"Of course, my lord." If he read Vlad's intentions, the knight didn't show it. Likely he didn't care. He knew better than to thwart his master.

* * *

Settling the Turks took Nicolai some time—he was uneasy letting in so many foreigners. Their leader, an older, dignified man, stated through a translator that they had pressed on ahead while the good weather permitted and were content to begin their talks as scheduled tomorrow.

Dusk had fallen by the time Nicolai sought Vlad in the northern tower. He did not fancy the errand. It was with deep foreboding that he broke the news to his prince.

"Not back. What do you mean, not back?" Thick eyebrows furrowed as Vlad stopped his pacing and glared at Nicolai.

Nicolai took a deep breath, then repeated his unwelcome information. "The lady Alina rode out this morning to picnic by the lakes, to take advantage of the break in weather. She and her maid became separated from the guards who spent several hours searching before some returned. They reported they'd discovered tracks into the forest."

Vlad's pale skin flushed red. "They left my wife and a maid out in the forest at night, with storms about to break and Turks in the castle!" As if to emphasise his anger, lightning flashed across the sky, followed by a deep rumble of thunder.

"We'll mount a search party first thing in the morning, my lord. Two of the guards are still out there searching." Nicolai strove to placate his Prince.

"I have enough to deal with, with the festering Turks and their blasted demands that'll no doubt come hard and fast on the morrow!" Vlad struck the table with his fist.

"Please, my lord—'

"Have those two imbeciles flogged and tied to a post. Let them see what it feels like to be left out all night! Better yet I'll flog them myself!" He dashed his goblet of wine to the floor and stormed out of the room, Nicolai trailing behind him.

* * *

Whipping the guards burned off some of Vlad's anger and he drowned the rest in wine. After a restless night, his head pounded the next morning, so despite learning that the search party had left at first light irritation plagued him as he dressed. Cream breeches and maroon tunic, with shining black boots, over which he donned a white ermine cape and a regal diamond-studded headdress.

I'll show them how a prince should look. Vlad examined his reflection in the burnished silver mirror and nodded, twirling his moustache in satisfaction. He deserved respect from the Turks but for that, he needed not just to impress them with his appearance, but to dominate the room with his magnificence.

Once he knew the envoy had been ushered into the hall, he entered, stalking up the steps of the dais and seating himself on the grand chair there. He listened to the flowery introductions and diplomatic speeches, relishing the fact that he didn't have to rely on a translator.

One day, Mehmed, you'll regret the fact that your father took me from my father. Everything he'd learnt during his years as a hostage of the Empire sat at the fore of his mind when dealing with his most dangerous neighbour.

The speeches continued. The leader of the envoy smoothed his long flowing robes then rested his hands on his sash. He called down Allah's blessings on the Prince and asked if they might be permitted to discuss the continuing peaceful relationship shared by the great Mehmed himself and the honourable Vlad Dracula.

The use of his patronymic reminded Vlad all too keenly of his obligations to the Order of the Dragon, sworn to fight against all enemies of the cross. His mouth tasted sour. Despite the Pope's backing and a tentative alliance with Hungary, Wallachia was merely a buffer state against the might of the Ottomans.

He gestured brusquely for the diplomat to continue. The speaker rattled on, lacing his words with compliments and continually alluding to the peace between Vlad and Mehmed the Second. The Sultan's affection for the Prince, his respect for the Voivodeship of Wallachia, and his fond desire for them to remain good neighbours, were translated for the benefit of the others in the hall. Vlad soon gathered the gist of the terms, and it blackened his already dark mood.

The Turks requested—*demanded*—as tribute, the payment of ten thousand ducats and five hundred men to be recruited into the Ottoman army. These figures had been floating around for some time now, but Vlad had stalled—not refusing to pay outright, but avoiding handing over money and men with the alacrity that the Sultan would have preferred. To do so would have been to shout to the world that he had bared his arse to the Turks and forgone all honour, credibility and duty to God.

As he formulated a diplomatic answer in his mind, he noticed Nicolai slip into the back of the hall.

"Excuse me," he interrupted the spokesman. "We shall have a short recess."

The spokesman's face showed no astonishment; he and the others bowed their heads politely. Vlad supposed they thought he prevaricated to buy time to think. He didn't care.

He was certain Nicolai had come to tell him that Alina was safe back in her apartments with no worse than a scare for having been out all night, and would welcome her husband's diligence in having sent rescue. He entertained a brief vision of the servant girl flinging herself on him with gratitude too. A smile crept under his moustache as he met with his knight in a side chamber.

"Well?" His tone was almost jovial, but no answering smile came from the other man.

Vlad frowned. *Were they hurt? Waylaid? I'll kill anyone who laid hands on them!* "What is it?"

"My lord," Nicolai's face was a picture of dread, and his speech came reluctantly. "We found their tracks in the forest, and followed them for quite some miles, coming out onto the northern road. We questioned a peasant as to whether he had seen a lady and her maid riding the day before. He told us that a pretty girl had asked him if it was the road to Transylvania, and he told her it was. He said she rode with a lady, hooded and cloaked. They rode north, he said. We whipped him for insolence and I sent most of my men after them on the road, while I rode back here as fast as I could to tell you."

Vlad stared at him. "What do you mean, 'they rode north' to Transylvania? Are they so empty-headed they have forgotten where they live?" He sneered. "The peasant lies or is stupid; they must have asked the way to Târgoviște. He's probably never left the pig-muck hovel he was whelped in!"

The tall knight's voice shook. "Forgive me, my lord, but after the beating we gave him he would not have dared lie. Many of the hoof prints have since been obscured by carts and animals, but it seems clear they headed north, and deliberately."

Vlad furrowed his brow in confusion. Lips tightened while rage mounted and his moustache quivered in fury.

"They've run away," he whispered, eyes flashing. "They've dared to run away from me, that whore of a maid and bitch of a wife. HOW DARE THEY?!" he roared. "What are they thinking? I did not give them leave. What wife abandons her husband and runs off like a slattern? Harlots! Sluts! I'll fetch them back and beat obedience into the both of them! Bring my horse! I'll drag them back myself if I have to!"

"But... my lord, the Turks..."

"THE HELL WITH THE FESTERING TURKS!"

Nicolai flinched. The Prince stormed back into the hall and drew his sword, his knight trailing behind him. He noted with satisfaction the polite expectation on the awaiting courtiers' and diplomats' faces turn to bewilderment and fear.

"I WILL NOT BE DISREPECTED IN MY OWN HOUSE! I will not be *dictated* to by a harem of *child*-molesting, *perfume*-wearing, *godless*, *heathen TURKS!*"

He took a deep breath and hissed, "You come here demanding tribute and soldiers," advancing on the startled Ottomans with a snarl. "You dare insult me by threatening war on my lands if I don't kiss the slipper of your master? THE HELL WITH HIM! He ruled me once, but he shall NEVER rule me again."

Most of the Turks quivered and clutched at their sleeves, but the eldest man, the spokesman for their group, eyed Vlad calmly and stroked his long grey beard. "We mean no disrespect, my lord. Please, put your sword away. We are a diplomatic mission. To harm us is to insult the great Mehmed, in whose name we speak."

Standing dead still, except for the tension visible in his sword arm, Vlad hissed through clenched lips. "Then in the name of respect, lift your hats to me."

Tension grew in the chamber. What Vlad asked was impossible and he knew it. The spokesman answered, "You know we cannot do that, my lord Prince. We wear these turbans in honour of the Prophet Mohammed, as you well know from your time as a guest of the Sultan. We cannot remove them, but we mean no disrespect."

The old man's voice stayed calm and his fingers stroked his grey beard as if to remind the Prince that he demanded respect, for his age, venerability and position as the Sultan's envoy.

Vlad locked eyes with him. "Seize them," the Prince whispered. Nobody moved.

"SEIZE THEM!" the Prince screamed, stepping forward and slashing his blade across the chest of the old man, felling him in an instant. Bright red blood sprayed across the rest of the envoy, spattering their ornate robes and sending them into a screaming panic.

Men all around the hall sprang forth to do their Prince's bidding, who howled like an enraged demon, "I WILL NOT BE DISREPECTED IN MY OWN HOUSE. I WILL NOT BOW DOWN TO YOU TURKS! IF YOU CANNOT LIFT YOUR HATS

TO ME THEN YOU SHALL NEVER LIFT THEM AGAIN!"

Vlad herded them out of the hall with his sword, vicious and unstoppable. They emerged into the main courtyard, where he demanded an anvil and nails be fetched from the blacksmith and set in the yard. The diplomats struggled and yelled that they had immunity, that they were under the protection of the great Mehmed and he would seek retribution a thousand times over should one hair on their heads be harmed.

Smirking, Vlad gestured for the old man he had killed to be brought out and set on a spike.

"Let Mehmed send his armies." He spat in one of their faces. "All of Christendom is against him. As a Knight of the Order of the Dragon I will fight to the bitter end rather than see his festering, swollen arse on my throne, or the punctured arse of my traitorous brother. Nail their hats to their heads!"

Screams broke in terrified panic as the Turks were held down and forced to place their heads on the heavy anvil. The blacksmith lifted a great hammer and punctured skulls one by one; each horrific shriek ending abruptly with a sickening crack, warm droplets of blood spattering across the faces of Vlad and his men. The Prince licked one droplet from the corner of his mouth, tasting vengeance.

The sounds of a brief, bloody skirmish echoed up the castle walls as Vlad's men hunted down the accompanying Turkish soldiers, who—taken by surprise—were cut down easily in their quarters.

Vlad bade all the dead Turks to be impaled and set upon the walls. He then ordered his horse and his cloak and with the grim light of death in his eyes, mounted and galloped out the gate. Nicolai and several other knights galloped after him. Townspeople scattered as hooves thundered down the road and many a small child was snatched from death as the Prince of Wallachia hurtled out in pursuit of his wife.

FIFTEEN

1459 AD

Nicolai rode hard, keeping right behind Vlad as they tore up the northern road in a fury. They caught up to his men in the early afternoon, by which time he could see the Prince's temper had been expelled through the energy of his horse. The men-at-arms were questioning a carter who quailed as they rode up.

"I swear, milord, I never saw nought. No wimen 'ave passed me, and I've been on tha road since dawn."

Nicolai watched Vlad lash out with his sword, cutting the man down, and the party rode on. When night fell they demanded lodgings at an inn and stabling for their sweat-streaked horses. Nicolai ascended from the common room to the private parlour where Vlad brooded over a cup of the innkeeper's finest wine.

Vlad noticed him waiting by the door, and gestured brusquely, grimacing "This has turned from a simple retrieval to a full hunt, Nikki. I'll look a fool if I don't catch them soon, and worse, I'll look weak if I don't catch them at all. And I'll be damned before that happens."

"We'll catch them on the morrow, my Prince, have no fear."

It was the wrong thing to say. Vlad flushed red and half rose from his seat. "I am the Prince of Wallachia! I do not fear a pair of treacherous bitches who have run off like gypsy sluts!"

The knight quailed. "Forgive me, my Prince! No one could ever doubt your courage or bravery, on the battlefield or off. Why, the way you spat defiance at the Sultan today will leave no man uncertain of your mettle." For this was his real concern, not this harebrained goose chase of an errant wife. His men could capture the wenches, sure enough, but the Prince was needed to galvanise the boyars whose country had been pitched into war.

His tactic worked—Vlad's attention was caught and Nicolai could see him recalling the events of that morning. "Hmm." The Prince sank back onto the chair and picked up his wine. "There's no doubt it had to be done. To have acquiesced would have been to cast shame on my father's name and all that the Order fights for. I will compose a letter to Mehmed, informing him that I will no longer have peace at the cost of my honour."

Nicolai privately thought that the murder of the envoy would send a clear message by itself, but then he was a knight, not a diplomat. His favourite language was that of the sword. He spoke that fluently. "Let me continue this search for you, my lord. You can return to Târgovişte and make ready for war with the Turks. This is a trivial matter." Holding his breath against another explosion of anger, he was relieved to see the Prince merely shake his head in dissent.

"No. We will catch them tomorrow. One day will make no difference and I'll not be the husband who cannot chastise his own wife. Have you any word from the innkeep about whether they passed through here?"

"Not him but a man came forth saying he witnessed two women riding north on the road from here this morning. Richly dressed, he said, and in a hurry. It is highly likely that it is them."

"Where do they think they can go that I will not find them? Is there a convent in the mountains they seek? Sanctuary will not stop me from dragging them out by their hair. I've half a mind to rape the servant girl and kill her on the spot just to teach my wife a lesson." Vlad's brow crinkled and he rested his chin on his hands.

Nicolai didn't try to persuade Vlad to turn back again. The best thing he could do right now was to find the lady Alina and her maid as quickly as possible so they could all return to the capital. Taking leave of his lord, he turned on booted heel and descended to the ground floor. He sought the landlord again to see if anyone else had come forth with information. He flipped a copper to the first informant and told him to return if he knew any more, but to beware of passing on any false information. Everyone knew how the Prince dealt with those who were dishonest—the tale of the golden cup in the fountain of Târgovişte was famous throughout the land. Wayfarers were welcome to drink from the cup, and thieves never dared to steal it because all knew Vlad would cut off their hands and then impale them.

* * *

Morning saw them ride out again, a party of twelve—Nicolai's men and the others who'd joined Vlad from the castle. Their best tracker picked up distinct hoof prints in the mud that was still drying in the early sun. "Still riding fast, my lord," he reported. "Not even attempting to conceal their trail. But we should overtake them."

The road rose sharply into the foothills of the Carpathians. This would slow their quarry down if they did not wish to wear out or lame their mounts. The fact that they were still riding so fast confused Vlad, though he did not let it show. He knew of no church or convent that would dare take them in and risk his wrath. *To where do they run?*

Midday passed, and the tracker confirmed that droppings left on the road were but a few hours old. They were riding up the Prahova Valley and it seemed the women had slowed on the ascent. Vlad pushed both men and horses harder, until all were covered in a lather that chilled quickly in the mountain air. The forest tucked itself in colourful autumn swathes around the stark grey peaks above.

Vlad's attention was caught as the man riding point held up his hand and halted. Dismounting, the man bent over and rubbed dirt between gloved fingers as he peered ahead. Trotting back on foot, he told the Prince that the hoof prints in the dust looked fresh. "I believe they're just ahead, my lord."

Vlad considered. Normally in a hunt he would stalk his prey quietly and with caution. *But women are not wolf or deer who can spring away through the woods.* "Go." He waved his hand forward and kicked his stallion into a gallop. His men launched their horses after his, leaving the tracker to scramble onto his mount and bring up the rear.

Thundering up the road, Vlad spotted the women. The Prahova River must have drowned out the horses' hoof beats, for it was only as his party drew close he saw startled heads turn at the sound of pursuit.

"Ride!" Vlad heard Alina cry out as she took off.

"No, my lady!" Gwyn the maid reached after her. Nowhere near as skilled ahorse as Alina, Gwyn was jolted dangerously to the side as she mis-spurred her mount. She clung on as Vlad's men surrounded her, her horse shuddering to a halt.

Vlad raced past with Nicolai, overtaking Alina's horse. He lunged and snatched her bridle, hauling both horses in. Her eyes met his in defiance and despite his anger, the thrill of the chase and success of her capture made him grin. He nudged his stallion closer and with both hands reached across to grasp her face and plant a fierce kiss on her lips. She jerked but then acquiesced, seeming to realise she had no way out.

She's lucky to get a kiss and not a beating. He broke free and she lowered her eyes, defeated, then drew in a sharp breath and turned her head, searching. Vlad followed her gaze to see one of his men dragging the maid from her horse. He stopped when Alina cried out, "No! Don't hurt her!"

They looked to Vlad. He waved his hand lazily and said, "Leave her be." He nudged his horse into a trot. His wife followed obediently and Nicolai brought up the rear.

"Well then," the Prince said, deep voice calm. "This mountain air is lovely but I've a hankering for home." He ignored their looks of astonishment—they obviously expected an outburst.

Some punishments are best given slowly. Let them brood. A grin flashed as his eyes flicked over the women, then he nudged his mount into a trot and began the ride home.

* * *

Gwyn found herself unable to get close to Alina as they travelled south. Vlad spared no consideration for the ladies, and scarcely any more for the men or overworked horses. Gwyn was forced to ride pillion with Nicolai, her horse tied behind.

Do they think I'm going to make a break for it? Or that I'll just fall off?

She wasn't unhappy about it though—not having to concentrate on the reins gave her time to think and plan. If only she'd been able to get to Alina in time. But she wouldn't have been composed enough to make the jump anyway. She'd tried to make the connection but the moment slipped away. Instead of that clear electric feeling, all she got was static. Now she was getting headaches and the pocket watch was itching in her palm. Was the thing malfunctioning? Michelle did say it was a prototype. Maybe there were glitches that no one knew about.

As soon as we get back I'll clear my head and we'll make the jump there. I'll have to improvise getting to Braşov. Dad's phone is on international roaming or I'll go to the police and get them to ring the hostel. It'll be a bit of explaining but if I can think of a good story maybe the pocket watch will help convince them. Except for Naomi. It doesn't seem to work on her... Whatever. Future Gwyn problem.

Her attention was jerked to the present as the horse halted. Peering over the tall knight's shoulder she saw they had stopped to water the horses and stretch their legs. Nicolai climbed down and helped her slide off. He wore a puzzled expression when he looked at her, and she concentrated on being dull and grey.

"I need to use the latrine," she said, tilting her head to the trees.

"Don't go far," Nicolai ordered. His look contained a warning that they would find her if she tried to run.

She nodded and clambered up the small bank, glancing back at Alina. The lady sat in her saddle, facing the other way, shoulders rigid. Gwyn sighed and wished she could get close enough to speak to her privately, but Vlad was monopolising his wife. She could hear him chatting cheerfully despite Alina's monotone responses. Gwyn felt like a coward for not making a dash to Alina and time-jumping out of here. But she didn't know if she could do it, and she couldn't risk getting it wrong.

At least my hiking boots are doing well. She trudged through muddy leaves to find a spot out of sight of the men. *Grey, grey, dull and grey*, she thought, seeking to dissuade any followers while she looked for a convenient tree. A sigh huffed from her as she relieved herself.

She lowered her skirts once she'd finished and stepped back around the tree. A noise made her glance up, and she froze.

A face was staring at her from amidst the branches. It was a man's face, rough stubble covering the chin, brown eyes wide. He stared at Gwyn, and Gwyn stared back. Neither of them moved until the man's eyes flicked towards the road, and Gwyn realised he was hiding from their party.

She put her fingers to her lips, indicating quiet. If he was hiding from

Vlad and his men then who was she to give him away? She wished she could climb into his tree and hide too, but she couldn't abandon Alina like that.

The man mimicked her gesture and nodded. Leaning against the tree, she muttered into the trunk. "Who are you?"

She heard the hesitation in his voice when he replied. "My name is Meric."

"Why are you hiding, Meric?"

"Uhh, I'm trying to get back to my village." He sounded shifty. While looking up at him she noticed a tattoo on the side of his neck, right below an ear that was half missing. The tattoo was a crescent moon.

"You're a Turk?"

He slapped a hand over his neck then lowered it. "No! I'm a janissary. I was born in Wallachia. I came with the envoy. But they're all dead. I escaped."

All dead... What is he talking about?

"I won't give you away," she promised. "Tell me what happened?" She didn't have long before Nicolai or someone would come looking for her.

When he described what had happed goose bumps prickled her all over. *Vlad just... lost his temper and murdered the envoy?* Disturbingly, it was the effect Michelle had wanted Gwyn to achieve.

War with the Ottomans... All the more reason to jump back to my time. But... Alina. She couldn't leave her to him. She wasn't going to abandon those she cared about this time.

Meric had gone silent and she buckled when Vlad's heavy hand fell on her shoulder.

"Argh!" She had time for one short yelp as she was shoved against the trunk of the tree. She tried to push back but her attacker was far stronger, pinning her wrists above her head. *Why didn't he warn me! Bastard!* Indignation turned to panic. It was all happening too fast—the Prince hiked up her skirts and she could feel cold air on her thighs. *No, no, no, no!* She didn't have time, this wasn't right! She needed to jump because she couldn't fight, she couldn't fade, it was going to happen and she couldn't stop it...

SIXTEEN

1459 AD

"NO!"

The weight on her back fell away and she crashed to the ground, scraping the skin on her legs and collecting bruises from the tree roots. Rolling over she saw *two* men fighting on the ground near her. At first, she didn't understand. Meric hadn't attacked her. He'd leapt down from the tree *onto* her attacker. Onto the Prince.

Vlad's shock was wearing off fast, but his ability to fight was hampered by his trousers being half-down. He was the better fighter though, and lashed out with the viciousness of a wolf at bay. Meric threw punches and kicks like his life depended on it. It did, Gwyn realised. The janissary could have stayed silent, and perhaps gone unnoticed while Vlad assaulted her.

The realisation empowered Gwyn. Taking a deep breath, she reached out with her mind to the pocket watch. *Got it.*

She ran towards the fighting men. "Meric!" she yelled. The man's head shot up and she grabbed his arm. The distraction gave Vlad the opportunity to take a swing but his hand never connected. Instead, it flew through blue cloud and he toppled over, overbalancing from the swing.

"What the devil?!" he growled, looking one way then the other, seeing no one.

"My lord!" Nicolai came hurtling through the woods. He hauled the Prince to his feet and brushed off the dirt and leaves that clung to him.

"Get off me!" Vlad snarled, lacing up his trousers, his face flushed a dark red. "Where did they go?"

"Who, my lord?"

"The girl, you fool! And the whoreson who attacked me!"

The knight looked around. He had heard the commotion and did not want to interfere, knowing his Prince could easily handle the wench. But then the shouts from *two* men had spurred him into action. The sight of Prince Vlad in the dirt, partially undressed, with no one else in sight, confused him greatly, but he didn't want to incur wrath by asking more questions, so he began casting about for tracks. There were none leading away from their location. "My lord..." he began hesitantly.

"Dammit, man, I can see they've gone. They just vanished!" The Prince drew up to his full height, moustache bristling. Several men-at-arms had followed Nicolai. They fanned out through the woods at the knight's signal, several making the sign of the cross.

The search turned up nothing and no one, so it was in incredibly bad humour that the party travelled on. Alina shook her head in dismay and confusion, and no matter how much Vlad yelled, she denied any knowledge of Gwyn's escape. She looked diminished as they rode on; a slight figure on her horse bowed down by loss and betrayal.

* * *

Flick!

The scene around Gwyn hardly changed, with one notable exception. Trees, bushes, even the mud on the ground seemed much the same, but apart from Meric, there was no one else in sight.

The peace was broken by the sound of retching. Gwyn hastily dropped the janissary's arm as he threw up. Heaving, Meric sank to his knees and steadied himself on the browning carpet of leaves.

"Are you okay?" she asked when he finished. The man sucked in air, pale under his tan. He looked exhausted. Judging by the contents of his stomach he was weak not only from time travel but lack of food.

"What... what happened?" he whispered, eyes darting. "Where is he?"

"Um, long story. Can you walk? You need some water, I think." She scratched her head.

"I'll kill him! Where is he?" Anger fuelled him and he grabbed Gwyn's arm, eyes wild. "Tell me or I'll kill you too!"

"Let go of me!" she snarled. "I just saved your life, you ungrateful prick!" *Holy shit, what have I got myself into?*

He let go, staring at her. "I didn't need saving, wench, I almost had him! He'll pay, that—"

"He's gone!" she shouted.

That shut him up for a second, and the evidence around them made him pause. "Where did he go?" Meric asked more quietly. "Tell me." It was still an order and Gwyn fought the urge to give him the finger.

"He… We're no longer in the same day as him, not here anyway." She might well have been speaking another language. He stared at her in confusion, anger mounting on his forehead again.

He doesn't seem like the nicest guy; for all that he saved you from being raped. Might be time to play the mysterious powers card. "I magicked us away. We are no longer in that time. We are in yesterday."

"Yesterday?" He stared at her.

"Uh, yep. I mean, yes. We travelled through time. To yesterday." *How is he going to take this…?*

Meric's hand twitched, as though he didn't know what to do. He finally said, "You do magic? You're a witch!"

Burn her! "Yes." She was emphatic. "And if you try hurt me, I'll curse all your fingers and toes off." She painted what she hoped was a threatening look on her face, concentrating on channelling her will through the pocket watch.

More hand twitching from the janissary. He went to speak, then halted, repeating the process several times. She concentrated harder. He sighed and deflated. "I was going to kill him. He deserves to die."

Probably. But I need him alive for now. "You want revenge for the men he killed?"

Meric paused a little too long, then spat vehemently, "Of course. He butchered them. He is a monster."

Gwyn eyed him thoughtfully, then took in their surroundings. "Is there a stream around here? I need some water, and I need to think. You want vengeance on Vlad, and I want to rescue Alina—his wife. There might be a way to do both those things."

"How?" he demanded, eyes lighting up and nostrils flaring. His expression combined with his torn ear gave Gwyn the impression of a street dog used to fighting.

"Let me think! We need a plan." *I can't let him kill Vlad, as much as the world would probably be a better place. But if I can use him to help me get close to Alina, then jump us all away...* She quashed the guilt she felt at tricking Meric. *Greater good.*

"There is a spring up there." He pointed up the slope. She followed him, marching in silence and then refreshing herself after him. He still looked pale and hungry, but he cleaned himself up methodically and efficiently. Meric looked to be of the same age as Vlad, not yet thirty but close to it.

"Where were you going?" she asked, watching him carefully. Making conversation bought her time while she endeavoured to put a plan together.

"My village, as I said," he replied shortly.

When he didn't expand on this she pressed further. "But you've been a soldier for... how many years? How old were you when they took you?"

"Eleven."

"Will your family even recognise you?"

He grunted and stood up, towering over her even when she also rose. "It doesn't matter now. What is this plan of yours that will let me kill him? He has insulted the great Mehmed, and I want to get to him before the Sultan does."

Pushy bastard, isn't he? She quelled her irritation. "Well, here in the woods is no place to stage an ambush with just the two of us. He's surrounded by soldiers and on guard, especially since you attacked him."

Meric grunted. "I should have waited until he was fully distracted."

"Excuse me?" Gwyn's stomach churned and rage inflamed her. "He was about to rape me!"

The tall soldier shrugged and turned away.

"Get fucked!" she spat, incensed. She rose and started to walk back down the hill. Banking the fury in her heart, Gwyn fought to control her breathing and her mind, reaching for the pocket watch to make a jump, the connection still familiar. *I'll go several months into the future—Vlad will have given up on me by then and will be too busy preparing for war.*

"Wait!" She heard Meric say.

Think of Gaius. He'd never stand by and let you get raped. The thought calmed her and she concentrated on when she wanted to go, not noticing as she did that she had slowed almost to a standstill.

As the blue haze rose up around her, a hand snagged her elbow.

Flick!

SEVENTEEN

1460 AD

"Get off me!" Gwyn shouted the second she realised Meric had come with her. He complied involuntarily, doubling over yet again, retching. She shoved him away. The sudden chill in the air surprised her, as did the sight of snow on the ground. *Crap. Didn't think about the change in seasons.*

Meric recovered quicker this time and straightened up, staring at her in awe. She faced him warily, on her toes in case he tried to grab her again.

"You really are a witch," he said, reaching out to touch a snow-sprinkled branch. He stared in wonderment as his fingers came away wet. The silence of the woods was broken only by their breathing; short puffs of mist escaping their mouths and clouding the air momentarily before dissipating.

Gwyn said nothing, not wanting to be distracted from his movements. He seemed to realise this and held up his hands placatingly. "I'm not going to hurt you," he told her.

"You said you'd kill me a few minutes ago," she retorted, "and you would have let Vlad rape me. How do I know you won't try anything?" *I wish I could cast a curse on him.*

He looked surprised. "I... I was angry. I almost had him, and you took that away from me. You have to understand."

"Get over yourself," she rolled her eyes. "I don't *have to understand* anything. He was about to gain the upper hand on you. And being angry is the shittiest excuse to threaten someone like that."

Meric frowned, about to respond, but Gwyn barrelled on. "You know I thought you'd jumped out of that tree to try save me because you wouldn't stand by and watch a woman get raped, but you're as bad as him! If you even think about touching me I'll... I'll..." She stopped. She didn't want to be a hypocrite and say she'd kill him. She was also becoming too cold to think straight.

Meric's mouth opened and closed a few times, and his hands twitched. He shivered. Neither of them were dressed for this sort of weather. At least her cloak was in better condition that the ragged one he wore. "I won't hurt you," he repeated, "on my honour as a janissary." He straightened. "I am not like him; I would never do to a woman what he was about to."

Her silence filled the air with scepticism as she pulled her cloak tighter around her, eyes narrowed.

"I meant it!" His indignation showed. "I... I do not like women."

The information clicked into Gwyn's brain. "You like men?" she wanted to confirm. *Not that being gay would stop him from hurting me in other ways.*

He drew himself up. "Radu the Handsome is also a lover of men, of Mehmed himself. There is no shame in it!"

Now it was her turn to hold her hands up in a conciliatory fashion. "I don't care who you sleep with, as long as it's not me. Who the hell is Radu the–" she twitched off as a snowflake hit her cheek.

"I will not hurt you in any way." Meric knelt on the frosty ground. "I swear it on my mother's grave." He looked up at her, earnest and shivering. "Please. You said you had a plan. I will help you rescue this lady from the Prince if you help me exact vengeance on him. You may be a witch, but you need my help I think."

I do need it. She grimaced. "Alright, get up. Can't have you freezing."

He stood with relief on his face, hugging himself for warmth. "Can you magic up a fire for us? We need to find shelter."

"No."

"But..."

"No, I can't magic up fire. My powers are... quite specific." *Decision time, Gwyn.* "I'll take us to spring, or summer. Come here." She reached towards him.

"Will I be sick again?" He eyed the proffered hand.

She huffed. "Probably. I can't help that, sorry. Are you coming or not?"

As Meric stepped towards her, she heard a low growl, then another. Both of them stopped and peered cautiously around. In the shadow of the trees, dark shapes emerged. They were slinking low to the ground but their aggression rose along with their growls.

Wolves. Gwyn's eyes widened and her fingers twitched, beckoning ever so slightly.

"Take my hand," she breathed. Meric's arm rose, but so did the snarls. With a split second decision Gwyn lunged for him. Something hit her back as the blue haze enveloped them.

Flick!

* * *

1460 AD

Smacking into the ground, Gwyn blinked furiously to clear her eyes. A wave of carrion stink and damp fur washed over her. Azure cloud dissipated as she pushed up then collapsed onto Meric. This time she rolled to the side and felt the wolf slide off.

She scrambled up, shrugging off the effects of time travel in an instant—unlike her groaning companion. The wolf was far less disoriented than Meric but it stumbled all the same, casting about in the bewildering change of smells. The temperature was the most noticeable difference; warm air flooded Gwyn's lungs, a sharp contrast to the icy chill of the snow from moments before. She backed away hurriedly and the wolf swung its head between her and the retching man on the ground.

The wolf leapt. Meric got his hands up just in time, scrabbling to push slavering jaws away from his face. Gwyn fought her instinct to run and leave him at the mercy of the wolf. Perhaps it was what he would have done. *But there's no guarantee it won't come after me,* a selfish voice muttered so she screamed a demented war cry and crash tackled the animal around its midsection.

As she did, time seemed to pause and a vivid memory flooded her mind. When Gwyn had been a few years younger she'd visited her grandparents' farm just after calving season. The cattle were in the stock yards; little bulls and heifers were tagged and in the case of the former, turned into steers. She'd abhorred seeing the rubber rings put on the little bulls' testicles, and was heartbroken at the frantic mooing that cascaded around the yard. That night the gates were left open for the cattle to wander back down to the river. The next morning Gwyn was horrified to find what she thought was the body of a little heifer lying by the gate.

It transpired that the calf wasn't dead, merely born late and too weak to follow its mother. Gwyn's grandfather loaded it onto the tray of the ute and instructed her to sit on it, preventing it from moving too much on the slow and bumpy ride down to the river.

At first, she'd been thrilled to touch such a weak and soft creature, but as the engine started and the wheels began to roll she was forced to wrap her arms around the heifer's neck as the animal began to panic. Lying down in the tray she had no way of seeing where they were and the trip seemed interminable. Time and time again she was almost brained by kicking hooves and thrashing head. Pitiful moos filled her ears as a huge, liquid eye rolled back and locked with hers and she cursed the beast for seeming so helpless when clearly it was not. It had been such a relief when they'd reached the bottom of the hill and the calf was reunited with its mother, and she vowed never to underestimate the strength of an animal again.

The memory of that experience was the only thing that kept her from being thrown right off the wolf's back as it bucked against her. It snapped at Meric but was now hindered by Gwyn squeezing its windpipe. Finally, it weakened enough for the man to throw wolf and girl to the side. He snatched up a stick to stab in the beast's eye.

It spasmed and yelped in anguish. Meric pushed the stick harder until the wolf twitched and fell limp. Only then did Gwyn relax her bear hug and breathe out a huge whoosh of air.

Meric looked at her strangely, then at the dead wolf. "You saved my life. Thank you." The words sounded reluctant to her at first, but then she saw he shook and his face was still pale under its tan. *The time travel,* she guessed, *not the wolf.*

"Second time in ten minutes," she giggled, feeling a little hysterical.

She wanted to cry and vomit at the blood stain spreading from the eye of the dead wolf. Would it haunt her dreams like the men she had killed?

Meric frowned, then pulled her to her feet.

"Let's not make a habit of it. I can take care of myself." He brushed her off, then clasped her shoulders gently. With sincerity in his voice, he said, "But I am indebted to you. I swear that I will help you and protect you, and together we will kill Vlad."

EIGHTEEN

2623 AD

Michelle brooded as she returned from her mandatory blood test at a local clinic. She didn't fancy another day in the archives. Brrrys met her in the hotel lobby. "Got news on our strange friends from yesterday." He waved a data crystal at her, his tail twitching with excitement.

She broke into a smile. "Ah! What did you find?"

They headed out to a café that served decent tea and had the sausage rolls Brrrys had taken a liking to. Not that they contained real meat— insects constituted the basis for most protein in diets. Even with rabbits, kangaroo and lizards replacing traditional livestock, consuming mammals, birds and fish became unsustainable by the end of the twenty-first century. Insect farming became the only viable source of food for billions of people.

None of this mattered to Brrrys as he happily consumed several large sausage rolls, informing his human colleague of what he had learnt. "Old family. Not at the political forefront anymore, though they were in recent centuries. They were against humans joining the Allied Planets. Favoured an Earth-based empire. As if this solar system is well-placed for any kind of interstellar trade. It's in the backwaters, as you humans say."

"It is a backwater," Michelle corrected. "Where do you pick up these sayings?"

Brrrys chuckled. "I did have to study human history to work in the Agency—I watched a lot of old holos." He ran his claws through the fur on his head, flattening his ears several times. "Anyway, these Fitzes seem to keep politically quiet these days, but they have a lot of credit. I sent a secure com to Grrrel last night and she ran a search on their banking. Lots of holding companies and whatnot, but she did trace funding of a certain lobby group back to—you guessed it—a trust of the Fitzes here on Earth."

"Interesting... Guess some of that research did pay off. But it's not a crime to fund political groups, even if you want to be anonymous. I bet it'll look clean tax-wise. We need to find out what they are planning, and get evidence to show Vivaldis."

The blue Mayash looked smug. "There appears to be a conference coming up in the southern hemisphere of this planet. A rehabilitation plan for one of your desert continents. An astonishing number of Fitzes are attending, along with some big business tycoons. Might be something in that."

She rolled her eyes. "And how are we going to get into that? Might look a bit peculiar."

"We're tourists, are we not?" he protested innocently. "This is my first time on Earth; I came here to keep you company while you recuperate. You can do your blood tests from anywhere, you know they just send the data for checking. We might as well see some of the place while we're here. It so happens that I have a fascination with deserts, seeing as we have none on my home planet."

"Hmm, and once we're there?"

His dark blue eyes glittered. "We split up. I'm the distraction—blue, alien and annoying. You can work out which humans don't like me and inveigle yourself with them."

She sighed. "It's the start of a plan. We'll work out the details on the way. Where did you say we were going?"

"Desert continent. Mostly wasteland. Called Australio or something."

* * *

Brrrys wasn't lying when he said he was fascinated with deserts. They had a fantastic view of the Greater Sahara from the upper atmosphere. For this kind of travel, a shuttle simply launched itself up into the thermosphere in a parabolic curve against the Earth's rotation. It then arced towards its destination with a minimum of low-atmospheric travel.

The Mayash spent half the trip staring out the window once the shields had been lifted after takeoff. Once the panorama of Africa had fallen behind, he looked up facts on their destination.

"It wasn't always completely desert," he informed Michelle as she tried to nap. "There were actually significant parts that were forest and farmlands. The coastal areas were quite habitable, though the population was always low considering the land mass.'

"Mmhmm.' His enthusiasm didn't actually annoy her—it was one of the things she liked most about him. She let his voice roll over her as she reclined in her seat.

"Looks like poor ecological management did it along with the change in climate; farming meat animals and crops that needed a disproportionate amount of water. Rather stupid actually."

"Yeah, my ancestors weren't too smart," she mumbled.

"Sea level rises drove most of the inhabitants off world. Guess it was cheaper to sign up to be a colonist than compete with everyone else on Earth. There are few outposts now left in the Province, and apparently some areas harbour outlaws. But the offshore colonies of sea mammals are the largest on the planet. The dolphins manage most of the seaweed farming."

"Mmm." Michelle was practically asleep. She preferred to set her unconscious mind a problem and let it work away while she rested. This conference might be legitimate and she and Brrrys might be on a rogue-comet chase. But it was the best lead they had. If these Fitzes were attempting to destabilise the Allied Planets by causing scandal and political upheaval, she had to find out. The news holos that morning contained increased criticism of Shanista leadership and the Time-Space Agency. That made her nervous, but she tried to put it out of her mind as she drifted to sleep. Brrrys continued to natter on about the current environmental status of the province of Australia; its sparse flora and fauna, and the current attempts to revitalise various areas.

* * *

They landed at the airport in the township of Sydney. What had once been the outskirts of a sprawling city were now host to dust and grit that blew in from the desert. The current town retained a rough but historic aura north of the immense harbour. The southern side was mostly silted, swampy and uninhabited. Great sea level changes in the twenty-second century had reshaped the shoreline drastically.

"Wow, you'd never believe this was once the largest city on this continent," Brrrys commented as they rode the shuttle to the town centre. The majority of buildings were underground, insulated against the dry air and howling desert winds that blew half the year round. This time of year wasn't too bad; an onshore breeze freshened up the streets, though the fierce sun meant Michelle and Brrrys didn't stay out too long. Falling into their agreed roles of strangers who'd met on the shuttle, they wished each other a good trip and split up to find accommodation. The conference was being held at the New Opera House Hotel, but when Michelle sought a room in her guise as an environmental research student, she was informed that everything was fully booked.

"Ah, probably a good thing,' she looked forlorn. "My research budget doesn't exactly stretch to it. I wanted to stay at this hotel, just to say I've been. Can you recommend somewhere?'

'Oh, surely you can find a room for this young lady."

It was a statement, not a question, and it came from a snappily dressed man in his thirties. He beamed at the clerk at the front desk, who promptly scanned his screen again and looked up.

"It appears we do have something; a modest room that should suit the Citizen's budget. My apologies for not seeing it sooner." His expression was bland, but it was clear that an unspoken order had been followed. Michelle pretended not to realise, and adopted a bemused expression.

"Oh! Are you sure? Thank you, Citizen." She smiled gratefully at the attendant and then at the man who had been the source of her good luck.

"Jaysen Fitz, at your service," he bowed. Then he also took her hand and clasped it gently. His skin was soft and fingernails were elegantly manicured.

How quaint. Hand shaking or clasping hadn't been used in mainstream society for well over a century. She let a smile creep onto her face as though she was charmed, rather than wary. "How did you manage that? Do they know you?"

"Oh, my family sponsored the conference, so it is our fault that the hotel is full. I gather they never normally get this much business, even in high season." His cavalier smile was no doubt meant to disarm, and she played along, altering her body language to complement his. "Are you here for the conference?" he asked.

"Kind of," she managed an embarrassed look. "I don't have tickets, but I was hoping to talk to some of the attendees. Rehabilitation of Earth's wastelands is the focus of my higher tertiary study. My tour of the planet happened to coincide with the conference."

"Ah!" He appeared fascinated. 'Perhaps you could tell me about it, once you've had a chance to settle in? It would be terrific to have some of our goals discussed academically. Of course we do have a number of professors speaking. Perhaps I could arrange a meeting with some of them for you."

"Really?' She looked incredulous. "I mean, I don't want you to go to any trouble. You've already done enough and I'm sure you're very busy with the conference—"

"No trouble," he cut her off with a wave of the hand, smiling. "The conference itself is all organised. I'm just here to try to make something come of it. I'd welcome the company actually—most of the professors and business people are a fair bit older than me. It'd be nice to have someone closer to my own age to talk to." Again with the charm. She pulled a face internally—he wasn't her type. But this was her chance to find out if there was more to this conference that met the eye.

"That would be fantastic," she put on the correct tone of restrained effusiveness, then pretended to notice the hotel clerk was waiting politely for her to check in. "Oh, I'm so sorry!'

Jaysen Fitz gestured for her to go ahead. "Perhaps you would meet me later and we can chat about the conference and your research. There is an opening dinner tonight—I'll have a ticket sent to your room." He didn't wait for her reply, merely flashed a charming smile again and strolled off. She noticed there was a reasonable queue behind her, and apologised profusely to the clerk and those waiting. A harassed looking manager appeared and started to check other people in.

"I don't think they're used to this many guests all at once," the Citizen behind Michelle commented, seemingly not bothered by the wait. Their demeanour was that of an academic, so Michelle decided not engage in conversation in case her cover was blown.

The hotel room was more than adequate for a seasoned traveller like her, with a spacious hygiene room and entertainment area of comfortable chairs. She stripped off, showered and lay on the bed in a robe reading articles about the conference and the history of the continent. *Should have listened to Brrrys more on the flight in.*

She was startled when the door chimed. She opened it to a robot proffering a crystal. Inserting it into the nearest reader, it identified itself as a ticket to the opening dinner that night.

Guess I'd better find something adequate to wear. While she didn't fancy spending too many credits, it was the perfect excuse to venture out and meet up with Brrrys.

NINETEEN

1459 AD

"Attendance at my university is flourishing, Radu." The Sultan looked out the window at his gardens, enjoying the view from his private reception room while he waited for a response from his friend, lover and confidante.

"Yes, oh Gracious One, and several of your latest building projects are almost complete. The city thrives under you." Radu was as careful as he was handsome, and never slipped into informal address when anyone else, even mute guards, were present.

"Yes," Mehmed frowned slightly. "Though we have had to permit the Greeks to return, or the streets would be half empty. We want life and learning and culture to flourish in this new capital of ours, and for that we need men."

This new capital of yours. Radu smiled without rancour. He loved his Sultan and would serve him in whatever he asked, but his ambition still called for his own throne, the throne stolen by his conniving, jealous brother.

"And the new tax?" Mehmed, second of his name, son of Murad, had a thousand different plans for his city and his empire, not the least of which was to rebuild the prestige and greatness of Constantinople. For this he needed money.

"The Jews and Christians are paying, and all incidences of harassment have stopped."

"I should hope so!" Mehmed frowned and turned away from the window. "We will have tolerance! If they do not convert, they pay, and if they pay, they are to be left alone. There are many ways to God."

Just some ways are more expensive than others. Radu hid his smirk. An avowed Muslim himself, his faith and loyalty were clear.

"Speaking of taxes, oh Gracious One, has there been any word from your envoy in Wallachia?" He burned to know if his brother had coughed up after several years of dancing around the issue of tribute, but he kept his tone casual. Mehmed wasn't fooled.

"Missing family, my dear Radu?" He stroked his light beard and raised elegant eyebrows as he considered the other man. "I'm devastated." He didn't sound it. "I thought you were happy here?"

Radu chuckled. "You know I am, oh Gracious One. You are my sun, my moon, my heart and soul. Without you I am a blind man, lost in the desert; a crippled sailor, adrift at sea—"

"Save your poetry," the Sultan cut him off and moved to sit on the cushions in the centre of the room. "You've never been to the desert in your life." A silent secretary handed him a document to peruse, while a servant plumped the cushions and offered cool mint tea.

"You have me there." Radu waited for the nod of permission and seated himself near Mehmed, joining him in refreshment. "But only because you know I'd shrivel up and all my good looks would be gone, and then where would we be?"

Their light banter was interrupted by a bowing servant carrying a missive. Mehmed beckoned the man closer and accepted the proffered scroll, breaking the ornate seal and scanning the contents. Radu watched him carefully, pausing from eating grapes. After a long pause his patience was rewarded.

"It seems your brother does not share your love for me, Radu." The Sultan's dark eyes flashed with anger and colour rose in his cheeks. "He has insulted me most greatly, refusing to pay the agreed tribute and murdering my envoy in the most barbaric fashion!"

Radu kept quiet, knowing that Vlad's education in barbaric acts had begun during his time as a guest and prisoner of the Empire.

"Nailing their turbans to their heads!" Mehmed did not froth, he was far too controlled for that, but his fury was plain to all in the room, guards, servants and slaves alike.

Radu swallowed. "He is an animal, Gracious One. He was always vicious, and cruel. He refused the enlightenment offered by your father, and now bites the hand that cared for him."

"He is ungrateful!"

"Unbelievably so!" Radu suppressed his glee beneath solemn words. "You gave him his throne and he betrayed you to the Moldavians and then the Hungarians. You offered reasonable terms to let him manage his affairs in peace, and now he throws it in your face."

The Sultan eyed his favourite. "You drip poison in my ear, Radu. You have always disliked him."

"Not always," Radu protested. "As boys, we were close, but he hated his time here. He could not see the benefits to a more civilised lifestyle." *And he was jealous of me but couldn't do anything about it. Instead, he took it out on others, like the bully he is. What was that boy's name, the one who cared for me?* He shook his head, trying to forget the horrible day Vlad had tortured that poor lad who'd done nothing worse than share a few kisses and caresses with Radu. The boy had survived and his ear had healed, but Radu never forgot the wanton cruelty, knowing that it was really him that Vlad wanted to hurt.

"Be that so, he was the best candidate at the time for the voivodship. You were too young." Despite his affection for Radu, Mehmed was a ruler, first and foremost

And you wanted me close. "I'm not too young now, oh Gracious One." *And my looks won't last forever.* While only in his twenties, like the Sultan, Radu was conscious that his nickname of "the Handsome" could easily be passed onto some younger, fresher man.

"What happened to being lost without me?" Mehmed's milder tone had returned, but Radu wasn't fooled. His ruler was a master politician, capable of playing any situation to his advantage, so his lover had to play the game too.

"Command me as you wish, my Sultan!" Radu leapt up and bowed with a dramatic flourish. "Keep me by your side, to recite odes to your magnificence, or send me forth in battle to smite down that treacherous swine who I am ashamed to call brother. Your wish is my heart's desire, be it far or near—I live only to serve you."

The Sultan's lips curled up at the edges, but he folded the missive with a hard fist. "Stay by my side, for now, my dear, for who else would make me laugh when my heart is sad?" He addressed the servant who had brought the news of Vlad's savagery. "Send Hamza Pasha to me."

Radu suppressed his anger at being passed over for the Bey of Nicopolis, but contented himself with the thought that Mehmed was merely playing other pieces on the board first. *My turn will come. Vlad has gone too far this time; he can't turn back. It will be war, and like a bug, he will be crushed.*

TWENTY

1460 AD

It would have surprised Radu to know that he had been in his brother's thoughts these last few months, as winter deepened and preparations were made for the war to come. The Prince nursed a bitter hatred for those who had inflicted captivity on him as a child and young man, but the loathing he felt for his popular, easy-going, good-looking younger brother eclipsed all other resentment.

Corrupting, effeminate, godless swine. He snarled into his wine cup, clutching the memory of discovering Radu's relationship with the Crown Prince of the time.

His eyes lifted to the form of his wife, picking at her meal at the other end of the table. Alina maintained she'd been tricked into running away with her maid, but he had beat her anyway. The bruises had faded, and since he liked his women pretty he didn't inflict any more, at least not where anyone could see. Her efforts at reconciliation finally bore fruit and he grew bored of punishing her. The fact that he was now often distracted by military matters also helped.

"I'll be riding out soon, my dear. Will you miss me?" He watched for her reaction.

"Of course, my lord." Her reply was toneless.

"I may be gone for months." His lips curled cruelly.

"I shall pray every day for news of you."

News of my demise, she no doubt hopes. Sipping his wine he lounged back in the heavy wooden chair, carved with the likeness of a dragon in honour of the Order.

"Yes," he snorted and swirled the wine in the cup. "I've no doubt you shall." *Don't ever think you will get away from me, Alina. You are mine.*

"My Prince," Nicolai entered the room and bowed to Vlad. "A messenger has come up from Giurgu. The Sultan has sent the Bey of Nicopolis, Hamza Pasha to seek terms with you."

"Terms! What terms does he think I will accept? I know what he will demand—even more ducats and men in retribution for his stinking envoy. Can he not face me in battle? Coward!"

"He is a coward, my lord," the knight agreed. The threat of invasion had loomed for so many years over Wallachia it had become a bugbear, like the tales of vampyres and werewolves that were used to frighten children. "But what about Corvinus? Will Hungary send men?"

This was not the right thing to ask. Vlad's face darkened further and he slammed a fist on the oak table. "Weakling! Corvinus makes all the right noises but hides behind my shield! So do the Saxons up in Transylvania, despite all the time I spent convincing them they must lend their support. Moldavia is the only one we can count on—marriage is good for something, I suppose."

He shot a sardonic look at Alina, who flushed and said, "My brother stands beside you, my lord."

"Yes." Vlad toyed with his moustache, one elbow on the table. He considered his wife sourly. "But even then we are vastly outnumbered. My knights aren't enough." It was the reason he had prolonged the diplomacy. Caught between Catholic Christendom in the west and the Ottomans in the east, he'd used every ounce of persuasion and intelligence he had to hold onto his throne. As it was, Wallachia wasn't even unified, and certainly didn't have the armies to hold its own against the Turks.

Alina pulled nervously at the fabric covering the scar on her right arm; a habit she'd acquired since her aborted escape attempt. Vlad found himself thinking of the occasion she'd acquired it. A slow, cynical smile spread across his face.

"We need more foot soldiers, Nikki." He swivelled in his great wooden chair and faced the knight. "Assemble some press gangs and start recruiting. Any able-bodied... *person,* over the age of twelve."

"My lord?" The directions were clear enough, but the tone left the knight confused. Alina gasped, her wit quicker.

Vlad's grin was feral. "You heard me! Any able-bodied person over the age of twelve. Man or woman, I don't care! Recruit them, shove a weapon in their hands and face them south and east! We'll ride to Bucareşti, then Giurgu, and show this Bey what I think of Mehmed's *terms.* You can be sure that whatever havoc we wreak we will have Turks on our tails when we return, so the city had best be prepared!"

"My lord… not women, please. Our Lord Jesus—" Alina clasped her hands and leant towards her husband.

"Our Lord Jesus can thank me for defending Christendom!" he shot back. "I swore an oath to the Order and I'm damn well fulfilling it!" *And I'll hold onto this throne by whatever means necessary. No one will dare plot against me.* He rose to glower down the table at his wife across the remains of their meal.

Alina gasped at the blasphemy but dared not argue further.

"It's war. They'll be calling me Vlad the Great by the time I'm done." A terrible smile lit the Prince's face. "Oh, and Nikki?"

"Yes, my Prince."

"Get rid of any beggars and other wastrels in this city. I can't afford to have them eating food meant for soldiers."

Nicolai nodded in approval. "How, my lord? Finding them all and sending them out of the city will take some time."

Vlad sat back down in his chair and poured himself another wine. "No, I've got a much better plan than that."

TWENTY-ONE

1460 AD

"That is a terrible plan," Meric announced. Gwyn bristled.

They were arguing in hushed voices in the corner of an inn. The taproom was noisy enough to mask their conversation, but not so crowded that they were shoved cheek by jowl as they sat on their benches. The façade was that they were farmers, husband and wife, so she was sparing with Alina's silver. It was only after she'd ordered them drinks with their turnip stew that she realised Meric didn't drink alcohol. He gave her a quiet lecture on the evils of spirits until she told him to shut up and listen to her plan. Now she had finished, he was disparaging that too.

"They have to come through the town," she pointed out. "We'll be waiting at the gates. I'll provide the distraction and get Vlad's attention while you slip through and grab Alina. I'll time-jump into another day, run towards where you are then jump back to now and grab you both. Then we'll all jump again into a safer time and get away. Easy."

It wouldn't be. The three jumps she'd made in quick succession had exhausted her. It had taken several days for her to fully recover and their progress had been frustratingly slow. Now that they were back in Târgoviște she wanted to time-jump to intercept Vlad and Alina as they returned to the city. Even as she talked her plan through, her stomach sank. She'd been trying to reach the pocket watch all this morning, but her mind's grip on it was tenuous and fleeting. She didn't know if she could pull off another three jumps in a row.

"It relies too much on luck," he was adamant.

"I happen to be lucky," Gwyn ground out through her teeth. *Are you,*

Gwyn? Really? The cynical part of her brain wondered.

I'm still alive, aren't I? she shot back at herself.

The soldier shook his head. "Your plan doesn't get me close enough to kill Vlad. I'm not so stupid to slip in amongst armed guards, because if your magic fails we are all dead."

She huffed. On their journey to Târgoviște, they'd been caught in a rainstorm and Meric had demanded that they skip to another time. She'd been forced to explain she was too exhausted from the previous time-jumps. He'd called her weak. It took a severe tongue lashing from Gwyn to force him to concede that he was ignorant of the energy required to perform such magic.

Winning that argument made Gwyn see that Meric wasn't so arrogant as to refuse to change his mind. So she bugged him to teach her some basic fighting moves for use against a bigger opponent. He'd refused at first, saying women didn't fight. She persisted until he agreed but then he mocked her lack of coordination and strength. After several days he admitted she showed discipline despite her exhaustion.

He'd taught her some basic holds and thrusts with a knife (always up from below, never from above). He'd also shown her how to hold a sword or axe to fend off the superior reach of an attacker.

"Which almost all men will be," Meric had said matter-of-factly. 'But many men are also cowards and won't hesitate to grab you from behind. You have to make them regret it, so grab your knife or even their sword."

She'd smirked and he'd burst out laughing when he caught her expression. "Well that would get his attention," he wiped his eyes. 'But probably not in the way you'd like."

"Not if I stuck a knife in it," she muttered darkly, while being absurdly pleased she'd made him laugh.

He winced. "True."

"Yes, but even with all these things, he's still stronger than me." She told him how Vlad had forced his way into Alina's rooms in the castle at Târgoviște. "Nothing I did worked." She flushed with humiliation.

He grimaced. 'You did all the right things. All I can do is show you a few more tricks but then you have to practise, and get strong. Lift things, stretch your limbs, run. Though I imagine it is more difficult in heavy skirts," he said, glancing down at her attire.

"I'll work on it," she assured him.

I might be lucky so far, but I don't want to keep escaping by the skin of my teeth. Her nightmares were worse since Vlad's attacks. She didn't ever want to be that vulnerable again, so she dragged herself from her blanket each morning and insisted Meric train her. *I want a training montage.*

She ground her teeth, remembering, then finished her tankard of barley water, indicating to the barmaid she wanted another one.

"Fine, you come up with a plan. And give me that wine if you're not going to drink it. The barmaid is getting suspicious."

Meric relinquished his wooden cup to her. "We would do better to separate the two. Kill Vlad first, then rescue your lady."

"Alina first." She was adamant. Her fear and jealousy wound through her stomach. She remembered the way Vlad had kissed his wife when they were captured. What if Alina didn't want to be rescued? She quashed those thoughts. *I have to get her away from him. She's clever and sensible—she'll know escape is her best chance.*

He scowled. "Very well, rescue your lady and then we kill Vlad. But no more than two works of magic at a time if you can't cope with more."

Gwyn pulled a face at the wine. It was sour, nothing like the finer stuff she'd become accustomed to in the castle. *Can't afford to waste this silver, though.*

"For that we need—"

"Ho there, innkeep, have you heard the news?" A man pushed in through the taproom door, stomping mud from his boots. The chatter lulled then bubbled up again as the crowd demanded to know the man's news. Someone bought him a tankard of mead when the newcomer feigned a dry throat, then he declared, "Our Prince has shown the Turks what happens when you threaten good Christian knights! That arse-licking Sultan sent another eunuch to demand money, and Dracula shoved him and his men on pikes!"

Most of the room cheered but several people muttered furtively and looked askance at their neighbours.

"He then crossed the Danube while it was frozen and slaughtered over twenty-three thousand Turks. He liberated the poor Christian

Bulgars who'd been forced to live under their yoke!"

All of the room cheered this time. Gwyn was staggered at the number. *Twenty-three thousand? That's…*

She saw Meric's face tighten and he hissed, "I told you he was a monster!" His fists clenched on the table and she placed her own hands over them to try to calm him. *The last thing we need is to get lynched.*

"Let's get out of here," she muttered, abandoning the rest of her wine. He trailed after her and they retreated to the street outside.

"The butcher!" Meric burst out after they had walked several streets and found a quiet courtyard. "Twenty-three thousand! How many of those were women and children?"

"Ssh! I know." *I guess Meric's not as callous as he first made out.* "It's appalling, but he's not here anyway—we need to go back to a time when he is! Maybe we can stop it from happening?" *Ooh, you risk messing things up now.*

Don't worry, she told herself, *we just need to grab Alina, we won't actually be killing Vlad. Michelle's mission is definitely accomplished—it is war!*

Meric plonked himself down on a bench, leaving Gwyn to lean against the well that graced the centre of the courtyard. He looked tempted by the idea but then shook his head. "It is better to wait until he returns here and have a plan for then. We can work our way into the castle, determine his movements."

She was relieved he didn't want to go back and change things but this plan didn't appeal to her either. "You can do that—I'm not going back into that castle unless I absolutely have to. Someone will recognise me." She pressed her fingertips against her temples.

"You're afraid," Meric accused.

She glared at him. Despite him being a good teacher when it came to fighting, their partnership was an uneasy one. Comments like this didn't help. "Of course I'm afraid," she snapped. "I'm not a big hulking soldier like you. I can blend in but I'm still vulnerable."

"Can't you curse them?"

"Of course no—" She halted, remembering how she'd threatened to curse him when they'd met.

To his credit, Meric didn't leap up and call her out for being a liar. He did look smug though, and said, "I thought not. You can't curse people at all, can you? What magic can you do?"

She fidgeted. He noticed.

"Allah help me, I'm not into women, remember? Even if you can't bring a plague of warts down onto me, I'm still not going to do anything to you! I swore it!"

Gwyn felt abashed for a second, then rallied. "Sorry, it's just—when you've come that close to being raped, you tend to be wary. It's different for you!"

A flash of hurt and bitterness from his eyes made her regret her words. The silence stretched out between them. She sighed and sat down next to him, gazing at the herbs growing in the windowsill across the courtyard. He didn't look at her.

"What happened?" she asked quietly.

He shook his head. She thought a moment.

"You know," she said quietly. "A few months ago a man tried to rape and kill a friend of mine, but I killed him before he could. I didn't mean to. I tell myself he deserved it but I see him every night in my dreams. Another man I killed also haunts me. And now even the Prince, who is not dead, finds me in my dreams and I am so *terrified*, I cannot even move."

"I've heard you cry out in your sleep."

Gwyn sighed. "That's why I don't want to go back into that castle. I'm so scared he'll find me, or some other man will get at me first. At least here no one bothers me because they think I'm your wife, but I *hate* how I'm not safe. My… magic lets me blend, but only if I am really calm, and I don't think I could stay calm around Vlad." She didn't admit that she was still fascinated by him, despite all he had done. She hated herself for that.

Meric considered this. "No. Neither could I. I want to kill him too much. When I was a boy, in Constantinople, he did this to me because he found me with his brother." He touched his ragged half-ear, and she tried not to shudder.

"That was just the beginning," Meric said. "He would have kept going if Radu hadn't stopped him. He said all sorts of vile things about what he was going to do to me. It was a relief when they sent him back here to be Prince. But he is still a monster."

But a necessary monster. Gwyn sighed.

They sat side by side as the sun went behind a cloud and Gwyn shivered. The sun had long since passed its zenith, and the last vestiges of sunlight were climbing up the wall, casting the courtyard into shade.

"Wouldn't it be better revenge for him to live knowing he's lost?" she tried. Maybe she could convince him that Vlad's downfall was inevitable. Despite his annoying traits, she did respect Meric for his determination. Now she also pitied him for his past. She didn't want the stain of betrayal on her conscience when she skipped out on him. *Better to convince him killing Vlad isn't worth it.*

Her respect for him was immediately strained by his look of disgust.

"Don't be stupid," he sneered, their moment of comradery lost. "Death and the devil are the only things good enough for him."

Gwyn rolled her eyes and rubbed her face, noticing smears of dirt that came away with her hand. *I really want a hot bath. But I can't give up now. I left Gaius and Adi. I'm not leaving Alina.*

She didn't know how she was going to explain a strangely dressed noblewoman to her parents. She'd need all her powers of persuasion to convince them into letting Alina stay with them for several nights while she worked out what to do. She hoped the pocket watch would work on them.

She has no passport, no birth certificate, and no funds. What do you intend to do with her, Gwyn?

I don't know, but I'll think of something. She was being irrational, in a way she had never been about Gaius, but she didn't know what else to do.

Her reverie was interrupted by screaming. Gwyn's head jerked up and Meric leapt to his feet, nostrils flaring as the acrid smell of smoke invaded the courtyard.

"Help! *Help!*" The screams were distinguishable now.

"Come on!" Gwyn ran, not waiting to see if Meric would follow.

She burst out from the laneway and saw the smoke immediately. A large house up the hill was on fire. Sprinting up the street she pushed past people fleeing in the other direction.

What are they doing?

"Help!" The screams were frantic, and shoving past two women Gwyn could see why.

There were people trapped in the burning building. They screamed for help through shuttered windows, hammering on the door which was... *barred from the outside?*

Men-at-arms formed a perimeter in front of the house, blocking anyone from approaching. The heat from the fire made them sweat—perspiration streaked through their soot-clad faces and arms. The fate of one who had tried to interfere was enough to deter others—Gwyn's stomach lurched as she saw the man's hacked body lying in the gutter. The guards had their weapons out and their faces were hard.

"Gwyn!" Meric snatched her arm and began to drag her away.

"What... what are you doing?" she demanded. "We need to help! I... you distract the guards and I'll try get in there and grab as many people as possible, and we'll jump to tomorrow—"

"Gwyn!" he shook her. "Come on, we need to get away, two of the guards are looking at us!"

"They're killing people!" she tried to yank her arm back but he inexorably pulled her along.

"Better them than us!" They rounded a corner. This street was quieter, but Gwyn could still smell the smoke. It was now tinged with a most revolting flavour.

"I'm going to be—." She heaved into the gutter. A corner of her brain noticed how the wine she'd drunk earlier tinted her vomit a lovely burgundy colour. Tears streamed down her face.

Meric waited till she expelled everything in her stomach, then hauled her along again. Gwyn staggered but kept up, breathing through her mouth and wiping her cheeks. The tears kept coming even as they halted back in the courtyard; she cried open-mouthed with loud, hiccupy breaths as she sank onto the bench by the well.

A dipper of water appeared in front of her. A few last shuddery breaths were expelled and her chest fell still. She felt hollow.

"Thanks," she mumbled, rinsing her mouth several times and splashing her face thoroughly, then drying it on her sleeve.

"They were Vlad's men, did you see?" Meric sounded angry. "Those people were locked in there on purpose. Allah only knows why."

"We should have tried to save them!" Gwyn rounded on him.

"How? What if your magic didn't work? They were killing anyone who got too close!" He shrugged expressively. "Stupid to risk yourself against such odds."

She stared at him, baffled. "How can you be so upset by the murder of people in Bulgaria but not also at the murder of people here? Is it the numbers or that these people are Christians and the Bulgarians were Muslim? Vlad doesn't care!"

Meric opened and shut his mouth several times, clenching his fists. "Perhaps. You're right. It's monstrous either way. But is it not worth throwing your life away on a lost cause. You want to save your lady, and I want to kill—"

"Who do you want to kill, lad? We need a few killers! You look like a fighter too." Two men-at-arms stood at the end of the laneway, grinning.

Gwyn leapt up at the same time as Meric and frantically tried to recall the few things he'd taught her. There was no other exit to the courtyard, something that both of them were stupid to have missed.

"Don't try it, lad," the other man cautioned. "Or we'll stick your missus, and ye won't like that. The Prince is calling for soldiers, and we've got orders to volunteer some." He gave a big, gap-toothed grin that showed what remaining pegs he had were yellow and black. Gwyn blanched, thinking rapidly.

"Don't take my husband, please!" She concentrated her will and felt the pocket watch warm in her palm. She kept her right hand on Meric's arm, urging him to stay still and let her do the talking.

It might have worked too, save for the fact that Meric pushed her backwards protectively and she tripped on the bench. She fell against the well, recovering quickly but it was too late—the first soldier had whipped out his sword and had it pointed squarely at her companion's chest.

"Don't try anything, laddie," he warned. "And tell your missus not to be afeared. Ye won't be separated."

What? Gwyn peered at him in consternation.

He laughed at her confusion and elbowed his mate while not lowering the sword. "I told ye the Prince wants soldiers. He ain't fussy about whether they're men!"

As they were shoved down the laneway, Gwyn gripped Meric's shirt with the terror of losing the only ally she had at this moment. They were joined by other involuntary recruits, hustled through the city gates and marched to a makeshift camp east of Târgoviște.

"Congratulations!" A knight roared. "You all have been given the honour of serving our noble prince!"

Gwyn swallowed and looked at Meric. He took her hand from the shirt she still clutched and grasped it in his. "Stay close to me," he said. "I'll keep you safe."

TWENTY-TWO

2623 AD

Jaysen Fitz was as good as his word. The opening dinner for the conference was hosted in the main hall off the hotel, under the ancient arched ceiling. Fitz stood chatting with several distinguished looking academics, but as soon as Michelle walked in he broke off from them to greet her with a large smile.

"Michelle! How good to see you! And don't you look lovely. Do all research students pack that kind of a dress when they're on study tours?" He chuckled and gestured admiringly at her shimmery blue number. It wasn't decorated with synthetic jewels like many of the Citizens' outfits were—there was a current fashion on Earth for sparkly coloured stones running up and down every seam line. Instead, it had a simply cut bodice with gauze sleeves and a long overskirt that caught the light as she moved, which concealed her muscles and more importantly, her footwear. Her boots were streamlined, not chunky, but while they could be dressed up in the right trousers and jacket, they looked incongruous in a dress. *Damned if I'm wearing silly sandals or heels, though.* She did notice that, unlike Vivaldis, humans here dressed along old fashioned binary gender lines, with a few notable exceptions like the Citizen who'd been behind her at the hotel reception. They were wearing a business shirt and bow tie, a flowing pair of slacks and a dainty pair of low-heeled sandals. Michelle smiled—she liked the combination.

She turned her smile onto Jaysen. "Oh no, I took the chance to go shopping. I try to collect a useful souvenir everywhere I go, so that often means clothes, rather than ornaments or holo-cards that you never look at anyway. It's not often I get to go to a nice dinner—I can't thank you enough for inviting me."

"It's my pleasure." He took her hand and drew her along to meet several people. She noticed that most bowed, but one or two, men and women, mimicked Jaysen and clasped her hand. It wasn't the personal space issue that bothered her—many of the times she'd travelled to had more tactile cultures—but she noticed after a while that the people who engaged in this habit were also the ones most conservatively dressed.

I wonder if that's significant. She filed it away and continued to play the part of an eager research student, slightly overwhelmed at her luck and grateful to be able to speak to such important business people, teachers and politicians.

Jaysen would flit in and out of groups, seeming to know everyone. He had a talent for making people feel like he really cared what they thought. *Maybe he does,* Michelle thought. *He comes across as genuine.* Her cynicism could not be allayed, so she kept one eye on him as he did the rounds. Quite a few of the people shared his light olive skin and curly brown hair and she guessed them to be other members of the Fitz clan.

Dinner was pleasant; indigenous insects and several other grubs cooked in a variety of innovative ways, with sauces and dips to add flavour. There was also a large selection of what Michelle assumed to be imported or synthesised vegetables. A hologram ensemble played quiet music in the background—another reminder of an earlier era. Michelle sat next to a rather imperious woman who lectured her on the weather patterns over Australia and how they might be manipulated to increase precipitation. Michelle half listened while making agreeable noises, but spent the rest of her time scanning the room and watching who was talking to whom.

Do you actually expect to discover a secret political sect? She was amused at her hope that it would be that easy. But if there was something dirty going on here at the behest of the Fitzes, or others like them, she would find out. *They don't know what's at stake.*

There wasn't much in the way of speeches. Jaysen welcomed everyone and gave an outline of the conference program; who was presenting when and what they hoped to achieve.

"A viable and comprehensive plan to begin rehabilitating this beautiful continent." He was eloquent, and showed passion about their purpose here. "We have assembled some of the best minds, the most stalwart politicians, the cleverest business people. I'm know that together we can build ourselves a launch pad for a better future!"

Applause met his words. As soon as he'd invited them all to mingle over dessert, chairs slid back and groups formed. Michelle identified the one thing that had been bothering her most of all. There were no non-humans. Granted, this wasn't unheard of, particularly since this was humanity's planet of origin and not a cosmopolitan centre like Vivaldis. Still, she would have thought a family with money like the Fitzes could have easily sponsored an off-world speaker. The Nolii were renowned desert dwellers and the Shanista were leaders in any cutting edge technology. This confirmed her suspicions that there was something off about this conference. She helped herself to a spun-ice parfait from a robot-waiter and wandered around the room, hoping to find something more concrete.

"Michelle!" Jaysen swept up with open arms. "Let me introduce you to some people—they might be able to help you with your research."

The rest of the evening was tolerable. She had to bluff her way through various conversations. Jay—as he insisted she call him—was never far, mingling and making sure people felt included. He was the best host they could have asked for, and she saw not a few eyes follow him appreciatively. If she was the naive, studious type she was pretending to be, she could have easily been seduced by his easy charm and thoughtful manner. She made sure she gave the impression that she was, though he made no move to get to know her more intimately. Perhaps he was in a monogamous relationship? After overhearing several people gossiping, that notion was soon banished. *Maybe he already has an assignation for tonight.* If he wanted her company, good manners dictated that he simply ask, and she could consent or decline with no further explanation. He clearly seemed to find her attractive, which amused her. He was older than her chronologically, but she felt a thousand years more experienced.

Probably a good thing. She excused herself and escaped to her room. She'd been invited to sit in on several talks over the next few days. Jay generously offered to speak to the University of Vivaldis about a discounted admittance fee for her. He later whispered in her ear that he'd only said that to avoid jealousy from all those who had paid to attend. She fluttered her eyelashes at him and giggled, but was glad her cover wouldn't be blown.

He is a little too perfect. But at least she didn't have to find out if that perfection extended to the bedroom—she wanted time alone to rest and think. And besides, she preferred Brrrys' cheerful camaraderie and soft blue fur to even the most dashing of human men, though her emotional attachment went no further than friendship. The Mayash was of the same mind, and the non-exclusive arrangement suited them both well.

She wondered what he had managed to find out in his guise as a tourist today. She'd been a little annoyed she couldn't find him earlier, but figured he was keeping a low profile. *Oh well, I'll catch up with him in a day or two and we'll compare notes.*

TWENTY-THREE

1460 AD

Radu surveyed the Ottoman camp from atop the low ridge. Thousands of tents were wedged into fields either side of the road from Bucareşti. The forest loomed close to the north but a perimeter of cleared land bordered that side of the camp.

Less than a day's march to the west was Târgovişte—a place Radu had never been. Born in Sighişoara like Vlad, he'd spent his formative years there and in the Germanies, gaining the education of a nobleman's son. He remembered little from that time. It was in Constantinople that his true education had begun; in love, politics and Allah.

He felt the stirrings of excitement that their goal, his goal, was so close. With an army this large, it was inevitable that Vlad would soon be brought before them in chains, or better yet, with his head on a pike. Radu couldn't decide which scenario he preferred and settled for imagining both. He smirked before kicking his horse into a canter and rode back down towards the centre of camp. His guards rode ahead, clearing men from his path until they reached the Sultan's grand marquee.

"The men are well in order, oh Gracious One!" Radu shouted, dismounting with a jingle of gold ringed mail. He stripped off his riding gloves and strode under the rich fabric of the tent. Mehmed sat on a travelling throne, reading dispatches and talking with various generals. A few of these generals eyed Radu with dislike; jealous of his position of favour and suspicious of his origins. He knew they regarded him as the Sultan's pet: pretty and paid but without substance. His comments about the status of the men were also inaccurate—anyone with any military experience could see that disease and hunger were beginning to take their toll. Vlad had avoided pitched battles thus far. Instead, he had swept in and out with brief, hard attacks, leaving behind scorched earth as he retreated towards his capital. The Sultan also learnt with disgust that infected camp followers were spreading sickness amongst his men. He forbade the use of whores, but with an army that numbered in the hundreds of thousands, it was impossible to prevent all outside contact.

Leaving Bucareşti and Snagov uncaptured in their wake, Mehmed was concentrating on Vlad himself. That meant Târgovişte. Radu hoped his report would cheer the Sultan. It was time to bring this war to a head.

"Very good, Radu," Mehmed replied absentmindedly. Radu hid his frown. It was hard to get time alone with his lover while they were on campaign—he had to show his dedication in other ways. He wanted to prove he was the reliable, loyal brother; one who could be trusted to take over the voivodship of Wallachia.

"Oh Gracious One," a general glared at Radu for the interruption and pursed his lips underneath his beard. "Tomorrow we can push on to Târgovişte and besiege the city. The Impaler will be trapped like a rat in a cage."

If you think my brother is going to wait for you to surround him, you'd be wrong.

"Lord Sultan," Radu broke in, "it's unlikely that Vlad will sit and wait for our forces to arrive. May I suggest a lightning attack tonight to cause confusion and disarray. Then you can bring the main bulk of your army tomorrow to pin him down."

"Lord Sultan, it would be best if strategy is left to your *experienced* generals. Under your gracious and all-knowing guidance, of course." The same general puffed up and his cheeks reddened, and his companions bristled alike.

Mehmed waved them all down like misbehaving puppies. "My strategy is guided by the Divine Allah. With His blessing, we shall move into place and begin the siege tomorrow. Too many of our auxiliary forces are still catching up."

Radu masked his annoyance with a smile and excused himself. The fact that the Sultan didn't even bother to try to make him stay piqued his anger more. *Do they think I have no knowledge of this country? Or do they not trust me?* He brushed aside the fact that he had not been north of the Danube since he was a boy, and instead chose to brood on slights, real and imagined.

Several hours later darkness saw him sitting alone at his ornate chessboard—a birthday gift from Mehmed several years ago. Radu toyed with the figure of the white queen between his elegant fingers, then tapped it against his teeth. He stared at the black king and queen, huddled together on the far side of the board. His dinner had long gone cold, and the camp was quiet. Mehmed had not sent for him and Radu raged silently even as his fears crept in with the shadows.

I'm getting older, less handsome. By the time I'm thirty he'll have found someone else. I'm no use to him as a general, and there are too many noble families to be kept happy to give me a real post in administration—not that I want to be a judge or a minister. If I can't convince him to give me Wallachia now I'll be pushed to the background, and will fade into obscurity.

His lanterns burned low and despite the warm summer air, Radu shivered as a draft crept in the tent. He used the white queen to flick the black king over. It rolled to the edge of the board and lay there, defeated.

If only defeating my infernal brother was as easy. Radu scowled and pulled the jewelled rings off his fingers, cracking his knuckles. The draft tickled his neck and he got up to go and tighten the tent flap, not wishing to call a slave and have his solitude disturbed.

The sound of a horse clopping quietly made him loosen the flap enough to peer outside. A dark figure sat erect; Radu could just make out the uniform of a scout in the light of the torch the rider held. Something about the horseman made him uneasy, but he wasn't sure what. Shrugging, he tied the flap down and made his way back across the tent, passing the chessboard. He paused, glancing down at the fallen black king, then at the black queen standing silently beside it.

His heart started to race.

* * *

The clouds rolled across the sky, stars peeping through the gaps. With no moonlight, the Ottoman sentries never saw the Wallachian soldiers who crept through the forest. An owl hooted, then another, then another.

The brightness came when torches flared in the darkness and hooves that had been muffled by rags thundered to life. Battle cries split the air as Vlad's men charged into the Turkish lines, setting fires and cutting down men. Then horses wheeled and the Wallachians retreated into the darkness of the forest. Screaming started from a different direction.

Radu's head snapped back and forth, trying to ascertain where the attack was coming from, but it was all confusion. Shouts from the Ottoman forces added to the din.

Mehmed! He remembered the strange rider. *He's going for the Sultan!*

He ran down the line of tents, sprawling as he tripped over a rope. He scrambled up.

"Protect the Sultan!" he yelled. "*Kaziklu Bey!* The Impaler is here!"

Shouts up ahead. The clang of steel and screams choked off in a gurgle. Radu realised he was completely unarmed and slowed his headlong dash. *It would be suicide to race into a fight so unprepared...*

But he rallied. Failing to save Mehmed would carry a fate worse than death.

He saw the rider, laying about with sword and spear, dealing out death to any who stood in his way. The savagery would have been enough to convince Radu of the identity of the man even if he hadn't seen his face. Vlad's eyes burned with hatred, roving back and forth as he killed viciously, searching for his goal.

Snatching up a spear from a fallen soldier, Radu hurled it at his brother. He missed by yards, but the action was enough to gain the Prince's attention and spur his horse towards Radu.

A heavy shape knocked him sideways and into the shadows. Vlad thundered past then wheeled to keep searching for the Sultan, ignoring his assailant. Radu struggled to his feet, pushing away the man who'd saved him.

"Hurry," he huffed. "He is trying to kill the Sultan!"

"Radu?"

The voice made him stop. It was familiar, and spoke his name as a question not to confirm his identity, but almost as if it wished him to recognise it.

"Radu, it's me, Meric. The janissary."

There was no light from the moon to shine on his features, but when he said his name Radu placed him. He'd seen the soldier from time to time. The man seemed to think Radu should know him though, and that irritated him given the situation. "Hurry then, Meric!" he exhorted. "The Impaler is trying to kill the Sultan. Let's go!"

He took off at a run, following the sound of hoof beats and screams.

* * *

"Meric, let's go!" he heard Gwyn hiss. They had heard whispers of the imminent attack. Deserting to the rear was impossible, but taking advantage of the confusion in the advance had been achievable. Joining those who were to break through the Turkish lines, they merely had to dodge their own side. Once in the camp, they encountered few of the enemy because of Mehmed's strict orders that no soldiers were to leave their tents.

Vlad had too much of a head start, however, so it wasn't until they were near the heart of the camp that Meric left Gwyn behind to catch up with him.

That was when he saw Radu.

In the light of the torches, dishevelled and looking frantic, he was still as beautiful as ever. He saw Radu throw a spear heroically at Vlad. The fact that his aim was atrocious did nothing to lessen Meric's esteem for him. Without thinking, he flung himself across the path of Vlad's horse to save the man he loved instead of taking advantage of the distraction to kill the man he hated.

And all for nothing.

"He didn't even remember me," he said, looking after Radu.

* * *

It took all Gwyn's composure to be grey, a ghost, invisible. She flitted from shadow to shadow, trailing her companion who sought to follow Vlad into the Ottoman camp.

"Meric! What are you doing?" Gwyn hissed, emerging from the pool

119

of darkness beside a tent and tugged on his arm. "Are you going after Vlad or not?"

She was playing a dangerous game. Once she'd seen she couldn't stop Meric from chasing the Prince, she stuck close, hoping that Vlad would lose them and no attempt on his life could be made. *Maybe I should ditch Meric and try to find Alina myself.* But she needed the protection his presence and fighting skill afforded her. She had no clue as to where she might find refuge in the army camp, or back in Târgovişte, without being harassed if she went alone.

"Come on." The soldier turned abruptly and set out away from the fighting. Gwyn hurried after him, cursing silently at fickle men who didn't explain what they were doing. She didn't dare risk speaking aloud and drawing the attention of the Ottomans, most of whom still huddled in their tents, raging against the orders that forbade them to venture out to fight or flee.

They were almost on the outskirts of the camp, dodging and weaving between tents and picket lines when Gwyn thumped Meric in the back to get his attention. He whirled on her but she couldn't see his expression in the dark. She whispered, "Horse?"

They were headed for the trees fifty yards to the north of the camp. To their right Gwyn could hear a large animal munching on grass. The mount must have lost its rider and fled the battle, but stopped to eat once it had calmed down.

Meric made a "hmph" noise and they changed course. Gwyn slowed and let the janissary approach the beast. He spoke quietly and held out his hands so as not to startle it. The horse stopped its grass cropping and raised its head, regarding him warily. Meric took the bridle and led it to Gwyn. She murmured and stroked the horse's nose, letting it snuffle at her.

Gwyn took Meric's hand and pushed it under her elbow, indicating she wanted a hand up. He gave her a boost then mounted the horse behind her.

They stayed low in the saddle, wary of catching a stray arrow. The action sounded several hundred yards away on both sides. Vlad's multiple attacks were succeeding in creating confusion.

By the time they were well away, carefully skirting around their own camp, Gwyn finally felt safe to ask, "What happened?"

Meric grunted, which she took to indicate that he didn't wish to discuss it. This infuriated her.

"Come on, I chased you into that bloody camp. You were hell bent on killing Vlad, then you just gave up? Not that I'm complaining; it was a suicide mission and I would have been lucky to try magic us out of there, but an explanation would be nice." She didn't bother to keep the sarcasm out of her tone.

"We got out, didn't we?" he muttered. She could feel how tense he was behind her. The horse clopped on, unconcerned.

"Yes, but only by going the wrong way first!"

"Forget it!" he snarled.

"No!" She tried to twist but they were wedged together in the saddle. It was strange to be so close to someone physically, but without any physical attraction. She found his closeness comforting even though he was annoying the crap out of her.

"Look, I know you don't know me that well, and I don't know you, but we seem to be sticking together for now so we should try to be honest!" *That's a bit hypocritical.*

"I said, forget it." He growled. A horrible, cynical part of her mind reminded her that his oath not to hurt her wouldn't stop him from shoving her off the horse and abandoning her in the dark. She subsided and they rode in silence—picking their way slowly along the dark road.

TWENTY-FOUR

1460 AD

"Oh Gracious One, are you feeling alright?"

The camp had been quiet for some hours now. As the morning sun broke over the horizon, a sigh of relief was breathed by those who were clustered in Mehmed's tent. Smears of dirt and blood marked some faces, painting the concerned masks they wore.

The Sultan himself was immaculate, not having taken part in any fighting. A quick-thinking guard had heard Radu's warning and corralled men into a silent wall of steel around Mehmed's tent. Their efforts were unnecessary as a rampaging Prince Vlad targeted the Grand Viziers' tent by mistake and was forced to retreat before a kill could be made.

"Told Mahmud his ostentation would get him in trouble one day," a voice muttered—Radu couldn't tell whose. He would have sacrificed a thousand Grand Viziers to save the Sultan, so he didn't care.

"Gracious One?"

Mehmed's head snapped up, eyes hard. Radu knew that this campaign had been more challenging than the Sultan had anticipated; advancing in Vlad's wake had meant burnt fields, poisoned wells and no livestock that could be pilfered to feed the army.

But the ruler who had besieged and captured Constantinople would refuse to be deterred by this annoying Wallachian wasp. Radu knew Mehmed would crush him, despite the sting, despite the losses of thousands.

"Tell the men to advance," Mehmed ordered. "I want to see Târgoviște laid siege to before nightfall, Inshallah." He brushed off any solicitations of assistance and stood, glaring at his commanders.

Dismissed, with the others, Radu hastened to get ready, ordering his horse and armouring up. He wanted to be there at his brother's downfall.

* * *

There was a terrible stench as the Sultan's party drew closer to the Wallachian capital, and a low, dull droning filled their ears. Radu's nose wrinkled and he pulled his scarf up to cover it. He wished he had a few drops of scent to perfume the fabric and cover the tangible smell that filled the air.

"Never smelt a dead body before?" It was the general, the one who'd vetoed Radu's input the day before. Grim-faced but with a small, twisted smile, he seemed to be taking a perverse delight in Radu's discomfort.

Radu ignored him and stopped squirming in the saddle. He'd seen dead bodies plenty of times before but always made the effort to keep distance between himself and them, fearing disease.

This smell, though… He was breathing through his mouth now, as the horses approached the last bend in the road. *There must be quite a few dead bodies to create a stench this bad!* Several flies batted his face and he waved them away. *And what is that noise?*

"Allah save us!"

Radu wasn't sure who exclaimed it, but even the battle-hardened generals echoed the man. The source of both the noise and the smell became apparent. Radu's mind boggled at the scale.

It… It's like a field of scarecrows. There must be thousands of them!

Skewered like pigs and left to rot, the bodies of fallen Turkish soldiers had been impaled and arranged on the outskirts of Târgovişte. Many had been part of the advance forces sent ahead to secure the way for the Sultan. Radu was revolted to see others were in a greater state of decay; bloated flesh and features swollen beyond recognition. He gagged, and took shallow breaths, head dizzy.

He wasn't the only one affected. A sheen of sweat covered many pale faces, and the Sultan himself lifted a shaking hand as if to ward off this hellish sight. Flies swarmed around the hand briefly, then returned to their corpse-bothering.

"The gates, Gracious One!" An advance rider galloped down the road from the city, scarf over his mouth like Radu. His horse reared as he pulled it to a halt. "The city is abandoned, oh Gracious One," the scout reported, fighting his mount's eye-rolling panic at the smell at the dead. "The gates have been left wide, and no living soul remains."

"The Impaler is g-gone?" Mehmed's voice shook, his iron control gone.

"Yes, oh Gracious One."

Radu could have cried with relief when the Sultan gave the order to turn back. He managed not to spur his horse into a gallop, but it was a near thing. Instead, he jostled with the generals and viziers as they followed the Sultan several miles back down the road.

Ugh, I want a bath, with myrrh and sandalwood, and slaves to scrub my skin and comb my beard and hair. I want fresh air and mint tea and I never, ever want to smell a dead body again!

Twenty-thousand was the count given as Mehmed's advisers clustered around him. No one particularly wanted to check—the figure was taken from the note discovered pinned to the corpse of Hamza Pasha. The Bey of Nicopolis was impaled on the highest stake amongst those adorning the city gates, as befit his high rank. At least, the note said it was Pasha. Radu clutched his chest when he heard how the silks worn by the dead man were rotting away along with the flesh. Skin that had once bloomed with vibrancy—everyone knew what a healthy, active man the Bey had been—was now grey and tight, stretching in a macabre yawn on a lolling head.

"We must go back," Mehmed muttered. A slave proffered scented moist towels but was brushed aside.

"My Sultan," the general who disliked Radu stood before Mehmed and claimed his attention. "We need to press on. The Impaler will have retreated into the mountains. We need to make sure he cannot reclaim the lowlands."

"We must go back!" The Sultan was wild-eyed. "He is not a man, he is a monster! Twenty-thousand—impaled on spikes and left for the crows for months and months!"

Radu saw the twist of the general's lips and remembered that the death count had been higher in Bulgaria. *Of course none of us saw that first hand.* He sat up straight and blew air out through his nostrils to clear them of any residual scent.

"Gracious One, your generals are correct," Radu stated, setting down his tea cup. Eyebrows shot to the ceiling as both Radu's nemesis and the other generals—most of whom had been milling like frightened chickens—looked astonished.

You think I'm a dandy, but even I know how to pick my battles. Something grim bolstered him as he went on. "How will it look if the greatest war leader the world has ever known," (*sorry Alexander*) "was to retreat from a defeated city? Târgoviște is yours for the taking." *Mine for the taking.*

"Defeated!" Mehmed was enraged. "It's a graveyard! How can I ask the men to fight after seeing this?"

"Because you *are* the greatest war leader in the world." Radu stood and pointed respectfully at the ceiling of the tent. "Is that not right, brothers?" He didn't wait for them to answer but ploughed on. "Allah's warrior on Earth, the man who conquered Rome of the East, the man who is building the greatest Empire ever to be seen!" His voiced deepened as he strengthened his rhetoric. "This is but a brief setback; we shall show the world that even death itself does not frighten you. We shall flush this pesky Prince out of his mountain cottages—he is a barbarian who has turned his back on civilisation, and on Allah, and he shall not go unpunished."

Most of the men in the tent stared at him, but the main general was not so easily flustered. "It shall be as you wish, oh Gracious One," he deliberately contrasted his tone to Radu's, speaking quietly. "We shall crush Vlad Dracula and all Europe will quail before you."

Carrot and stick. Radu hid the smugness from his face. He watched Mehmed gradually pull his emotions back under his skin, mouth twitching and eyes becoming distant until his face was still and his composure regained.

They would not be retreating today.

TWENTY-FIVE

2623 AD

Michelle found the conference speakers interesting. She formulated several intelligent questions in case she was called upon, but happily, attention did not stray her way. Sitting at the back of the lecture hall she pretended to take notes on a small computer. She didn't see Jay at any of the talks that morning, or even when she slipped out of the hotel to find some lunch and look for Brrrys.

She found no sign of the Mayash in any of the cafés or shops close to the New Opera House Hotel. Her guise was one of seeking something cheap to eat, so she didn't search too long. *Probably gawking at tourist sites,* she chuckled as she selected an ant-based protein smoothie flavoured with tropical fruit syrup. Many insect species flourished in this harsh climate and she wondered how the proposed changes would affect their habitats.

Afternoon sessions were not as long as the morning ones, so once finished she opted for a swim in the hotel pool. It was underground, like most of the building, but with a fantastic holo-relief to give the impression they were paddling under the old bridge that had once graced the harbour here. Again, she noticed a level of conservatism that would have been unheard of on Vivaldis, or even European Earth. Bathing costumes were the norm, so she donned a black one-piece rather than swim naked as she would have preferred.

"Ah, there you are Michelle!" Jaysen Fitz looked as handsome in a swimming costume as a suit. Her smile of appreciation was not lost on him. *Hmm, he's attractive and he knows it.* The realisation was a decided turn off, though she made sure such sentiment was not visible.

"Hi Jay," she paddled to the side of the pool. She was a strong swimmer but she acted hesitant and smiled gratefully when he reached a strong arm down to assist her out.

"How have you found the talks so far? I can't attend them all—there is so much to take care of, but my assistant makes sure I get the gist."

"Oh, they're wonderful! I can't thank you enough for all you've done for me." *Don't gush too much,* she cautioned herself.

"Like I said, it's my pleasure." They strolled around the poolside and sat down on some lounge chairs. She towelled herself off while they chatted.

He queried her background. She was ready with a false story, decked out with plenty of real detail: her orphaned childhood, study at the University of Vivaldis. He admired her self-advancement. "I've always had such a large family." He rolled his eyes. "Aunts, uncles, cousins, siblings, in-laws. In some circles, there's almost no one I'm not related to or connected to in one way or another." He said it simply, without boast, and she wondered if he found all these relations and connections onerous.

"Must be nice, always having someone you know?" she ventured.

"Ha! Yes and no. Family is supreme in my parents' eyes, but there are so many obligations. I envy you, having the freedom to do as you wish." He looked wistful.

"Well, you'll have to come and visit me on Vivaldis—take a break from them for a while," she smiled. "Or do your family extend there too? I suppose they might well. It is the place to be!"

He bristled then covered it with a smooth shrug. "Oh, I don't know. My family don't like to leave Earth. I don't know how I'd go with all those aliens there."

"What do you mean?" she laughed. "Technically you'd be the alien, having not been born there."

"You know," he smiled conspiratorially. "Non-humans. I've heard there are quite a few, for a supposedly human planet."

Michelle quelled her instinct to punch him in the face. *Must get my aggression checked.* She mimicked his shrug and rolled her eyes in return. "Oh you know, they're everywhere. What can you do, though?"

"Not here they're not." He leant closer and lowered his voice. "What if you could do something? Earth is a human planet. Maybe if more leadership was shown, things might change. But the people in charge have to be told."

She nodded slowly, as if his words made sense. "That's true. But how could I do that? I'm just a research student. And besides, I saw a Mayash on the same flight in here as me. So there are some, even if they are just tourists."

A sneer painted his features. "The cat ones. They might be tourists now, but wait until they start coming in hordes, wanting to live here like they do on your planet. And there are others. Wouldn't it be better if they started regulating who could come and go, and give preference to the ones who deserve to live on Earth and Vivaldis?"

She shrugged again. "I guess so. I mean, you're right." *No, you're not, you bigoted piece of filth.* "But there isn't much I can do about it. Wish there was." Behind her projection of reluctant apathy, her attention was tuned to him like a tight-beam scanner.

He sat back and gazed at her thoughtfully. "You never know, maybe there is. All it takes is the right people to make a world great again."

"You think? I do hope so. Hey, do you want to grab something to drink?" She signalled the robot waiter who rolled on over from the bar. "I'm really enjoying the juice here."

He shook his head and climbed to his feet, well-muscled torso gleaming in the artificial sunlight. "I have to go. Duty calls! Maybe you'd be free for a real drink later?" That charm was in play again as he grinned down at her.

"That'd be great!" She scrambled up. 'Where shall I meet you? In the lobby?'

"How about I come to your room at eight? I have a VIP pass up to the rooftop bar. The view is incredible at night. Wear that sexy dress again." Winking, he turned on his heel and strolled away.

That seemed like a definite come-on, she mused as she sat back down and sipped her juice. She sighed. *The things I do in the name of duty. Wonder if I'll be able to claim that dress on expenses?*

TWENTY-SIX

1460 AD

"Get down!" Meric hissed, yanking Gwyn by her dress. She sat down with a thump and glared at the soldier as he peeped through the bushes.

A troop of armed horsemen trotted past on the road below. Only after the last jangle of harness had faded in the distance and birdsong had resumed did they relax and look at each other.

"They're heading away from Târgoviște, not towards it," Gwyn muttered.

"Mmm, but they were packed for travel, not fighting," Meric replied.

She frowned. "They had weapons and all."

"Yes, but only a few within easy reach. The rest were stowed for easier transport by the horses and none were in heavy armour. They aren't looking for the Sultan. I'd say they are heading to the mountains."

"But why? Vlad's been inflicting all sorts of losses on the Ottomans. Why run away now?"

Meric shook his head. "You saw the rag-tag bunch of 'recuits' we were thrown in with. His knights have been inflicting losses because he strikes like lightning then disappears. Disease and not enough food will be taking their toll but you saw but a fraction of the men the Sultan has to command."

"Oh." There wasn't much she could say to that. It had been several week of her time since she had seen Alina, and disillusionment was passing into despair. Escaping conscription was one thing, but now they were on the road, directionless, and having to hide from every passer-by. She'd been mentally touching the pocket watch for the last few hours, reassuring herself that she could make a jump. *Maybe I should forget about*

Alina… She sniffed a tear away, feeling pathetic.

It didn't help Gwyn's mood that they hadn't eaten much since they skipped out of camp last night. Reminded, her stomach chose that moment to rumble. Meric started, then realised what it was.

"What?" Gwyn crossed her arms over her stomach defensively. "I'm hungry. Apple and cheese doesn't quite cut it, sorry."

He laughed quietly. "You'd make a good soldier," he said, "always thinking about your stomach."

She half smiled at this. His good moods were sudden and fleeting, but infectious all the same. "I don't know about that. Despite everything you've been teaching me, I can't even fight."

"You've killed men."

"They were lucky hits." Her hands clenched.

"First time is the hardest." He tensed and peered down from their hiding place at the road. "Hooves," he said, all seriousness again. "If this keeps up we'll have to wait until nightfall to move." He glanced back at their horse, munching contentedly on grass a little further up the glade. They'd stripped the Ottoman finery from the saddle and bridle but nothing could disguise the quality of the breeding. An Arabian, high-shouldered and proud-necked, with black hair that should have been glossy but instead was mud-spattered and mussed. Neither Gwyn nor Meric wanted to abandon the animal as a means of transport, but it would hardly blend in if they were to pose as refugees and not deserters.

Gwyn peeped over his shoulder then gasped as her heart leapt.

"Shush!"

"Look!" she whispered excitedly. "It's Vlad. And Alina!"

Alina was riding right up the front with Vlad, stone-faced. Vlad looked cheerful and Gwyn's lip curled. Nicolai rode behind them, looking disgruntled as his eyes swept over everything. Knights and men-at-arms followed. This was the largest party she'd seen today and she saw that Meric was right. They were abandoning the capital and heading for the mountains. *Of course!* She recalled Alina mentioning the citadel near Poenari, on the River Arges; a defendable retreat, haunted by the ghosts of those who had died building it.

"This is our chance!" she turned to Meric, eyes alight.

"What? Are you mad? There are a hundred knights down there!"

"I'll jump—I can do it! I'll grab her and jump to another day, then come back for you. Just stay here!"

"You'll never get close!" He grabbed her by the shoulders.

"I'm not leaving her with him!"

The lead horses were almost level with their hiding spot. Gwyn wrested free and pushed through the bushes, sliding down the small slope. Vlad had already passed but Nicolai reacted and drew his sword. Her eyes widened, knowing that she could walk through time but not through sharp metal.

From behind her, a blood-curdling cry made everyone on the road jump. Gwyn saw Nicolai's head snap up and Vlad whirl his horse, drawing his sword in one swift movement. Spears and bows raised as knights and soldiers searched frantically for the attacker.

Meric was evident the next instant, screeching horrific war cries and waving his arms as he leapt from the bushes. He jumped up and down at the top of the small slope and hollered in Turkish Arabic.

Gwyn moved. She bolted towards Alina, ducking behind Vlad's stallion and praying the beast wouldn't kick her. Inspiration struck and she laid hands on both Alina *and* her horse, then she activated the timepiece with her mind. The blue haze rose up around them.

Flick!

* * *

She jolted backwards as the horse reared but Alina stayed on. Her short scream matched the mare's frightened whinny. Gwyn landed in mud and rain pelted down on her face.

"Dammit!" The cold thick mud smeared up her forearms and elbows and with it a burst of fatigue hit her.

"Woah!' She heard Alina cry out. It was hard to see in the dark and the rain, but the horse and rider were right in the middle of the road.

"My lady! Alina!" Gwyn hauled herself up and went to grab the reins.

"Stay back! My husband is the Prince and if you lay a hand on me he will skewer you alive!"

"My lady! It's me," she shouted and managed to catch the bridle. "It's Gwyn! It's okay!"

"What?" Alina was addled, probably by the time-jump, the sudden change from day to night, and the rain. "Gwyn?" She peered down and furiously wiped water from her face.

"Just hang on!" Gwyn stroked the frightened horse's face and blew air gently into its nostrils. The animal shied away, as distressed as its rider, but gradually calmed enough for Gwyn to lead it off the road and under the trees. They went slowly to avoid slipping on the muddy slope. She wiped her hands on her skirts and used her scarf to dry her face as best she could.

"Gwyn, how did I get here? Where is Vlad? How is it you're here? You disappeared last year—I thought you were dead!" Alina got down off the horse and looked about nervously. The interlocking limbs of several great trees meant that this small patch of grass was relatively dry. This helped calm her frightened mount, though the lady herself just looked confused.

"It's hard to explain." *What are you doing? You need to get back to rescue Meric!* She quelled her skittish thoughts and reassured herself that time wasn't an issue. "I have a kind of magic that let me get away from Vlad. The Prince. We are still in the same place, but in a different time."

Alina gaped.

"Look," Gwyn pressed Alina's hands with her own. "Trust me. We will escape this time, I promise." *Please don't bolt.* "Just stay here. Please?"

"I... I will stay here," Alina stuttered, dishevelled but beautiful. Gwyn's heart filled with admiration for the lady's self-control. Gwyn leant forward and kissed her on the lips, pressed her hands once more and said, "Good. I won't be long."

She left the lady astonished and squelched back onto the road. The rain poured down. *Argh, why isn't there some way of telling what weather you are going to jump into?* She was soaked to the skin and tired. *At least this thing is getting charged. Okay, concentrate.* She faced down the road and stepped carefully to the spot where Meric would be.

Taking a deep breath she tried to ignore her saturated skin and pushed back the hair that stuck to her face. The familiarity of the moment she was in and the one she'd jumped from stood out in her texture of the timeline, like bumps in a piece of long string. She thought herself along to just after both bumps, holding the moments in her head, one in front and one at the back. It made her brain ache, and she was afraid of mixing the moments up. She concentrated fiercely and reached...

Flick!

* * *

"Kill him!"

When Gwyn had stupidly given away their position, Meric knew he'd have to improvise. Not wanting to make a target of his back, he'd run *towards* the horses when someone fired an arrow at him. Then he'd leapt up and down like a madman when he saw the blue cloud envelope Gwyn and the lady.

He'd refused to let any hesitation show, but at the back of his mind he wondered if Gwyn might not reappear and he would be cut down, or worse, captured and slowly tortured to death.

Something hit him hard in the back and he felt that stomach-wrenching lurch. He was pushed forward as an arrow whizzed through the space where his head had been.

Blue filled his vision, clearing as he hit the road with his knees and outstretched hands. The cold of the rain filled him with shock and he gasped with nausea. His head spun. He realised that Gwyn had knocked him over but bounced off him when he hit the mud. She lay on the road. Her hand rose in a feeble attempt to fend off the weather.

"Gwyn? Gwyn!" He looked around. It was night and there was no one else in sight, not that that meant much, given the poor visibility. Gwyn tried to get up, slipped and groaned.

Was she struck? He couldn't examine her properly for wounds but he felt gently.

"M kay..." she mumbled." He lifted her carefully and she flapped her hand back up towards their hiding spot in the dell. "Lina."

The rain lightened and he was grateful for the lull. Then it came down every harder and he hurried towards the cover of the trees.

"I'm okay." This time, Gwyn managed to sound more coherent. "You can put me down." Meric ignored her request but stopped when he heard the whinny of a horse.

"Gwyn?" A lady—the lady—spoke. A shadow detached from a larger pool of darkness.

"Here," Gwyn struggled weakly. "My lady, this is Meric. He helped rescue you."

"My lady," Meric spoke and the shadow that was Alina stopped. He continued. "Gwyn, we need to get somewhere dry. Can you take us to a time that it isn't raining? And maybe with a little light? Pre-dawn perhaps. It's going to be too hard to make a camp in this.'

"I'm too tired," he heard her whisper. "I don't know if I can."

"I don't understand," said Lady Alina, closing the gap and touching Gwyn's arm. "You said we had gone to a different time? How is that possible?"

Meric replied confidently, "It's a magic she has. She saved me from your Prince too, when he would have killed me." A gust of wind blew a shower of raindrops down through the leaves, and they all shivered. "Please Gwyn, you have to try, elsewise we'll catch sick or break an ankle in the dark."

He could feel her sigh. "Alright. Horse," she said.

Meric carried her to the horse, feeling herself tense as though steeling herself. He wondered how she worked the magic to move them through time.

He would have been surprised to know she was wondering the same thing as she searched for a time to go to. Past moments felt like Braille as her mind swept through them. But how could she know the weather? She didn't want to pitch them into sleet or snow, a thunderstorm or a freezing gale. She sank deeper into her meditative state, trying to find some clue in the computing mind of the pocket watch.

There were layers to it, and more intricate workings than those she'd previously accessed. Either she had more intuition than she realised, or the device had an unspoken artificial intelligence that was learning from her and supplied the information that she wanted. Or so she hoped. It was like speaking another language and only half understanding the conversation.

"Everyone touch," she breathed, her eyes closed. She felt Alina's hand grip her wrist, Meric's warm bulk against her and the wet hair of the horse.

Everything seemed incredibly heavy. The rushing feeling was slow to rise, but then finally...

Fl...ick!

Sunlight burst through her closed eyelids, painting them red. She passed out.

TWENTY-SEVEN

1460 AD

Gwyn's dream irritated her. Justin and Naomi were bickering as she tried to sleep, but when she went to tell them to shut up, her tongue refused to move and she was choking. Her hands flailed as her mother stood over her, mouth moving but no words came out, only grass.

Grass? Her eyes flew open and she gulped air. It was the horse that stood watching her, equine expression not flickering as she chewed. The bickering continued, however. She turned her head from side to side to see Meric and Alina sitting several metres apart. Her neck ached and she felt behind her—the saddle had been her pillow. When she sat up the ache ran up into her head and down her spine.

She groaned. She was still damp from the rain. "What happened?" She sneezed and her back went into spasms of pain. Both Meric and Alina rushed forward then halted, eyeing each other off. If Gwyn hadn't been in complete agony she would have laughed at the standoff, each party's face a portrait of fearful mistrust.

Meric stepped back and gestured graciously. Alina closed the gap to Gwyn, helping her to a sitting position. The pain eased to a dull throbbing that pounded her from temples to toes. She took a careful breath.

"What's going on?" she managed.

"This Turk—" Alina began.

"I'm not a Turk!" Meric retorted. They glared at each other until Gwyn broke in.

"He's not, actually. He was born in Wallachia and taken with the same levy that took Vlad. Um, the Prince." *Why do I care about his proper title?* But she didn't want to risk alienating Alina after going to so much effort to rescue her. Her previous fears played across her mind again.

"Well, then," the lady sniffed derisively. "This *man* who claims to have been born in Wallachia but fights for the Turkish army said he helped you take me from my husband."

Take. Not rescue. Gwyn's heart sank. "Yeah, that's right. He also saved me from being raped by Vlad." She didn't bother with 'Prince' this time.

"We cannot trust him," Alina hissed, not caring that Meric could hear. "He will try to ransom me—"

"Alina. My lady." Gwyn was abrupt. *Resolve this now.* "Do you wish to escape your husband, as you told me you did? He is a violent, sadistic monster, and with no heir he will not hesitate to be rid of you one way or another, you told me so yourself. Do you wish to be free?" *Do you wish to be with me?*

The sunlight through the green leaves played across Alina's face as her eyes darted from side to side. "Yes," she whispered.

"Then this is your chance." *Our chance.* "Meric can help us; he and I have a deal." *One I hope he will keep.* Gwyn tried to stand up but collapsed in pain again. "Argh! What the hell happened to me?"

"You fainted." This time, Meric did step forward, kneeling to assist. Alina drew back. The soldier lifted Gwyn carefully under the arms until she half stood, half leant against him. He wrapped his arms around her. "Just relax your body, and take a deep breath, then breathe out. Again. And again."

With each slow breath out he squeezed her spine. The tension in her back uncurled with each crack and the spasms eased. She managed to stand on her own two feet, but held onto his arm all the same.

"I'm so tired," she said. She looked about. They were still in the dell by the road. "When are we?"

Alina and Meric exchanged a glance. "We were hoping you could tell us," he said.

"The leaves are green and the flowers are well in bloom, so it looks to be summer," the lady volunteered. "We have not ventured out to the road yet to see if there are any who might tell us. It would look strange." She fidgeted and Gwyn realised that neither of them had wanted to abandon her. Whether it was because they feared what the other might do or because she was their ticket out of whenever they were, she didn't know.

"Um." She searched her mind and reached for the pocket watch.

She found nothing.

Her distressed look must have triggered concern in her companions, but she held up a hand to forestall their questions. She concentrated harder, not noticing she swayed as she did so.

There was... a faint connection. Like a dim light in place of the electrical surge she normally experienced. She tried to push along it but was bounced back, and the connection fizzed...

"No!" she jerked and stared at her left palm where the pocket watch lived. It was there, melded into her skin as living metal, but there was something wrong with the spiral. It wasn't wound down, it was... reversed.

"What's wrong!" Alina's voice broke into her thoughts.

"Nothing," Gwyn stated automatically. "I... I'm having a little trouble working out when we are. Give me a minute." Her stomach churned and Meric had to grab her as her legs gave way.

"Sit down.' He set her on the ground. As she sneezed again her eyes watered then wouldn't stop. She was panicking, she knew, but couldn't help it. Tears leaked out her eyes and dribbled down her cheeks and nose, turning her into a snuffling mess.

"Gwyn, what is the matter? Calm down!" They were on either side of her, their enmity forgotten as they crowded her with concern. She hiccupped and sniffed inelegantly, wiping the back of her hand across her face.

"It's not there!" she wailed. "I can't use it! We're stuck! I don't know when we are and I can't get us out!" *Get a grip, girl!*

But everything hurt too much; she was too tired and achy and damp and cold. "I want to go home..." she murmured pathetically. *You might as well say, 'I want my mother!' What would Michelle think of you now? Whimpering in a soggy heap on the ground!*

I don't care what she thinks! It was Michelle's fault she was here and there was little chance that the arrogant future-woman would be coming back to rescue her this time.

"Calm down," Alina ordered. Gwyn jerked her head up in shock.

"Give her a chance!" Meric intervened. "I'm sorry, Gwyn, I shouldn't have asked you to make that final jump. It was too much for you."

"That's done now." The lady's tone was stern. "We need to dry off and work out a plan or we might as well lie down in the mud and give up. We don't know when we are, so we will have to be careful, but at least it's not raining."

Alina was right, but Meric kept a protective arm around Gwyn and glared. Gwyn sighed and said nothing. All her energy was drained. She was happy to be told what to do, not caring how pathetic she was being.

Meric said, "This dell is protected enough from the road, especially with all this foliage. You ladies would be best to strip off and lay your clothes in the sun while I go and scout."

Alina bristled at his presumption but Gwyn laid a calming hand on her shoulder. "It's alright, my lady. We don't need to fear him."

Meric nodded and rose to leave. "I'll try to find some food and more clothes. We aren't far from Târgoviște, so there are plenty of farms nearby. I won't be gone long. I'll whistle three times when I return so you know it's me. If it's not me..."

"We'll hide," Gwyn managed to get up and shoo him away. "Go on, if I don't get out of these clothes I'm going to catch a cold." As if to emphasise her point, she sneezed again.

When he was gone, Alina rounded on her. "How do you know he won't sneak back to spy or even try to ravish us? Two ladies in a state of undress are more than enough temptation for any man, let alone an enemy soldier!"

"He's not the enemy!" Gwyn snapped back, dismayed that Alina mistrusted her judgment so much. She forgot that it had been months since her mistress had seen her and instead went on. "He saved me from *your* husband raping me and he risked his life to save you. He hasn't once been inappropriate to me—"

"He seemed pretty familiar just then with his arm around you, like a two-bit whore in the street!"

Gwyn's face hardened. She barely recognised her own voice. "Since coming to this godforsaken time I have been harassed, assaulted and almost raped *numerous* times by supposedly Christian men. I've tried to save you from that *monster* you call a husband, and the only man who has been decent is the 'enemy' soldier," she made quotes with her fingers, "who was kidnapped from his home, brought up in a different religion, and... and...' she couldn't think of a third thing. "And he doesn't even like women!" She blurted out even though she felt it was beside the point. Not liking women in bed was no guarantee of respect.

She shook her head, exasperated, and started to struggle out of her dress. After a few moments, Alina helped her. Gwyn assisted Alina in turn and they hung their garments over low tree branches where patches of sunlight came through from overhead. Judging by the sun and shadows it was late morning and quite warm. They reached their woollen shifts and after a moment's hesitation, Gwyn stripped that off too, squeezing out the residual water and lying down in the sun on the grass next to it so she could pull it back on in a hurry if she needed to. She felt extremely self-conscious but steeled herself. *Better a bit of embarrassment than pneumonia.*

The self-consciousness heightened when Alina copied her, and Gwyn tried not to let her eyes slide sideways. She felt her nipples harden when the lady slipped an arm around her, cuddling against Gwyn's back.

"What's wrong?" Alina's voice in her ear sent shivers down her aching spine. She intended to say how the pain in her body was making it difficult to relax, but the lady continued. "We'll warm up faster like this, like we used to do in bed."

"Mmm." Gwyn didn't trust her voice. She felt warm between her legs and hot where Alina's skin touched hers.

"Does he really like men?" the other woman wanted to know, her voice curious. "That is a sin.'

Gwyn blushed. "Ahem, yes, well, your brother-in-law Radu is also known for it. Seemingly they are more tolerant there. Where I come from people are more willing to accept that men love men, and women love women. Or both." She stopped her babbling.

They lay there for what seemed like forever, Gwyn getting warmer and warmer but unable to move. Alina's silence was killing her.

"Is that how you love me?"

Gwyn froze, but she couldn't ignore the question. She was grateful she was facing away as she said hoarsely, "Yes."

She felt Alina tense... then pull away. Both women sat up. Gwyn wanted to say something, to explain, to tell Alina that she loved her, and couldn't she give them a chance? The words choked in her mouth and her stomach threatened to climb up through her throat. Nothing showed on Alina's face, no disgust or horror, but the stiffness of her jaw as she pulled her shift back on spoke volumes to Gwyn.

She'll never let me touch her again.

Hurt fought with anger in her heart. *I stayed here for you! Risked my life to rescue you from that bastard. How dare you not... not...*

She wanted to beg but knew it was pointless. As she dressed herself words buzzed like bees in her skull, loud but threatening to sting her if she grasped them. So she ground her teeth and blew air out hard through her nostrils, stopping the tears before they could squeeze out.

It was several hours before Meric returned. Each woman was chastely dressed but with outer layers still drying in the sun. Meric wore a different shirt and had managed to find a couple of blankets, as well as some turnips.

"Everything's burned or looted," he reported. "I was lucky to find these."

"But where should we go?" Gwyn felt lost. Her plan had been to rescue Alina and simply jump into the future and... she didn't know what.

"Moldavia." It was Alina who spoke. Her tone was firm and decisive. "We will go to my brother."

Meric baulked. "Moldavia is hundreds of miles away! There could be armies between us and your brother, whoever he is!"

"He is the Prince!" Alina drew herself up haughtily.

Gwyn sighed and reflected that while Alina was timid around Vlad, anyone else who crossed her, like the priest back in Kronstadt, received the full force of her noble disdain.

"I thought Vlad was the Prince," Gwyn interrupted, not wanting them to start fighting again. Her head ached and the prospect of only turnips to eat made her stomach rumble. They both looked at her, taken aback.

"My lord Vlad is the Prince of Wallachia. Stephen is Prince of Moldavia. They are cousins," Alina replied shortly. "My brother arranged the marriage to bring about an alliance."

"So neither of them is Transylvanian?" This question had been bugging her for some time now.

Alina huffed with impatience. "My lord was born in Transylvania – I don't see how this is helping us!"

"Just curious." She was tired and over it all. "Whatever," she said. "You want to go to Moldavia, you can go to Moldavia." *I'll go wherever you go,* she thought, but she couldn't hide the bitterness in her voice.

"*We* will go to Moldavia." It was an unmistakable order, and both Gwyn and Meric bristled.

Alina ignored their reaction. "You took me from my husband, magicked me through time and left me without servants, soldiers or luggage, so you will take me to my brother in recompense."

Gwyn was gobsmacked. This wasn't the Alina she knew. Meric sputtered and shot Gwyn a filthy look, as if to say, *This is what you had me risk my life to rescue?*

But she couldn't deny Alina's logic, as highhanded as it was. She hadn't asked Alina if she'd wanted to be rescued. The first time they escaped Gwyn had influenced her with the help of the pocket watch. Maybe, away from Gwyn, Alina didn't want to leave Vlad? Or at least didn't want to leave her comfortable lifestyle, fraught with its own perils but predictable to a certain extent.

I should have found a way to ask her what she really wanted, rather than just thinking about how I wanted her...

"You don't have to stay," she told Meric tonelessly. "I'll take her. You can go wherever you want."

"Don't be stupid," he barked, "you wouldn't last half a day without me. Besides," his face softened. "Where would I go? I'm a traitor to my birth country, a deserter to my adopted one." He grimaced. "I'll be executed or conscripted if I'm caught. My only chance is to leave here and find work as a mercenary somewhere. Might as well be Moldavia. Besides, I said I'd protect you."

A moment of understanding flitted between them and Gwyn was grateful he wasn't abandoning them.

Alina watched impassively, and despite her bruised heart Gwyn appealed to the common sense she knew was there. "What if your brother sends you back to Vlad?"

Brushing stray curls back from her face, still achingly beautiful despite the dirt that patterned her skin, Alina simply said, "He won't. I won't let him."

Easier said than done. But she didn't argue, merely turned to the horse and started loading it up with their meagre possessions.

"Let's go to Moldavia, then."

TWENTY-EIGHT

2623 AD

The view from the rooftop bar was good, but not spectacular. Michelle made appreciative noises as Jay pointed out features of the town and constellations above. She supposed this view was impressive for someone who'd never been off world. He'd confessed as much, though by his tone she took it as an admission of pride, and she didn't bother to hide her incredulous look.

"Not even to the Moon?"

"Not even to any of the space stations!" He was emphatic.

"Fair enough…"

He chuckled and topped up her drink himself, rather than waiting for the robot to do it. Their ornate little table—made to look like old-fashioned wrought iron but most likely a recycled plastic composite—was near the edge of the balcony. The whole deck had been cut into the sail-like roof of the New Opera House Hotel, which had been modelled on the original building. It overlooked the water, looking towards the pillars of the long dismantled Harbour Bridge. There was hardly anyone else up there—clearly the VIP status meant what it said.

"You weren't raised here," he told her. "You can't understand how important Earth is. It is the centre, the home of all humans, whether they are born here or not. It is important that it takes its rightful place as leader of civilised space. True leaders don't need to go around checking up on everything. They have people who do that. Why leave a perfect planet to mingle with lesser beings?"

"True…" she pursed her lips as if pondering the value of his words, even as she wanted to laugh at him for his wilful ignorance. *I have seen the top of my anthill, what other anthill could possibly be better?* "I know I'm lucky to get to come here—so many students would kill for a trip to Earth."

"You could stay here!" he leant forward eagerly. She managed not to flinch from the alcohol on his breath. She had tipped half of her drink over the balcony when he wasn't watching. Most Vivaldans didn't consume alcohol. She didn't think it was even that widespread on Earth, but again here was a throwback to the past, like the conservative dress and hand clasping.

"I could? No, I have to write my paper and present it." She giggled. "What an idea, though!"

"Not just an idea, Michelle," he said earnestly and took her hand. "When I met you I couldn't believe you weren't from Earth. You seemed so normal, so keen to do good work here with the environment. You belong here. It's not all provincial towns like Sydney. Greater Milano has some of the best culture in the universe, and London is full of history."

"I do like history," she interjected before she could help herself.

"Earth is the richest planet for history. Where you come from, it's tainted by the influence of aliens. Here it's pure, but we need to keep it so."

He's insulted my planet, my friends and me in a few short breaths. But he thinks he's paid the highest compliment. That I am good enough to stay here! And all this from a spoilt git who has never even stepped out of his own residence! He has no idea how remote Earth is from civilised space. It's got history alright, amazing history, but in political and cultural terms it's still a backwater…

"You're right." *You're wrong!* "But how do we make that happen?" She spread her hands wide in a gesture of helplessness.

"I have friends," he tilted his head forward and raised an eyebrow, reclaiming her hand. "And my family is powerful. We have links and connections and influence, even off world. We are trying to make things better for Earth and for all humans. But you must know people on your planet, like-minded people, who will jump at the chance to improve their lot. No more being subordinate to insects, cats, turtles and slugs."

She stifled a gasp as her eyes widened. "Wow," she clenched her teeth into a smile. She'd never heard anyone speak such blatant and disgusting slurs about the other species of the Allied Planets. Not to mention it reinforced the mentality she'd encountered so often in her time travels; that human beings were superior to other organisms, rather than a privileged species whose cognizance and sentience gave them a duty to care for their environment.

Hang on. That didn't quite tally with the environmental front this conference presented. Unless that was all a sham? It seemed legitimate from the talks she'd attended that day. Or was it real but being used as a cover?

Realising he was waiting for her reaction she picked up her drink and took a decent swig. "I'd like to meet your friends if they can make something like that happen!" Her voice was louder than necessary. She chimed her glass with his and giggled again. He smiled in return, and she pretended not to notice a calculating look in his eyes. He was rubbing his thumb over the back of her hand. When he saw her looking he raised it to his lips and brushed it gently, eyes looking at her in question.

"Maybe you can meet them," he said. "But I'd like to get to know you better first. What say we take these drinks back to my room?"

* * *

She was surprised that his room was so many levels down.

"Don't you get a penthouse?" she asked playfully.

"It went to one of the guest speakers." Leaning close he brushed her hair back from her face, looking intently into her eyes. He hadn't made a serious move yet, just little touches and looks. It was somewhat unusual for Michelle. On Vivaldis people knew to ask clearly for sex, and answer clearly in return. It was basic good manners. But men in other times had done this ambiguous courtship dance too, so she knew how to read the signs.

They stepped out of the lift and down a lit hallway. He held her elbow—tighter than necessary—and guided her to a plain door, using palm-scan to gain entry.

The room was dark, and Jay stepped behind her. He wrapped his arms tight around her, and she forced herself to stay relaxed, despite her instinct to throw him off. *Either he has some non-standard tastes or this is not going to be a romantic interlude.*

The lights flashed on and she blinked. Brrrys sat strapped to a chair, unconscious, dark blue blood matting his fur. His tail was bound to the frame.

"What the?" Michelle jerked in shock, but Jay's arms held her tightly.

"Recognise him?" he hissed in her ear.

"What? No! What are you doing, Jay? I thought we…?"

"Don't lie!" He squeezed her tighter.

"Ow! What are you talking about? I don't understand. Why is this Mayash here? What's happened to him?" She imbued her voice with fear and confusion.

"You came here with him! You're a spy for those time-meddling agents! What did you think you would find?"

"I'm serious, Jay!" She struggled and managed to twist around to look at him. She looked at him pleadingly. "I don't know what you're talking about! Please! Why are we here? I thought you liked me!"

He grabbed her head and forced her to look at Brrrys. "How could I like someone who sleeps with aliens? You're disgusting!"

"Jay!" She stomped hard on his instep, the edge of her boot jabbing through his soft dress shoes, and whirled around as he released her. "You're crazy! I thought you were a nice guy! This is disgusting, bringing me here and showing me this! What is wrong with you?"

She stared hard at him, bewilderment on her face, and he wavered for a second. *Got you,* she thought.

"What is this all about?" she whispered. She placed her hand on his chest. Her eyes flicked to Brrrys in the chair and back to Jay, then she drew a short breath and placed her hands on his shoulders.

His expression softened and the line of his mouth twitched. Then his eyes hardened. "I can't let you leave…"

He wasn't ready for the crack of her forehead against his nose.

"Ugh!"

Michelle didn't reply, merely kneed him viciously in the groin. As he doubled over she assisted him to the ground face first and bent both arms behind his back. She knelt heavily on his spine. "What's the go, Jay?" she hissed.

"Let me up, you bitch! You don't know who you're dealing with!"

"You told me. Big powerful family, lots of connections, xenophobic attitudes. But you're about to tell me a lot more." She bent his wrist and elbow back hard and he cried out.

"Argh! You'll... get... nothing... Ow!"

"Fine." She flicked her knife out of her boot and showed it to him, then pricked the point under his ear. "You won't say anything as a corpse either."

"What?" His eyes went wide. "Are you crazy? What are you doing? Ow!"

"I'm killing you, Jay, unless you talk. You have three seconds to start. One. Two."

"No! No, no, no! What... what do you want to know? Please don't kill me!" Tears leaked from his eyes and she smelt urine. Her nose wrinkled.

"Who's who? Who's calling the shots, who's connected, and where? Talk fast, my hand isn't too steady when I've had a few drinks."

"My father! Frederick Fitz! He heads the Earth First Party. We own companies, charities, but it's all secret."

"Details!" she barked, activating the wrist com contained within her pretty bracelet.

He rattled off the names of various organisations and their key members. She was surprised how much he knew. Whether it was accurate or not was another thing, but that was for others to verify. When she'd garnered all the evidence she thought she'd get from him, she tore a long strip from the hem of her dress and bound his wrists and ankles together. She left him on the ground, face down and he twisted his neck to see her, demanding to know what she was doing. She ignored him and went to check on Brrrys. The furry blue Citizen opened a bleary eye and sighed as she cut his bonds.

"You aren't keeping very nice company," he muttered.

"No, it would appear not," she replied as she helped him stand. "What happened to you?"

"Not sure. Bag over the head. Knocked around. You were right about the xenophobia. They weren't very polite. Didn't ask anything though. I didn't give you away."

"No... I think they knew we were coming. Everything was a little too convenient on my side. Now what to do about you." She considered Jay on the floor and played the knife between her fingers. His eyes flickered with agitation.

"I told you what you wanted to know!" he pleaded.

"How do I know you didn't lie?" she lifted the knife.

"I didn't! I've implicated my whole family! Please!" His voice cracked and she noticed the stain of urine on his trousers grow.

"I can't have you calling security." She had already stripped him of his wrist com and done a quick pat down to ensure he didn't have any panic device concealed in or under his clothes.

He was so focused on her he didn't see Brrrys creep around quietly and whip his tail out with one swift crack. Jay slumped back to the floor.

"Thanks." Michelle put the knife away in her boot. "Come on, we have to get you out of here."

The Mayash panted. "My stuff is back at my hostel."

"Ok. I have to try to get you up to my room and clean you up, then we need to leave here, fast. This place is not healthy for off-worlders, human or not."

She hauled Jay up and placed his hand on the palm scanner. The door slid open. Two men stood with their backs to the door, guarding, but they obviously weren't expecting an attack from within. The blow Brrrys gave with his tail was weak, but it sent one man reeling. Michelle kicked the legs out from under her target and knocked his head against the wall, rendering him unconscious, then grappled with the other man.

"Watch it!" Brrrys wheezed as the man crashed past him. Michelle didn't reply, she never did in a fight. She merely kicked the man in the guts and then grabbed his skull to tap it against the floor. He slumped and was still.

"Aren't you ever afraid you are going to kill them?" Brrrys asked, pulling himself upright. His normally dark eyes were pale.

"Not usually," she replied, relieving the men of wrist coms, palm-sized stunners and ID. "Have had a lot of practice. Don't want to get arrested for murder. Not in this time anyway."

"No wonder you and Grrrel get along so well," he murmured as he swayed. She steadied him. "So bloodthirsty."

"You hold your own. Come on, stay with me." She kept talking quietly as she supported him on the way to the lift. It was a miracle no one saw them but it was late. Back in her room, she placed him in the shower and bathed him gently. The water made him wince awake, but he drifted off to sleep as she laid him in her bed, doing her best to bind his injuries.

* * *

She returned several hours later, after retrieving his bag from the hostel. She'd told the irritated security guard that their Mayash guest had gone to hospital from heatstroke and she'd been sent to gather his things. He hadn't wanted to let her in at first, but after she showed him the key crystal and handed over an anonymous chip for some credits, he relented.

She scooped up Brrrys' possessions then stopped briefly at a twenty-four hour medical centre on the way back to the hotel to pick up some first aid supplies. She sent off her blood sample at the same time.

As she crept along the corridor back to her room a quiet voice startled her. "Agent Michelle."

She had her knife at the speaker's throat in a second. She shone a light from her bracelet in their eyes. It was the Citizen from the lobby, the one who had been standing behind her. They held up their hands and said quickly, "I'm a friend! I'm here to warn you!"

"Warn me about what?" She kept her voice low.

"Your cover is no good; the Fitzes know you're a Time-Space Agent. They are suspicious as to why you're here and plan to deal with you and the Mayash Citizen," they whispered urgently and Michelle lowered the knife.

"Come inside," she ordered and grabbed Brrrys' bag with the first aid supplies in it. Once through the door, she was still quiet, motioning to Brrrys' sleeping form on the bed. "Who are you and why the warning? Who do you work for?"

"My name is Eddie, I'm a police officer. I was sent by Beijing—we received a tip-off from Vivaldis that two Citizens were seeking information on an unsavoury political group called Earth First. We've been monitoring them for months now, but could never find anything illegal. There's been an increase in activity since the scandal at your

Agency. We think they either had something to do with it, or are seeking to capitalise on it."

Michelle sat down. "Well, this would have been bloody handy to know before we threw ourselves into their hands at this conference. Why didn't anyone contact us and fill us in?"

Eddie ran a hand through their long, wavy hair. "EF have anticipated every search, every warrant, every plant we've tried so far. We took the chance that you might get further than us, and then we could make contact."

"They knew we were coming. You said so yourself. So that was obviously a crap plan." She didn't bother to hide her derision.

"We had a mole. That was the other benefit of not making contact earlier. We kept the tip-off very quiet and monitored the communications of all who knew. We caught the mole—they've been dealt with. But I had to warn you."

"You were too slow. Have a look." She guided Eddie silently to the bed and gestured to Brrrys' face in the dim lamplight. The police officer gasped quietly and asked, "What happened?"

"Ssh." They returned to the seats by the door. "Like I said, they knew we were coming. I need to get him out of here but he isn't well enough to travel by normal means. Maybe you can help us with that."

TWENTY-NINE

1460 AD

A brother and sister begged near the church, wary eyes on the road. They had their backs to the graveyard wall that ran crookedly up the hill. It was fortunate it was summer, for they were ill-clothed and had thin, dirty faces that made them look older and more careworn than their tender years should have allowed.

The girl spotted the small party approach and nudged her brother. He sighed and picked up his begging bowl, shamed but too hungry to hesitate. His sister had taken to stealing lately and he knew that if she were caught she would be beaten to death, what with food being so scarce. Then he would be alone.

The girl knew the risks she took but preferred stealing over trading their bodies for money or food. She'd seen more than one corpse in a ditch on the road as they fled the lowlands. No one cared what happened to a whore, especially not a child one, and if anything happened to him she would be alone.

This village played host to the refugees escaping Turkish and Wallachian armies alike. Many had never left the fertile river valley of the Danube, and felt hemmed in by the mountains that marched away to the west and north, but it had been the traditional retreat since Dacian times. This group approaching now was just another from whom the children might beg a coin or crust.

The girl thought these three looked less desperate than the usual creatures that dragged themselves up the road. The man, neck and head swathed in a scarf despite the warm sunshine, was tall and strong, and the two women appeared tired but not destitute. One woman rode the horse as though she was used to it, which spoke of money. The sweat-streaked beast was not any old nag used for dragging a plough.

"Some food, master, mistress?" The boy kept his eyes low, holding out the wooden bowl. "A coin?"

"Please." His sister was bolder; she stood and implored. "Our parents were murdered by Turks. We are starving."

"Please," her brother echoed. Her belly rumbled as if to emphasise her words.

The young woman who walked ahead of the horse strode on without looking at them, an anguished look on her face. The man exchanged a look with the horse-rider who pulled a small half loaf of black bread from her saddlebag, passing it down to the girl. Her hands were reddened and scratched, not callused like a commoner's. Her fingers were far softer than the bread crust as they brushed the girl's grubby hand.

Later, she said to her brother that the horse rider was the most beautiful woman she'd ever seen. He scoffed even after only the memory of the bread remained. It had been their last good meal before he started to suffer from first watery, then bloody, bowels. The girl cursed the bread, knowing nothing of dysentery and other water-borne diseases that marched through victims in times of war. The priest had refused them entry to the church, so they huddled in the lee of a gravestone up on the hill as the boy burned up in fever. He ended up lying in a pool of his own muck before passing into unconsciousness and then death, leaving his sister alone with every other refugee who was trying to escape the war.

* * *

Gwyn didn't comment on the lack of bread with their meal. Guilt crept like a spider from her heart down into her stomach, souring the taste of the pottage. Bread would have made it heavier. They'd left that village several miles back, choosing to camp in the forest away from the hordes, trusting to Meric's experience as a soldier to conceal themselves from desperate thieves. While Alina clearly expected him to protect them should it come to a fight, Gwyn insisted on half an hour of combat practice every morning and evening, forcing her tired muscles to learn grips, holds and blows. Meric accommodated her, even if he became impatient with her lack of skill. Alina mocked her and called her mannish, then complained because she was hungry and no one was readying the food.

"You have arms and legs," Gwyn shot back and Meric smiled. The relationship between the two women was rocky, strained by the rough conditions and awkwardness of getting to know each other on a different level to lady and maid. Alina also quite obviously avoided physical contact whenever she could, and Gwyn felt spurned.

They had been on the road for half a week, covering only as much ground in a day as walking pace could manage, much to Alina's disgust. The day after they left the village with the begging children, the lady put her foot down.

"I'm riding again today," she announced as they broke camp.

"You rode yesterday." Gwyn answered before Meric could, and kept her tone reasonable. Surely Alina could see the importance of conserving the horse? She was intelligent and sensible.

"It's *my* horse," Alina argued when Gwyn stepped between her and the horse. "Get out of my way, Gwyn."

"Stop acting like a brat," Gwyn snapped, surprising herself.

Alina slapped her. Gwyn went bright red and furious tears leaked out of her eyes. She turned on her heel and walked away, refusing to speak to anyone for the rest of the day.

* * *

Gwyn could tell Meric was exasperated. She knew he thought Alina was a liability but he'd confided to her that perhaps Prince Stephen would take him on as a mercenary. He also told her he was glad at least, aside from the one slap, she and Alina didn't brawl like some of the idiots he knew. She wanted to explain to him that this wasn't the real Alina, that it was the difficult conditions that had the lady behaving like this. Then she became annoyed at herself because she wondered if it was true.

"That's enough for tonight." Meric signalled the end of their practice session. He hesitated, and then said, "You're getting better. Well done."

Gwyn was startled then offered a tentative smile, the first all day. It fell as she heard Alina's snort of impatience.

"Oh, I'm sorry? Did we miss the bell to dress for dinner?" Gwyn's voice was bitter. All her fear and frustration threatened to pour out through the cracks. Meric had not pressed her about the time travel after she'd declared so adamantly that they were stuck, but every second she wasn't thinking about Alina, it filled her mind.

"Stop," Meric ordered. "Stop it, the both of you. You've been at each other's throats with your bickering. I'll help you cook dinner, Gwyn. Lady, you can clean."

Mutely, Gwyn started meal preparations. She fished out a pot and several bowls they'd acquired from a burnt-out cottage near Pucioasa. A scant bag of millet porridge and summer apples scavenged from orchards followed. Gwyn had been astonished that Meric and Alina had never heard of such traditional Romanian foods such as potato and mamaliga, but then she felt stupid and remembered that neither spuds nor corn had yet been introduced from the Americas, it was decades before Columbus' famed voyage.

As she poked twigs into the fire, she pointedly ignored Alina. It was easy. She knew exactly where Alina was all the time so she simply faced the other way. Her body was a compass, her heart the needle that swung true no matter which way she turned.

As she watched the moon rise that night, she shivered as the howls of wolves echoed across the hills. This countryside was raw and real, with storybook dangers as well as more mundane threats, like twisted ankles and bug bites.

At least I'm not trapped in one place like I was at Masada. Even learning how to throw a punch makes me feel like I'm achieving something. Just not the things I wish for.

A footstep from behind roused her from her self-absorption and she started to tell Meric to sod off, even though she knew it would be rude. She hated this surly version of herself but didn't know how to shake out of her funk.

To her surprise, it was Alina, not Meric, stepping daintily over the log and seating herself beside Gwyn. About to snap, "Yes?" she managed to halt her tongue and instead satisfied herself with a raised eyebrow. *You are like a puppy begging for a treat,* her brain told herself in disgust.

"I'll take first watch," the lady offered, picking up Gwyn's empty wooden bowl and fidgeting with it, working it round and round with her hands.

Gwyn raised both eyebrows at this. Alina had not stood a watch the whole time the three had been travelling together, declaring herself to be a noble, not a guard dog. Meric had rolled his eyes, his exasperation with the ways of the nobility clear. Gwyn hadn't argued, still caught between playing the maid and trying to win back Alina's affection.

"Gwyn..." the lady hesitated, then plunged on, "How you feel... it is wrong. A sin in the eyes of our Lord God."

Gwyn stiffened and half turned to look back at the fire to see if Meric was listening. He was nowhere in sight. *Must have gone to the loo or something.*

In a low voice she answered. "Love isn't a sin." But as she said it out loud, she wondered if she did love Alina. She didn't like her much right now, as much as she was still crazily attracted to her. *Maybe it's just physical?*

As if to confirm her thoughts, Alina touched her on the shoulder and Gwyn jumped. "That kind of love is meant for marriage between man and wife."

Gwyn didn't know if she wanted to kiss the other woman or shove her off the log. "Like the love between you and Vlad?" she couldn't keep the sneer out of her voice. *"That's* a greater sin than two people being kind and affectionate, man or woman." She stood and looked down at the source of her infatuation, wanting to say more. "Don't worry, my lady, I won't bother you again." Bitterness etched into her soul. "Watch until the moon is above that tree, then wake me. Enjoy."

She turned on her heel and managed not to trip over the log, but only just, ruining the effect. Her face flushed with mortification and her heart hurt. She brooded until she was swept into sleep.

* * *

"Gwyn, wake up!" Meric shook her out of her dream and Gwyn opened blurry eyes to look at him. She was used to sleeping on the ground again.

Her body had re-accustomed itself with surprising swiftness despite the weeks of sleeping in Alina's bed. Walking all day exhausted her physically, so where she slept mattered not. But surely she'd only just finished her watch? Why was Meric waking her?

"Huh? What's wrong?" She rubbed her eyes. Her dream had been so nice; Alina had declared herself wrong and come to Gwyn with those beautiful grey eyes and they'd…

She shook that thought away and looked around their camp. It was before dawn—the moon was close to setting. The starlight barely illuminated Alina's sleeping form huddled close to the dying coals, gleaning what warmth she could since she refused to let Gwyn sleep next to her.

"Shh," Meric put a finger to his lips. "I heard something."

Gwyn stiffened and looked about. "A wolf?" She couldn't zap them out of this quandary, though sometimes she felt a niggling in the back of her mind like the pocket watch was there, just out of reach. She surmised that she'd burnt out by attempting so many jumps in a row, with so many people. And a horse.

"No," Meric breathed in her ear. "Men. Too noisy for wolves. Go guard your lady. I'll pretend I've gone to make water and circle around."

"Don't—" *Don't leave us!* Gwyn wanted to whisper, but he'd already moved away. She crawled on her stomach to Alina and lay alongside. Normally she would have rejoiced at the chance to be near the other woman, but fear crept up from her stomach and squeezed her chest. She tried to breathe calmly, not wanting to wake Alina and have her cry out.

Several long minutes passed. Alina snored quietly and Gwyn almost snickered. *I don't remember her snoring back in the castle.* The waiting was threatening to make her hysterical. Unlike all the times when she had to act without thinking, this was far worse because her mind conjured up all sorts of possibilities.

Then she heard a crunch of twigs and she peered down the length of her body, seeing a man walk carefully into their camp. *Meric!* She breathed a sigh of relief but then realised the way the man looked about marked him as a stranger. She lay still, hoping he'd ignore them. The sky was getting lighter and it cast the man's face in shadow but she sensed something predatory as he bent over their supplies and rummaged.

A grunt from the trees made his head snap up, and the silence that followed was punctuated by Alina's soft snores. The man drew something from his belt, stepping to where the women lay. Gwyn waited till he bent down then kicked his knee as hard as she could.

"Argh!" the man yelled. Gwyn dived at his legs but he recovered and shoved her off easily. Gwyn rolled away from him and pushed herself up, shrugging her cloak away.

Alina woke and screamed, distracting the attacker. Gwyn circled away and yelled, "Hey!" in the deepest voice she could manage. She was hoping the dim light would disguise the fact that she was a woman and make her a bigger threat than Alina. It must have worked because he darted towards her quicker than she'd expected. Forgetting all Meric's training she turned to run and tripped over the same damn log from the night before… and went flying.

He was on her in an instant, and she struggled in vain against his much heavier bulk. He hauled Gwyn to her feet as torches burst into light—six, seven—she lost count as the campsite filled with people. Then a voice so indignant as to almost make Gwyn laugh, cut through the melee.

"Let go of me! I am Alina, wife of Prince Vlad Dracula, Voivode of Wallachia, and sister to Prince Stephen of Moldavia. Unhand me at once!"

Gwyn's head stopped spinning and she focussed on Alina standing by the campfire. The noblewoman was being held by a large man whose spectacular moustache and braided hair made Gwyn think of a Viking raider. His roar of laughter didn't inspire confidence, but his joviality made her hope he wasn't about to kill them.

"Oh pray excuse me, *my lady*," he chuckled. "I didn't realise we were dealing with *nobility*."

His companions laughed. They were rough men who searched the travellers' meagre luggage swiftly, exclaiming disgust over the poor pickings but making appreciative comments about the horse and Alina. Gwyn felt a stab of annoyance that no one thought her looks worth commenting on, then realised how stupid that was.

"This one's a fighter." Two men hauled an unconscious Meric into the circle of light, and Gwyn gasped. He had a bloody bruise on his head. The leader looked at him, then Gwyn, all the while holding a furious Alina.

"Looks like she's a feisty one too," he nodded. "Who are you? The Pope's mistress?" This got a laugh, and Gwyn rolled her eyes despite her fear. *Keep laughing. Better than raping and killing.*

"I'm her maid," she indicated Alina, then Meric. "And she really is the Prince's wife. He's our bodyguard. The Prince was sending us to Kronstadt when we were attacked by Turks and everyone else was killed. If you deliver us there he'll pay a good price to ransom us." She breathed deeply and concentrated on being calm and confident.

The leader cocked his head and pulled on his moustache. "Ransom, eh?" A few other ears pricked up. Alina looked furious but Gwyn glared at her, hoping she wouldn't give them away. The hope of ransom might keep them alive and unharmed and get them to where they wanted to go. Or where Gwyn wanted to go anyway.

I'm sure if I can spend more time with Alina she'll come around, then maybe…

She shook the impracticality of it away and ignored the fact that she still couldn't reach the pocket watch. Best to deal with the current problem.

"Ransom of Turkish booty," she continued on. "You know the Prince won a great victory against the Sultan near Târgovişte?"

The leader looked confused. "That was almost a year ago. The Turks have overrun the lowlands. Your precious Prince has fled to Moldavia last I heard."

A year ago? That meant she must have jumped them further forward than she'd intended. It was all a confusing memory—she'd just been trying to get them out of the dark and rain.

She bluffed. "He took the spoils with him to his cousin, Prince Stephen," she flicked a look at Alina and received a slight nod in return. "Prince Stephen is my lady here's brother. He would also pay for her safe return. Safe and *unharmed.*"

At that the leader released Alina's arm and she pulled free, hugging herself tightly. She still looked regal despite her mussed hair and travel-stained cloak.

"What my maid says is true." She managed to look down her nose despite the fact that she was shorter than the bandit leader. Her voice was haughty. "My lord husband and my brother will want to know I'm safe, and they will... pay." She coughed reluctantly over the final word.

Eager to capitalise on her companion's cooperation, Gwyn continued. "And with whom do we have the pleasure of travelling?" She spoke as if the ransom deal was a done thing, and these men merely chose to escort them rather than attack their camp before dawn.

This seemed to tip the balance in their favour. The bandits were either so puzzled at having the situation reversed on them or the idea of a ransom simply won them over. The leader shrugged and gave an elaborate bow.

"Petro Petrovich at your service... my lady," he chuckled again and bowed to Gwyn also. "If you'd follow me?" He remained bowed. Alina sniffed and Gwyn followed her—the man who'd captured her fell in close behind, and the implication was clear. They were prisoners, even if they were unbound. Meric was tied with a length of rope and thrown over the horse.

They stumbled half a mile through the woods before emerging into a circle of wagons well hidden from the road.

"Gypsies!" Gwyn heard Alina mutter in disgust, and Gwyn was fascinated immediately.

"You're Roma?" she asked her captor.

He grunted and pushed her towards a wagon. "We are Secani. From Little Egypt. Sleep here. No run."

Alina was bundled up behind Gwyn. "What about him?" Gwyn asked before they shut the door on her. They both looked at Meric who had woken up and was frowning darkly in the flickering torchlight, assessing his surroundings.

"Sleep under," the Roma man replied shortly, then turned to the man leading the horse and said, "Tie him up well. He looks like trouble."

When Meric didn't react Gwyn realised it had been said in a different language. *But I can understand it...* It seemed that the pocket watch's ability to translate was still working. She kept quiet, not wanting to give her new knowledge away.

"Meric, don't cause trouble," she called softly as the Roma tied him to the axle of the wagon. "They are going to ransom us." She had a thought, then concentrated, muttering the only Arabic she knew,

"Inshallah. Meric, can you understand me?"

He jerked. "You speak—?"

He received a clip to the side of the head from one of the Roma. "No talk!"

Gwyn was shoved inside the wagon. She heard the clunk of a solid wooden bar shutting them in. There was a scuffle outside, but it didn't last long. Meric must have trusted her enough to cooperate. *At least until I can work on a way to get us out of here.*

She didn't really want Vlad ransoming them. She even wondered if he would. Prince Stephen might be another thing, but if the two Princes were working together to marshal forces against the Ottomans, they couldn't avoid the former Prince while seeking the latter.

Either I get this damn pocket watch chrono-thingy working again, or I need to think of something else.

She turned to look at Alina, but with shutters over the windows and a barred door, the wagon was completely dark. "Alina?" she ventured. Maybe now they were thrown together the lady would thank Gwyn for her quick thinking and let her sleep next to her again…

"What?"

The sharpness of the tone cut her, but she tried again. "Are you alright, my lady?" Was that the slightest hint of pleading in her tone?

"No. I'm not. I'm filthy, sore, hungry, cold and tired. We've been captured by gypsies and my husband will *never* pay a ransom for me, but he might kill everyone here, so I suppose that's something. Even if my brother pays, if my lord is there, Stephen will hand me straight back to him and I won't get a chance to persuade…"

"Persuade what?"

"Never mind!" Alina snapped. Gwyn heard her lie down, and the lady's voice was muffled as she faced the other way. "This is all your fault," she said.

Gwyn felt miserable because Alina was right.

THIRTY

2623 AD

The hovercraft was docked in a cave in the sandstone cliffs that graced the northern side of the harbour entrance. They'd left the New Opera House Hotel under the cover of darkness, exiting through a service portal at water level and zipping over the bay on a small private hydrofoil. Michelle hoped Brrrys was strong enough to handle the move, knowing it was more important to get him away from this place than allow him time to recuperate. He woke when they zoomed into the cliffs and managed to board the hovercraft under his own steam.

"Captain Asha here will take you to the islands of Aotearoa," Eddie advised. "Earth First will be expecting you to run for the safety of a spaceport, not somewhere more remote. The mountains there are a good place to lie low while your colleague recovers."

"You have evidence now," Michelle argued. "Why not start arresting the pricks?"

"Some evidence." Eddie had accepted a copy of Michelle's recording of Jay's confession. "It needs to be verified or they'll slip away. Let the police do their work—I need you two safe as witnesses."

Michelle wanted to dispute this, but she bowed to the other Citizen's authority. She wasn't used to having to follow laws when she travelled through time, but she recognised she'd broken enough now and had to let the police do their work if she wanted to retain her credibility.

I don't have to like it, though. She itched to get back to her real work, chafing under the restrictions of the present. She felt guilty as she checked over Brrrys. The hovercraft slid out from its berth under the cliffs and whirred over choppy waves in the dark, its bow aiming for the sunrise. He had collapsed again, and as she accessed the ship's first aid facilities she realised his injuries were more extensive than she'd first thought. She didn't have enough knowledge of Mayash physiology to be confident of her treatment and didn't have the time or resources to educate herself.

Finally she thought he was as stable as she could make him. She spoke to Captain Asha and informed her that they needed to find a doctor as soon as they made landfall, preferably one who had experience treating non-humans. The Captain nodded but stayed silent, eyes never leaving the horizon that brightened by the minute. Exhausted, Michelle left the bridge.

Sleep overcame her as she lay in one of the narrow pods in the main cabin. Brrrys lay in another pod, asleep but groaning occasionally. She'd treated his head wound with antiseptic sealant, but was concerned he might have internal injuries. Bad dreams plagued her: she'd grown a tail like a Mayash but it strangled her while Brrrys laughed; Commissioner Hera fired her from the Agency and she was turned out onto the streets; the girl from the past, Gwyn, stood over her and declared she was a better Time-Space Agent than Michelle ever was, and when Michelle tried to argue that Gwyn had no training, the girl poked out her tongue and disappeared in a blue haze.

The sound of an alarm penetrated her consciousness and she tumbled out of the sleep pod in panic. Red light flashed through the cabin, and the warning siren told her something was wrong.

"What's going on?" She lurched to the portal that led to the bridge, staggering as the floor bucked beneath her.

There was no one at the helm.

"Asha? Asha!" Michelle hollered, casting about. *Where the hell is the captain?*

A groan from behind her sent her dashing back to Brrrys' pod. "Stay put!" she yelled above the sound of the alarm. "The captain's gone. I have to see if I can get this thing back up in the air!" The lurching of the ship was caused by the buffeting waves of the ocean outside. She could see the smash of foam on the helm window. The bow plunged under the dark green water before breaking free to gasp at the sky.

There was no sign of the captain. *She betrayed us!* Michelle knew she couldn't dwell on that now. She had to stop them from sinking.

Throwing herself into the pilot's seat, she looked at the helm computer, forcing herself to think clearly.

"Shit." A flurry of fingers over the screens and touch pads silenced the alarm but resulted in nothing else, only a computer message informing her she did not have permission to access the manual pilot. No sooner had that message flashed across the screen, another appeared in bold lettering:

VESSEL IN DISTRESS—SHIP STABILITY COMPROMISED.
PLEASE EVACUATE IN AN ORDERLY FASHION.

Well, that's bloody brilliant! Frantic tapping in an attempt to override the computer lockout failed, and with the next almighty crash of waves on the bow Michelle was pitched from the chair.

"Fuck!" she screamed. She could hear Brrrys groaning in the main cabin. *Okay, time to get out of here—where are the escape pods?*

She hauled herself back into the main cabin and scanned for their means of evacuation. Flashing red arrows had appeared on the swaying floor, pointing to the exit at the stern of the ship. She made it to Brrrys' side and helped him up, steadying herself against the next roll of the deck. His tail gripped her waist tightly, and together they staggered past the other sleeping pods, the food dispenser and the head to find...

An empty escape pod bay.

Michelle swore again. *Unhatched, tail-eating, treacherous*—her thoughts were cut off by Brrrys gripping her arm so tightly his claws dug in. His fur had puffed up with adrenaline but she knew he could collapse any minute...

"Back into the sleep pod!" she yelled over the groan of straining metal. Suddenly her voice echoed into a disturbing quiet, and the rocking and swaying were minimised greatly.

They looked at each other. "What's going on?" the Mayash whispered, eyes wide and diamond shaped pupils expanded with fear.

The hull groaned again, but with a deep resonance that vibrated even through the plastic flooring under their feet.

"We've gone under," Michelle breathed. They clutched each other, both trying to think of what to do. She could feel Brrrys shaking. She knew he could swim, but right now he was in no state to, and outside was the wild, restless ocean.

"Pod. Now." She helped him back into the main cabin. She pushed him carefully but firmly into his sleep pod. Grabbing their gear, she stuffed it in with him then raced to the kitchenette facility and punched in a function that spat out several packaged meals and beverages. She threw them in, ignoring Brrrys' cries of protest as the parcels hit him.

She slammed her palm on the hygiene niche that nestled between the food dispenser and the head. Everything was tiny and close together, as befit a transport vessel with limited space. This worked to her advantage. Every second she wasted meant the hovercraft was sinking further and further underwater...

She leapt backwards as sanitising liquid sprayed out and all over the floor. The ship began to tip, finding its heaviest point at the stern and slowly changing equilibrium. Michelle staggered the few steps back to the pod, taking a moment to tap on the computer that managed the capsule's capabilities.

While Asha had locked her out of the ship's main pilot computer, the captain had obviously not approached her sleeping passengers in case they awoke during her desertion. All sleep pods were independent of the ship's main systems. If the ship was damaged and hull integrity or life support systems were compromised, and escape pods were damaged or inaccessible, passengers or crew could lock themselves into the sleep pods, send out a mayday and await rescue. It was a last resort, but one that had saved many space farers and planet dwellers alike over the centuries.

For this reason, the pods were detachable, in the event that rescuers could not operate in a safe environment (such as the vacuum of space) to retrieve those stranded. Each pod could 'pop' its couplings and be removed from the wreckage of the ship to be brought on board another, with the ability to supply oxygen and liquid food via input channels.

Michelle popped the capsule, grunting with effort as she manoeuvred it out of its holdings and sliding it easily across a deck slickened with sanitising liquid. She angled it towards the stern.

"Are you going to get in?" Brrrys demanded. He sounded afraid.

"In… a… second…" She pushed and the pod gained traction and slid quickly. She managed to hang on and was dragged along with it as it crashed through the portal and into the empty escape pod bay.

The sleep pod was much smaller than the escape pod had been, but its weight was sufficient to alert the computer that something was there. The ship was fast heading towards vertical now, and several loose items from the main cabin began sliding and crashing down around them.

"Get in!" Brrrys yelled.

Michelle didn't waste breath replying, merely tapping in one last command to the escape bay computer and scooting in next to Brrrys. It was a tight fit but she didn't want to risk being separated. The lid closed with a hiss-snap.

"Sorry," she said as she was squished against Brrrys. He winced. They were practically standing now; the ship was almost on its end. She wrapped her arms around him in an effort to protect him as the whoosh of pneumatics ejected the pod out of the ship and down into the frightening deep blue of the open ocean.

Still, Michelle didn't relax. She didn't know if they made it out in time to be angled away from the hovercraft. She craned her neck to peer through the clear lid of the pod. The silence was eerie, broken only by their breathing in the confined space.

They began to rise. The stored oxygen and highly durable but lightweight materials of the pod meant it would float.

A dark shadow caused them both to flinch as the hovercraft came into view. Michelle held her breath and felt Brrrys tense as it neared, descending towards their rising pod. She couldn't judge distance underwater and with the distortion of the lid. *Will it miss us?*

Whoosh! With a stream of bubbles, the hovercraft plunged past them with only metres to spare, gathering speed as it dived towards a dark and watery grave. They spun in its wake but continued to rise slowly instead of being dragged down with it. The pod gained momentum and flattened as it reached the surface.

"What are you going to do? Even if we send out a mayday the Fitzes will be looking for it." Brrrys was hugging his tail to his chest, the very picture of a child trying to comfort itself, even though she knew that it was so he didn't squash it against the side wall.

"I'm going to send out a different mayday," she replied, reaching over him and into the tiny storage compartments behind. "One which I hope someone else will hear. And I'm going to sedate you. You'll be more comfortable."

"I'm not sure…" his voice trailed after she jabbed the pin-prick of sedative into his neck.

Sorry, my friend, I need to concentrate. She hoped he would survive. If they weren't rescued quickly it was likely his internal injuries would become far too serious to recover from.

Working awkwardly around him, feeling increasingly nauseated as the pod was subjected to the surface swell of the ocean, she managed to instruct the computer to emit a series of distress calls—not via any of the sophisticated channels by which normal transmissions took place. Her mayday was using a far more basic form of communication.

Sonar.

THIRTY-ONE

1461 AD

"Why are you bothering? They won't let us out." Alina's accused sulkily.

"I want to see," Gwyn replied as she peered through the window. The cart bumped over a rock and she was almost jolted off her perch, but she managed to hold onto the wooden bars.

"There's nothing to see."

"Sure there is. Trees and wagons and Roma dudes riding up and down the line." Gwyn was fascinated by their hosts. *Captors.* "We'll have to persuade them to let us out to ride or something."

"As if they're going to permit that. It's been days and they've hardly let us leave this wagon!" Scorn was evident but Gwyn ignored her. *We aren't walking so stop whinging! I wish I knew where we are, though. We've gone a lot further north than Braşov I'm pretty sure.* None of her history subjects had covered the Romani folk—all she knew is that they travelled throughout Europe and didn't integrate with non-Roma communities.

"Just wait and see. I hope Meric's getting on okay." The big man was nowhere in sight and hadn't responded to any of Gwyn's calls when the jolting of the wagon had woken her that first morning. She'd seen him at a distance when they were let out each evening to eat and stretch their legs but hadn't been able to get close enough to talk.

"I'm hungry," Alina complained.

Reminded of food, Gwyn sank to the floor and considered their surroundings. There was nothing to eat in the rattling, crowded wagon. Trinkets, rugs, cups and horse tack filled the small space, hanging from hooks and adorning the floor. Their nights were reasonably comfortable thanks to the rugs, and despite Alina's best efforts she couldn't avoid lying back to back with Gwyn due to the confined space. The girl had silently rejoiced—her success at persuading the Roma leader Petro to take them as hostages had given her a new boost of confidence.

As the days passed, however, that confidence was wearing off. Their guard refused to speak with them and what conversations she overheard amongst the Romani consisted of obtaining a new charter for safe passage through Hungarian lands. She didn't quite understand, but gathered that they'd fled slavery in Wallachia and were hoping to join their kin in the north of Transylvania. They were expert metalworkers, and she often heard them discussing offering their skills to King Matthias Corvinus in the same way their forefathers had once served Emperor Constantine.

I need to talk to Petro Petrovich again and see if I can persuade him to change direction... Unless he does intend to take us to Moldavia. Argh, I want to get out of here and find out where we are and what's going on!

As if in answer to her thoughts, the wagon rocked to a halt and she could hear voices outside. Before Gwyn could leap up to the window again the door opened. A Roma woman, bedecked in dull red and brown scarves and jangling earrings looked in imperiously at them, then gestured for them to exit.

"Come," she ordered, then rattled off a series of instructions to the man beside her, which Gwyn understood were orders to bring Meric to join them. They were led past other members of the clan. Gwyn counted twelve adults and several dark haired children who participated in the activities of setting up camp.

"Wait," she put a hand on the Roma woman's arm. "Can we please use the toilet? Um, make water?"

The woman said nothing, only lowered her eyes in disapproval to Gwyn's hand, who removed it hastily. The woman sniffed. "Make water this way. No run. Men hunt you."

After attending to their needs, they were brought before Petro Petrovich who was sitting on a box beside the largest and most ornate wagon. Using a dagger to cut his nails, the leader considered them for a long moment before roaring, "Bring a seat for the ladies!"

A small boy appeared with a couple of three legged stools. Gwyn sat down but Alina stayed standing. "I demand you release us at once."

Gwyn couldn't help but admire Alina for her continued confidence but leapt up all the same. She tugged Alina gently onto the other stool. "What my lady means to say is thank you for your hospitality and for taking us to Moldavia, where you will be richly rewarded in exchange for our safe passage. Prince Stephen and Prince Vlad will be delighted to know their beloved sister and wife is alive and well."

Petro sheathed his dagger and huffed a laugh. "Bring us some wine and food, my dear," he said to the woman who had brought them over to him. Gwyn touched Alina's arm and raised her eyebrows to indicate to let her do the talking. Alina glared at her but remained quiet.

Meric appeared at the same time as the food. He sat on the ground by Gwyn's feet and Petro indicated that they should help themselves to the bread, cheese, stuffed fowl and vegetables placed on a low table set in front of the stools. Gwyn wondered if there was etiquette to follow, but as Petro didn't join them in their meal she gave up and simply ate as neatly as she could manage with her hungry belly. She kept one eye on the Roma man, who stared at Alina most of all.

The food disappeared all too quickly and Meric let out a belch. Gwyn glared at him for a second but was pleased to see her companion unharmed apart from the fading bruise on his head.

"Thank you, Petro Petrovich," Gwyn said formally.

"Hmm." He watched Alina, who ignored him. "I do recognise you now, my lady—I saw you giving alms to the poor once in Târgoviște. Do you believe your husband and brother will reward us if we bring you to them?"

"Of course they will," Gwyn was eager to keep him on side. *Come on, Alina.*

The lady struggled to pull down the sneer that had been creeping up her face. "Yes." She was short. Gwyn pinched her leg and the lady glared. "My husband will be most eager to have me returned... and my brother will pay for my ransom." Gwyn could almost hear her thoughts stating that they'd be lucky to get one ransom out of Stephen, but not to count on payment for an immoral servant girl and her janissary companion.

This appeared to be good enough for Petro. "We are heading north away from the wars, but I suppose we could detour to the east."

Gwyn capitalised on this. "Perhaps a message could be sent?"

Petro looked at her with a raised eyebrow. "Do you happen to have a pigeon hidden under your skirts?"

She blushed. *Yeah, Gwyn—it's not like they can text Stephen.*

"No," Petro said. "Your man can go instead. I'll even permit him to take a horse. You ladies will be safe with us, I give you my word."

"Wait," Meric protested but Gwyn overrode him.

"We'll be fine, Meric. Petro seems to be an honourable man."

Meric stared at her in bafflement. She closed her eyes for a second and concentrated. *Inshallah.* "Just do it," she said in Turkish Arabic. "Try to bring back help from her brother, not her husband."

Meric frowned in consternation and she held her breath, hoping he'd understood and she'd actually spoken that language. "I… I will take a message to the Prince." He stood up. "Shall I leave at once?"

Gwyn raised an eyebrow at Alina, who pursed her lips. "Yes."

"Excellent!" Petro leapt up and offered his hand to Alina. She looked at it as if he'd held out a fresh horse turd. Gwyn bumped the lady's arm up and Petro pulled Alina to her feet. He held onto her hand a little longer than necessary and Gwyn felt a burning stab of jealously.

Too late for that now. I hope Meric keeps his wits about him and gets a message to Prince Stephen and not Prince Vlad!

THIRTY-TWO

1461 AD

Meric would have liked to gallop away from the gyspy camp and never look back but he had sworn to protect Gwyn and he owed her his life. The precious noble lady could stay with the gypsies for all he cared. It angered him to see the way Gwyn fawned after her.

Wasting her heart on that one. He nudged the gelding into a trot and ducked under a low hanging branch—already shedding leaves as the season got colder this high in the mountains. The track wound through the trees and passed a few cottars' huts. Stopping to question a man hoeing vegetables, he ascertained that these were the lands of one Countess Báthory, of Castle Csejthe which could be seen in the distance.

More nobles. He grimaced briefly and his thoughts drifted to the only noble who'd ever shown him kindness. *Radu.* But even he had forgotten Meric, forgotten the love they'd shared when they were young.

Radu. You turned out to be just like the rest.

* * *

Radu considered his appearance in the polished silver mirror and wished it was glass. *This place is such a provincial backwater. I'm going to turn this place around.* It had been months since Mehmet had returned to Constantinople and Radu's heart twinged a little, missing his lover. But being installed as the new Prince of Wallachia made up for any personal sadness and Radu intended to make the most of his Ottoman-backed power.

His eyes slid to the letter sitting in a bronze dish on the table beside the mirror. It was heavy vellum with thick red wax and a cloth of gold ribbon. The seal of Matthias Corvinus, the Hungarian king, was still recognisable—he'd cracked it open carefully. Radu was pleased that several months of negotiations and secret messages were about to pay off.

He returned to the mirror and tweaked one more hair into place. Straightening up, he set his features into what he imagined was a wise but fearsome appearance. The Wallachian boyars might have backed him over Vlad and helped tip the siege at the Citadel on the Arges in his favour, but he was under no illusions that he could trust them. *Slippery, two faced and uncouth. Surely some of them must have known about the secret passage that allowed my devil of a brother to escape.* He didn't let those thoughts show as he descended the stairs and entered the main hall of the castle.

The chatter died down as the lords turned to face Radu. Eyes were watchful and many hands stroked beards as they considered their latest Prince.

Radu waited until he had everyone's attention then spread his arms wide. "We have won a great victory here, my lords!" He smiled magnanimously. "I am your new and rightful Prince, and you shall be rewarded!" *You won't be thrown off the castle walls for a start, even those of you who were late to show your support.*

Murmurs of agreement broke out, but one voice rose above the throng. "We know your brother will not relinquish his hold on Wallachia so easily, my lord. How do you intend to stop him raiding without hosting a Turkish army on our lands? They've already taken back their cannons." Several beards bobbed up and down as other lords agreed with the speaker, a grizzled noble in rich robes.

You pledged your support for me when it looked like I might gain the upper hand and because you hate Vlad. But you won't do your part in finishing off the menace and instead want me to conjure up a solution!

He smiled. For the first time, the boyars noticed a slight resemblance to his feared older brother. The almost foppish features were eclipsed by hardness. Several wondered if they'd traded the devil they knew for another, more capricious.

"It's all in hand, my good lords, you need not fear." Radu looked them all in the face one by one, taking his time. "We will strengthen our own armies and my voivodship will usher in a new era of peace between the great and gracious Mehmed and Christian Europe."

Before anyone could protest that he'd not answered the question, and ask if that meant new taxes, a minor lord who'd been paid to stand back in the crowd and wait for this very moment shouted, "Hurrah! Hurrah for Prince Radu!" The lord clapped vigorously and another bribed boyar closer to the front joined him.

The other lords joined in slowly but gained enthusiasm as they saw the guards standing along the walls brandish their spears and thump them on the floor in a cheer. "Hurrah! Hurrah! Hurrah for Prince Radu!"

Radu permitted himself the tiniest curl of a smile and congratulated himself. While Vlad ruled through fear and violence, he, Radu, would shine through diplomacy and intelligence. He would deal with vastly different faiths and rulers, carving his own little niche in the process.

And as for Vlad, well—Radu had a plan for him.

THIRTY-THREE

1461 AD

Michelle was dozing uncomfortably when the solid bump against the pod jolted her awake. It wasn't the slap of a wave, though many had washed over the pod as it rode the swell. Trying to sleep was the best way to avoid being seasick. Brrrys was unconscious so it wasn't as if she had anyone to talk to.

The bump came again and several dark fins slid past her line of vision. She pressed her hand against the clear lid and started when a streamlined head burst from the water beside her. A large, dark eye considered her intelligently.

Whew. She sighed with relief, knowing they weren't safe yet, but better than being cast adrift in a lonely grey ocean.

The dolphin chittered briefly then dove beneath the surface, joining her companions as they surged protectively around the pod. After a while, a much larger shape hove into view and something like a Biblical nightmare took place as immense jaws closed around the pod. Lodged in the whale's mouth, Michelle could feel the pod accelerate as their rescuer swam southeast.

* * *

All day and another night passed, and a new pod of dolphins took over from the whale when they neared the coast. Michelle signed her gratitude to them when she saw the fern-marked hydrofoil come out to meet them. The whole sleep pod was lifted into the vessel and she breathed the unfiltered air with relief as she clambered out. She was stiff and clumsy, but human hands steadied her, helping her into a seat.

"My friend is injured," she told their rescuers. "Please don't move him from the pod."

"Understood," one of them replied. "Do you need first aid?"

Michelle waved them off. "I'm fine for now."

"Where are we?" Brrrys voice was hoarse. He'd managed to drink a little when he'd woken.

Michelle looked around. The fern sigil was emblazoned on the inside of the vessel as well. "Aotearoa?" Her rescuers nodded as they secured the pod. "Some large islands east of the Australian continent. Where we were originally headed. How are you feeling?"

He winced. "Not great." He didn't look good. His fur was lank, his normally bright eyes were dull. She tried not let her worry show.

"You'll be alright," she tried to reassure him. "I'll find someone to have a look over you once we get there."

He subsided back into the sleep pod as they closed the final short distance to land. They docked in a cave at the foot of one of the most incredible mountain ranges Michelle had ever seen. A broad-shouldered man with greying temples and an incredible array of tattoos on his face and arms greeted their party and assisted the Mayash out himself. Brrrys perked up, tattooing being unheard of in Mayash culture (although fur plaiting and beading was common), and asked several questions as they boarded a small spherical vehicle that whirred along rails through round tunnels. Michelle wondered if it was to distract himself from the pain.

"I am of Maori heritage," the man, who introduced himself as Henare, told them, pointing out various tattoos and explaining their significance. Michelle listened while trying to keep track of where they were, but the tunnel arced up and down and veered around. With no external landmarks she was lost. She felt like they had risen in elevation, which Henare confirmed when the vehicle stopped in a large cave.

"There was significant geographical change here several hundred years ago. The land is mostly stable now, and we've found this side of the mountains provides excellent sites for the communities that make their homes here. A lot of the lower land slipped into the sea, bringing the shoreline much closer to the peaks."

She wasn't interested in the geography except to learn where she was, and she was unsure how much Eddie might have told this man about them. So she asked.

"What's your understanding of why we are here, Henare?" She looped an arm under Brrrys' shoulders to help him rise from the seat. His tail wrapped around her to steady himself. "We really need a doctor—Brrrys has suffered some injuries and I'm not qualified to treat him."

"The doctor has already been sent for," the man reassured her. "Officer Eddie contacted me, stating you and your colleague are witnesses in a very important case and you require somewhere to lie low and recuperate. I was expecting you to arrive yesterday, but the dolphins informed me your vessel sank."

"We met with an accident." Michelle tightened her lips.

Henare frowned. "I'll get a report from you. I am part of the local police, insofar as Aotearoa has one. We were once a nation of many warriors, centuries ago, but we are quite peaceful now."

This man likes his little history lessons, she thought ironically. "Good," she said.

She followed him across a cavern several dozen metres across, into a smaller cave which was equipped with several beds, computers and a medi-bot nurse. An infirmary. It was brightly lit, so she could see how much worse Brrrys looked as she helped him lie on the bed, positioning him half on his side so his tail wasn't squashed.

"I'll leave you for now," Henare advised, "and sort out some food and accommodation for you. Ah, here is the doctor." A woman walked in through another opening and bumped foreheads gently with Henare before turning to assess her patient.

"Kia Ora, I'm Doctor Quinn," she was business-like but friendly. "May I touch you to assess your injuries? I will also need to take blood and run a number of tests. Do I have your permission?" It was standard procedure for those of a medical profession, and Michelle was gratified to see she didn't appear surprised or concerned about treating a non-human.

As if she'd read her thoughts, Doctor Quinn smiled at Michelle even as she nodded Henare out the door. "I'm a qualified doctor of humans, Mayash and Nolii," she spoke to both Michelle and Brrrys. "I've worked on Mars, Ganymede and Saturn Station One, as well as doing extra study on Vivaldis. It's actually quite fortunate that I'm here visiting family for several months or you would have been hard-pressed to find someone who could help you." This was to Brrrys, who had relaxed even as he nodded permission for her to proceed.

Her examination and scans revealed Brrrys did have internal injuries which could have been quite serious if left untended. He accepted sedation so she could inject a team of nanobots into his system that would repair and heal him from the inside out. Michelle was directed outside the cave to await Henare's return.

A bubble of guilt gnawed at her. *He could have died. How can I tell him I thought they might attack us, but chose to use him as bait anyway?* She was so used to operating solo, safe in the knowledge that whoever she used had died hundreds, if not thousands, of years before she was born, and therefore didn't really matter. *Or do they?* She remembered Gwyn's shock and horror when faced with the Masada suicide, and her attachment to the Roman boy. She had dismissed it as over-sensitivity. *The girl might have time travelling ability, but she's got nothing on my experience and efficiency.* But her experience and efficiency had almost killed Brrrys.

Her thoughts halted when Henare returned and gestured for her to follow him. The infirmary cave had been sealed by opaque forcefields, so she felt reasonably safe leaving Brrrys there. Her guide took her several levels up to a common dining cave that had one side open to the mountainside. The impressive view distracted Michelle, so it took a moment for her to realise she'd been surrounded.

"Hi! How are you, Citizen?" several voices chorused as she looked around her, startled. A handful of teenagers milled about, smiling greetings and bowing. 'Come and have something to eat, you must be starving!"

"Henare, can she stay with us?" one boy asked.

Henare smiled nonchalantly. "I've already assigned her to Harret's group," he pushed gently through the young people and sat down on a bench with a view of outside.

Michelle found herself ferried along and seated at a table with some sort of protein cereal and vegetable juice. *Of course, it's breakfast time.* That was why the other caverns and tunnels had been so empty. She realised how hungry and exhausted she was. A tall, muscular teenager with long brown braids noticed. "Eat up, then I'll take you to the dorm," she encouraged. "Henare said you are in witness protection, and were rescued by dolphins and whales when your hovercraft crashed. You're safe now, don't worry. Our family will look after you."

"What Harret says," nodded an older lad, refilling her cup. "We'll look after you. You can rely on us, Henare."

"Good." The policeman rose, drained the last of his juice and snatched a roll from the basket at the centre of the long table. "I have to go to work now; don't anyone be late for jobs or study. They'll keep an eye on you," he told Michelle, who was bewildered. Was he leaving her with a bunch of kids? "Get some rest, and tell Harret here if you need anything special, and she'll find me or my partner."

With that, he was gone and her fatigue was catching up with her fast. The girl called Harret chivvied her into finishing her cereal, then flapped her hand at the others to shoo them away. "She's tired! Get to your work and study! You can talk to her later!" She was by no means the oldest person there, but seemed to have some position of seniority. Why, Michelle couldn't tell. Her natural wariness kept her quiet but she nodded her thanks when she was escorted into a tidy dorm room and offered a bed at the far end of the cave.

"No one will come in and disturb you," Harret told her. "Sleep as long as you like. Hygiene room is through there." She indicated another doorway, then dimmed the lights using a computer panel by the main door and left.

Michelle fought her weariness long enough to pace about the room. There was an additional exit through the hygiene room, but the forcefield was up and the computer didn't respond to her attempt to open it. Same with the main door's forcefield, and Michelle had the uncomfortable feeling she was trapped.

Still, there was nothing she could do about it right now and nothing would be achieved in her current state. She took off her boots but nothing else, and lay down on top of the bed covers, sending her mind into a pre-sleep meditative mode. Within seconds she was snoring.

Her sleep was surprisingly restful, and she woke feeling refreshed until she remembered Brrrys and her inability to leave these rooms. She had taken Eddie's offer of extradition because it was the quickest way out of a dangerous situation. Now she was unsure if she'd traded one danger for another. She didn't know anything about this place.

All my missions back in time involved extensive study, training and familiarisation with the people and environment of the time, she thought irritably. Once again her resentment of the freeze on the Agency boiled to the surface, so it was unsurprising that her expression was quite fierce when Harret entered the room, wearing a backpack.

"Oh good, you're awake! Oh. What's wrong?" the girl held her palms up in a placating gesture. "You look pissed off."

Tactful, not. Michelle schooled her features into a more agreeable expression. "Nothing. Well, lots of things, but nothing I care to discuss right now. Can I visit my colleague in the infirmary?" It was a question but came out more like an order. To her credit, the teenager didn't quail under Michelle's authoritarian tone.

"Sure thing. Would you like to clean up and change into some fresh clothes first though? Probably a good idea if you are going to the infirmary. In fact, Doctor Quinn will insist on it. She is a stickler for hygiene. She complains about the dirt here. 'We live underground!' I tell her. She's been in space too long." The girl laughed and slung the backpack off her shoulders, pulling a pair of trousers and all-purpose adjustable shirt out, offering them to Michelle.

Michelle accepted them silently and turned to enter the hygiene room. Harret followed her and chatted while Michelle showered, asking questions which Michelle deflected or ignored. Harret's good nature wasn't deterred by this rudeness and Michelle figured that if the girl was going to talk incessantly, she might as well provide useful information, so she began quizzing her on where they were and who lived here. At least the girl showed none of the prudishness she'd witnessed at the conference in Sydney.

What Harret disclosed surprised Michelle. It was a family-oriented community, but young people were actively encouraged to travel on Earth and off it in the course of their studies or work. They usually returned home in their early thirties to start having children of their own and re-integrated into the community, often teaching if there was no call for their career of choice here. They farmed seaweed off the coast and administered the vast marine conservation areas around the islands, working with the pods of dolphins and whales in the area.

Finishing up her shower, Michelle dressed and memorised the route to the infirmary as Harret continued to talk. The girl was in training for a leadership position—her talents for emotional intelligence had been fostered early and she would soon spend time in other communities throughout the islands, getting to know the people and learning how they dealt with issues and problems. With this kind of a career she would never spend extensive time off-world, and while she didn't seem to resent this at all, she was curious about space travel and non-humans in a way that marked her as the opposite of Jaysen Fitz. She was proud of her home, but recognised there were other ways of life that weren't necessarily superior or inferior, just different.

Michelle also noticed Harret barely managed to curb her excitement at seeing a real live Mayash. Doctor Quinn permitted the girl to enter the infirmary alongside Michelle. It was late in the day now, and Brrrys remained under sedation, but his colour and fur had improved, and his breathing was far steadier.

"He'll be fine," Quinn told her. "Just needs some rest now the nanobots have done their work. Can I give you the once-over?"

"Yes, actually," Michelle belatedly remembered the requirement that made her submit a blood sample for testing of time lapse. "Are you able to send a blood reading anonymously? I have a reporting requirement, but I'm not keen for anyone to know where I am."

"Of course," the doctor gestured her to sit on a bed. "Patient confidentiality is a priority, and patient safety even more so. I'll send it via Beijing—they can handle whoever needs to see it."

That task done, the Doctor gave her a clean bill of health. "Except for your stress levels. Those are extremely high. I'm not surprised, as I understand from Henare you are in witness protection, but you are safe here, so try to relax and recuperate."

If you knew what was at stake you wouldn't relax, doctor. She merely nodded and tapped Harret on the arm.

"Come on, you can talk to him when he wakes up. He loves attention." *Especially from human women, but you are probably too young for him, even if you are of legal consent age.*

"Are you happy to talk to the others?" Harret bubbled with excitement. "They haven't been off-world yet, but some are due to leave for university study soon, and have so many questions."

"Sure,' Michelle was taciturn.

Ugh, I'm going to be surrounded by perky teenagers for weeks. I need to find a way to ditch this place and go and do something useful.

THIRTY-FOUR

1461 AD

The Roma had decided to camp a few days and Gwyn was keen to show Alina that they weren't the thieving vagabonds the noble lady called them. Unfortunately, she never got the chance as they were mostly confined to the wagon where they slept. Their guard was reticent and ignored her questions, so she desisted, not wanting to slip into his language by accident and give away the one advantage they had.

Alina was as bad at first but then thawed and let Gwyn brush her long black hair with a wooden comb from their saddlebags. Gwyn revelled in the touch but kept her expression neutral and stayed quiet, wishing Alina would relax instead of sitting so stiffly.

"What is your brother, Prince Stephen, like?" Gwyn asked. The day had warmed up and they were sitting beside the wagon, enjoying the sunshine. Well, Gwyn was enjoying it—Alina continued to sulk.

At first she thought the lady was going to ignore her. Then Alina spoke, "He is a good brother. A good Prince. Not as warlike as… as my lord, but a brave warrior in his own right, and clever with his nobles. A good Christian too—he is very devout, and has built many monasteries and churches. I can see why my lord has gone to him. Stephen would never consider making peace with the Turk."

"But do you get along? I mean, will he hand you straight back to Vlad?"

"He will do what is right," Alina informed her tersely, and Gwyn sighed.

The rest of the day passed slowly. Alina's conversation was restricted to complaints about the lack of cleanliness (Gwyn didn't think the camp or the people were dirty—no more so than anyone else who lived on the road and certainly not more than some of the peasants she'd seen) and lack of wine. She wondered how Meric was getting on. It had been several days and she worried he wouldn't be able to find them when Petro decided to move his people on.

They were fed, though not abundantly, and an uneasy truce was arrived at in the wagon, with Alina permitting Gwyn to lie back to back under the same blanket for warmth when they went to sleep. Gwyn tried the door every night but it was always bolted from the outside. Tonight she gave it a cursory try then gave up and attempted to get her whirling mind to rest.

She didn't know at what point her convoluted thoughts slipped into dreams. It seemed like only seconds before she flew awake to the sounds of screams and men yelling.

"What's going on?" Alina demanded. They scrambled up and peered out the window. It was dawn; the frost glittered on the ground. Dark circles were cut into it by horses' hooves. Men in armour were rounding up bewildered and frightened Roma. An indignant Petro pulled on a shirt and tried to calm his people. No one seemed to be getting attacked but there was definitely menace from the warriors who had their swords and spears out.

"I'm not sure." Gwyn was bumped aside as Alina tried to look out—there wasn't enough space at the window for both of them.

Alina gasped. "It's him!"

"Who?" Gwyn managed to squeeze back in. Then she saw what Alina meant and a wave of relief washed over her. "Meric!" she yelled. He looked over and pointed out Gwyn and Alina's wagon to one of the men beside him. A man-at-arms rode over and unbolted the door, releasing the two women and escorting them back to their rescuer.

Meric was on a bay gelding—not the scraggy one given to him by Petro, who had declared Alina's fine black mare unfit for a long journey and in need of rest and care. Alina had muttered they sought to steal her horse but in the same breath she stated it was fortunate that Meric hadn't been given her horse, as he was likely to make off with it. Gwyn couldn't help but give Alina a triumphant little smile at Meric's return—much sooner than she'd expected and in the company of…

Who is that?

A lady sat beside him on her own horse. A noble lady to be sure; her riding clothes were beautifully cut and stitched, dark green velvet sables with sable collar and matching hat. The lady's polished style matched her looks. Gwyn supposed she was pretty—the way she carried herself on the horse was a testament to her confidence—but the woman's stern beauty paled beside Alina's intensity, despite the latter being travel-worn. *Alina would be beautiful even after being dumped in a pig pen.*

Gwyn envied the newcomer her warmth. This early in the morning it was quite chilly, though as the first rays of sun peeped over the horizon the promise of a fine day was made. The lady noticed her shiver.

"Two cloaks!" she ordered. Garments were quickly shed from a couple of her men and presented deferentially to Gwyn and Alina.

"I am Countess Elizabeth Báthory, and you cigány are on my land without leave," the Countess glared down at Petro. He seemed less self-assured now that he was on the pointy-end of the stick. "What's more, you are keeping two women prisoner, one of whom purports to be the Lady Alina, wife of Prince Vlad of Wallachia."

"May I have leave to speak, noble Countess?" The Countess frowned but the Roma leader barrelled on. "We rescued this lady, her servant and their guard and were escorting them to safety—sending the guard here to take a message to the lady's noble husband as well as her brother. They asked us to take them with us, and promised us reward. We could not leave them so unprotected and under-supplied as we found them." He shot a wild-eyed look at Gwyn, who pitied the man.

I don't think the nobles are particularly sympathetic towards Roma. This Countess looks like she might cut them all down, the women and children too.

"It is true, my lady Countess," Gwyn burst out. "They meant us no ill and we did promise reward." *Argh this is all going pear shaped and someone's going to cop it.* She could see Meric frowning and she took a deep breath and concentrated on exuding calm. The warmth in her left palm reassured her and yet again, Gwyn knew she had to think fast in order to talk their way out of this predicament.

"Oh forget the gypsies, Countess, and just take us away from here," Alina startled everyone by interrupting. Everyone turned to look at her. She wore impatience all over her face. "My guard may have been over zealous in describing our situation, but I'll be glad to send these people on their way. My brother, Prince Stephen, tells me to be charitable towards those with less, and I think it will suffice not to punish them for a mere misunderstanding." Chin high, the lady strode up to Countess Báthory and looked her full in the face, clearly showing she considered them to be equals. Gwyn closed her gaping mouth and exchanged a look with Meric who raised his eyebrows and sat back in the saddle. She peeped sideways at Petro, who seemed to be holding his breath along with the rest of his family.

The dour lines of the Countess' face contorted into an odd smile. She reached down for Alina's hand—who clasped it—then said, "Very well. You shall be guests of mine until your noble brother can be told of your whereabouts. Word from Wallachia was that you were dead, Lady Alina, so no doubt your husband will rejoice to hear you are alive and well." She gestured to several of her men, who dismounted and knelt on the grass to offer a step into their horses' saddles.

"My own horse is here," Alina informed Countess Báthory imperiously. She looked down her nose at Petro, who gestured hurriedly towards the picketed beasts under the trees.

In a remarkably short amount of time Gwyn was seated behind the soldier who'd lent her his cloak and they had left the Roma behind. Her riding companion was short so it was easy to see over his shoulder up to the front of the train. Meric rode up beside her—he caught her looking ahead at Alina, who trotted her horse next to the Countess. He shook his head. "Nobles stick together, Gwyn."

She frowned and tore her gaze away. "Thank you for getting help," she said, ignoring his comment. "You were quicker than I expected."

He shrugged. "Lucky. I used her name and that got me in front of the Countess, who was quick to want to help. She's got a reputation for protecting women and girls in these parts."

Gwyn was chuffed. *How fantastic—a Countess who actively helps women even back in these times!*

The thought gave her hope.

THIRTY-FIVE

1461 AD

Gwyn didn't see much of Meric over the next few days. She was so busy playing lady's maid to Alina again—choosing gowns, doing her hair, taking walks with her in the castle gardens—that she felt a little guilty when she caught a glimpse of him in the training yard, mingling with the other men-at-arms. The cooler weather up here in the mountains meant it wasn't unusual that he wore a neck scarf all the time, which hid his tattoo.

He seems fine—well fed and keeping active. The story was that Meric had taken part in various battles against the Ottoman forces before being assigned to guard Alina. On one of the few occasions that Gwyn got a chance to speak to him he told her he was teaching the castle garrison Turkish fighting methods. His skills as a fighter and a teacher earned him the respect of the castle guards and she excused herself from worrying about him.

Besides, her persistence sticking to Alina's side was paying off. The lady was still aloof but they'd returned to something close to their original relationship and Gwyn was glad to be able to sleep next to Alina again. Their conversations became less stilted and the old, kind Alina gradually returned. Perhaps she had forgotten Gwyn's declaration of love or was less disgusted by it when she saw how devoted Gwyn was to her. Gwyn hoped it was the latter.

They saw Countess Báthory every dinner time in the great hall of the castle. Halberds and swords decorated the cold stone walls, interspersed with the heads of boars, wolves and stags.

"My late husband's triumphs," Elizabeth waved a beringed hand carelessly at the walls. "I should take them down and hang some nice tapestries instead, but they remind me of him."

"How did he die?" Alina enquired.

"Hunting accident. Ironic tragedy," the Countess said, her nasal tone unaffected by grief. "It was quite some years ago, and we had no issue. This castle and its lands remained in my family, since it was part of my dowry."

"Is that so?" Alina was the epitome of polite and gentile conversation as the fish course was served.

A manservant poured wine for the ladies then, at a signal from the Countess, made his way to the table below the dais and poured for Gwyn. She bowed her head in thanks for the show of favour.

Báthory smiled and continued speaking to Alina. "I'll have my tailor measure your maid for another dress. I do like to see a young girl look pretty. How fortunate that we are of the same size and you could wear a gown of mine."

"Your kindness does you credit, Countess," Alina replied, lightly touching the black velvet dress she wore.

Gwyn agreed. A small voice in her head said it a little *too* kind but the rest of her was too busy comparing Alina favourably to Báthory. They were dressed almost identically, from full white sleeves to broad lace collar, but Alina had a warmer and more natural beauty than the Countess. Báthory's tight braids and heavy jewellery accentuated her white skin and delicate features but she was stiff and her smile never quite reached her eyes.

"My lady is vain, and rightfully so," murmured a thin, bald man seated on her right. Gwyn glanced at him and he smiled, showing blackened teeth. She started and looked in his rheumy blue eyes instead. That made her feel even more uncomfortable and she chided herself for being so shallow. *He can't help his looks.* But she wondered if he could help his sulphurous breath—she took a gulp of her wine, burying her nose in the scent of that instead.

"She is very elegant," Gwyn replied, hiding behind her goblet.

The man took this as an invitation to continue, introducing himself as Thorko, an alchemist. He made inane conversation as the dinner wore on. She took to glancing towards the ladies on the dais in an effort to discourage him and was disturbed at one point to see a hungry look on Báthory's face as she looked at Alina. Her companion drew her attention and when she looked up again the Countess' face was politely neutral.

The alchemist's continued nattering and praise of the Countess' good looks bored Gwyn and her responses became non-committal as the meal dragged on. She preferred instead to watch the way Alina's hair shone in the candlelight and how her lips met the wine goblet.

Thinking about where else those lips might touch made her hot and flushed so she set down her wine and glanced along the lower table. Half the household had already risen, so she caught her mistress' eye and begged to be excused. Alina dismissed her with a flick of the fingers and returned to her conversation with the Countess.

Whew, I need to lay off the wine or I might make a move I regret. She was terrified of another rejection. *Play it slow, Gwyn. You'll win her over eventually.*

The heat in her body had her venturing outside and up onto the curtain wall. She stood between two merlons and braced herself against the wind. It was fresh against her flushed cheeks, but her head still felt dizzy.

"Gwyn!" a voice hissed and she jumped.

"Meric, you scared the hell out of me!" The soldier was standing right behind her. She thumped his chest and blew out her breath. "What are you doing creeping up around here at night? Have they got you doing guard duty?"

"No." He caught her hand and led her to an alcove away from the edge of the wall. A real castle guard strolled past and eyed them suspiciously. Meric winked and slid an arm around Gwyn's shoulders and faced her as if they were about to kiss. The guard chuckled and walked on.

"And what's so important that you have to pretend you like women?" She wanted to shrug his arm off on principle, but it was nice and warm. She leant into him. She was finding it hard to keep her balance and his support was welcome.

"I had to talk to you." He sounded annoyed. "I'm supposed to be looking after you, remember? I couldn't stroll on up to the ladies' apartments, and you didn't come looking for me!"

Guilt blossomed in her heart. "You seemed fine!" she protested.

"I was hardly going to act otherwise," he retorted. He must have felt her shivering, for he drew his cloak around them both. "I've only been allowed out of the castle once and that was just to the village. We're trapped here."

"Hardly," she retorted. The cold was cutting through her slight wooziness. Why had she come up here without a cloak? *Oh yeah, to cool off. Stupid wine.*

"We are!" he insisted. "There's something funny going on here— none of the men here will say what. I don't think they even know themselves but there are rumours. I think we should leave."

"Rumours?" she scoffed.

"Haven't you noticed there are no young women working in the castle? Or have you been so occupied chasing your precious lady around you haven't opened your eyes? She sees you as a servant, nothing more." His words cut her more sharply than the wind could.

"Are you sure you like men?" His embrace suddenly felt too hot and she pushed away. "You seem awfully concerned with young women." *Myself included.* The old fear rose up in her and she felt sick. What if she'd trusted Meric all this time, thinking he wouldn't see her that way, and he turned out to be more like her than she realised, liking both men and women?

"Gwyn, stop it. Listen!" He grabbed her arm. She used his weight to yank herself forward and kneed him solidly in the groin. "Urrgh!" He doubled over and she wrenched free, running to the stairs and flying down them. It wasn't until she was back in the relative safety of the guest quarters that she managed to slow her breathing and calm herself.

Just like the others! She looked around the apartments—big old tapestries adorning the walls, heavy wooden furniture—and frowned. She did feel trapped. Her eye fell on the jug of wine sitting on the table and she shook her head. *Bad idea.* Instead, she changed from her dress into the old breeches and shirt she'd begged from a servant and began doing some push ups and crunches to get warm. She ran through all the moves and holds Meric had taught her to fight off an attacker. It was hard with no actual opponent but she improvised as best she could. She then stretched before stoking the fire and heating water to bathe. Alina still hadn't returned from dinner and it was late, so once she was tolerably clean (bucket and cloth bath was better than nothing) she went to bed.

* * *

The fire had burnt low and Gwyn awoke cold despite the heavy furs on the four poster bed. Something was wrong. The hour must be quite late, she felt sure, but Alina still had not returned. Tucking herself into a ball, she cursed her mistress' absence. She didn't want to get out from under the covers but knew that she had to build the fire and heat the room once more.

"Fine!" After several minutes of trying to pretend the cold would go away, she leapt out and hurried to the hearth. Her feet nearly froze on the flagstones. She alternated between hopping into her stockings and poking several more logs on the fire, willing the flames to take hold faster. After a while she stopped shivering enough to look around and call out tentatively, "Alina? My lady?"

No answer.

Turning so her back could enjoy the warmth, she considered the room. It appeared exactly as she'd left it when she'd gone to bed some time ago.

Did she stay up talking to the Countess? Every other night the noble ladies had retired early, and Gwyn assumed this was a habit. She wished she had her phone or a watch—then realised she did, of a sorts.

Nothing. Her connection to the pocket watch was still absent. *Why?* She raged silently. *Stupid thing must be broken.* If she ever got a hold of Michelle she was going to throttle her for sending her on a dangerous mission with faulty equipment.

Muttering curses, she moved away from the fire's warmth long enough to get her clothes and bring them back into the tiny semi-circle of heat. She dressed, remembering to grab a thick cloak this time and calmed herself. She needed to be grey. She didn't fancy explaining herself to anyone wandering the halls at this time of night—especially if, as Meric said, young women weren't common in the castle.

Why would he say that? She padded out of the guest quarters and down the dark stairs with a candle for light. It was true she hadn't paid much attention to the composition of the staff here, so focussed on Alina she had been. But what did it matter?

Now that she thought about it, she couldn't recall seeing many women at all here. She hadn't explored much, but even the servants who brought wood and food and drink to their rooms had been men.

Weird. She shrugged. *But that's why we are close again. Alina can't replace me with some castle girl.*

Another part of her puzzled, *For a noble with a reputation for helping young women, why aren't there any living under her protection then?*

The great hall was empty; remnants of the meal had long since been cleared away. What little light there was came from her candle and the banked hearth fire. She touched the top of an unlit candle—the wax was cold.

OK, where would Alina be in the middle of the night since she's not in our rooms and she's not stayed up talking?

The chapel? She had prayed a lot back in Târgoviște, and spent time here in front of the castle altar. Gwyn sighed with annoyance and retraced her steps. Instead of ascending the stairs to their rooms she took a different stairwell down to the level that housed the chapel. Built into the hill itself, Castle Csejthe had all sorts of uneven floors and passages that rose and curved. A person might start out on one floor, ascend two flights of stairs, go outside then through a tunnel cut into the rock and end up back on the *same* floor but at the other end of a hallway. Gwyn had found this entertaining at first, but now, in the dark and with the breeze gusting past her and threatening to blow out her candle, she resented the fact the place resembled a rabbit warren.

Trying not to check behind her every five seconds, she took two wrong turns then found the chapel. It was empty and as cold and silent as a tomb.

Except... she thought she could hear something. An eerie, crying noise that stopped as she paused to listen. Holding her breath, she strained her ears.

Nothing. Then it came again. A keening, faint at first but then more definite. *Someone crying? A woman by the sound of it. Or a child maybe.* It was high pitched, and she shivered from more than the cold. She moved closer to the altar to identify the direction it was coming from. She wasn't sure if she wanted to find and comfort the person or run away.

She had to stop several times, listening carefully as she crept past the altar and into the room behind it. She closed the door quietly behind her, checking first to make sure the bolt was on the inside with her. *I've read too many books where people go snooping and get locked in somewhere!*

She wondered if there would be a secret passage, then scolded herself for being dramatic. The light of her candle revealed several chests, a table and a low door towards the back. When she pressed her ear against it, her heart sank. The wail began again and she knew that she'd have to go through the door to find it.

The cry sounded more than miserable. It sounded afraid. It wasn't hard to imagine a vampire crypt or Dr Frankenstein's laboratory somewhere in the castle, with tortured prisoners waiting to be sacrificed in the name of the devil or science.

"Don't be ridiculous!" she whispered harshly, fighting to ignore the prickling of her skin. *It's probably some servant crying over a broken heart and hiding away where the rest of the castle can't hear.*

She took three slow breaths and steeled herself, pushing open the door. It swung easily, not with the god-awful creak she'd expected. More than that, there were torches burning in brackets on the wall at intervals, providing enough light to cast deep shadows. Gwyn blew out her candle, wanting to save it. She wrapped her fingers around the hot wax and used the pain to jerk herself into action.

The cry came much more clearly, if less frequently now, as if the person emitting it was exhausted. The passage dipped and swung left, then descended a poorly lit set of stone steps. Gwyn felt her anxiety build up in her until she could hardly bear not to turn tail and run back upstairs to hide under the covers.

It's definitely a woman. In fact… Cold horror gripped her and she crept as quietly as she could down the last few steps.

The door at the bottom of the stairs was open. Gwyn took a breath and peered inside. This room was well lit, which made the scene even more frightening. It was a dungeon: iron hoops were bolted to cold, slimy stone, with partially rusted manacles hanging from both wall and floor hoops. At least, she hoped the red stains on the metal were rust.

Gwyn saw the source of the awful keening—it was the sole prisoner of the cell. Lovely black hair askew, grey eyes full of tears and lips that Gwyn had dreamt of kissing, lips that were split and bruised.

It was Alina.

THIRTY-SIX

1461 AD

Gwyn rushed to Alina's side. "What are you doing here?" she asked, frantic. The lady's eyes focussed on her in alarm.

"Help me, Gwyn! Free me, please!" Alina begged.

Gwyn cast about, looking for a way to release Alina from the chains. Then she whirled, cursing herself for not realising sooner. It should have been obvious—all the doors had been unlocked, the torches lit.

There was someone else here.

Countess Báthory smiled ghoulishly and rose. She had been reclining in a cushioned chair, a goblet of wine within reach on the carved chestnut table. The furniture was a disconcerting contrast to the rest of the dungeon, but the thing that really caught Gwyn's attention was the thin stiletto in the Countess' hand.

"I was going to save you for later, girl," Báthory said. "But since you've decided to join your mistress, or whoever she really is, I'll have to do you now."

Gwyn stared at her, confused and horrified. She stood, Alina at her back in an attempt to protect her, no way of getting around the blade to the door.

"I told you," Alina moaned, "I'm Lady Alina, wife to Vlad Dracula, sister to Prince Stephen of Moldavia. Please let me go!"

"What the hell have you done to her?" Gwyn demanded. "Are you nuts? Vlad will skin you alive when he finds out about this!" *He really would, too.*

"Lady Alina is dead," Countess Báthory answered calmly. "She threw herself from the walls at Poenari rather than be captured by the Turks.

We heard about it months ago. I don't know why you thought she could impersonate her."

"I *am* her!" Alina wailed as Gwyn insisted, "She *is* her!" but the Countess just laughed. It was actually quite a nice laugh—a gentle chuckle, not the demonic cackle that would have suited the situation far better.

"It wasn't a bad story to try to escape those cigány vagabonds, especially since I am known to protect women. But no true lady would allow her servant to speak for her and travel with just one guard. The real lady Alina would have sought out protection from her husband immediately had she been attacked by Turks, not disappeared for months then resurfaced in Transylvania. Are you thieves, or players, or just whores?"

Alina gasped and began to cry again, and Gwyn couldn't deny the Countess' logic. Never had it been more important to try to talk her way out of a nasty situation.

But she was not given the opportunity. Countess Báthory swept to the door in a flurry of thick skirts and backed through it, stiletto pointed at Gwyn. Realising her intent Gwyn shouted and rushed to the door. She was brought up short by the blade jabbing neatly into her left shoulder. Horror stopped her more than pain, for she felt nothing at first, then a sharp burning set in. The Countess pushed her backwards and pulled the door shut. Gwyn hit the ground at the same time as the heavy bolt thunked solidly into place on the outside of the door.

"No!" she exclaimed weakly, unsure if she meant the door, the knife wound, or both. Pressing her hand to her shoulder she saw that it came away bright red. "Shit," she said, turning to look at Alina, who stared.

"What happened?" the lady asked, aghast. Smears of blood coupled with the bruising to make her face both pitiful and nightmarish.

Gwyn shuffled over on her knees. "She stabbed me." *Thank god the torches are still lit. I think I'd panic if it was dark.* "I need you to help me bind it." It was cold where her knees touched the floor, even through the fabric of her skirt.

"Wh-what? I'm chained here, Gwyn, I can't help you!"

Gwyn looked at Alina, tears threatening to fill her eyes as she struggled to control her voice. "Alina, I need you to help. I'm going to get us out of here, but I need you to stay calm." Calm was the last thing Gwyn felt—she was enraged that Báthory had injured Alina so. She wanted to reach out and stroke that beautiful face but the pain in her shoulder demanded attention. "We'll tear a piece from my skirt, then I'll hold it in place while you tie it. Please."

The lady sniffed and nodded. They worked together—the sudden pressure on the wound when Alina pulled the cloth tight made Gwyn dizzy. She put her head down between her knees.

"Gwyn? Gwyn!"

Gwyn waved a hand feebly. "I'm okay, just a little faint. Fuck me, it's cold in here." The pain and her fear made her careless with her language. Alina didn't even seem to notice.

"Gwyn, I'm afraid. Why is she doing this? Why doesn't she believe who I am? There was something in my wine, it made me... woozy. She told me we were going to pray, but then she pushed me down the stairs and laughed! She cut me too. Everything hurts." She babbled on like a frightened child.

Gwyn shuffled closer and wrapped her arms around Alina, mumbling, "It's okay. It'll be okay. I'll get you out of here..." before her vision tunnelled to black and the dizziness swept over her head. She was aware of Alina clinging to her and weeping on her uninjured shoulder before she could resist unconsciousness no more.

* * *

Gwyn woke shivering and clung to the only spot of warmth she could sense.

"Ow, Gwyn, you're hurting me!"

"Huh? Wha?" Gwyn grimaced and pushed herself upright. She peered about in confusion. Barely burning torches cast flickering shadows and she recalled her disastrous circumstances.

Oh yeah. Crazy Countess. Alina chained. Me stabbed. She winced and flexed her left fingers cautiously as she leant back against the wall. Her hand moved satisfactorily, and the pain in her shoulder was a dull ache—irritating, but not insurmountable.

"We need to get out," she breathed. How long had she been asleep?

"How long has it been?" she asked Alina, whose puffy eyes could still be seen despite the shadows.

"I don't know. You fell asleep and I did too," Alina sniffed.

Gwyn was annoyed. "I fainted," she corrected sharply. "I had just been stabbed."

"She *cut* me and pushed me down the *stairs!*"

Gwyn was abashed. "I'm sorry. Is anything broken do you think?"

"No." The reply was sulky. "I don't think anything is broken but everything *hurts*. I can't stand up because of these chains." Alina lifted her arms and the iron chinked.

"Okay." Gwyn thought aloud. "She'll be back at some stage. We have to be ready when she does. Did she chain you herself or did someone help her?"

Alina stared at her. "A man helped her. A servant. Can't you... can't you magic us out of here?" She was desperate, pleading.

I would that I could. "I can't." Gwyn's reply was terse. "I don't know why. I haven't been able to since we did that last jump. Trust me, I've tried."

Have you, though? A strange little whisper at the back of her head made itself heard. She went to push it aside then stopped. Something about it made her think it was important, but she didn't know what

Enough of that. Concentrate on your current dilemma.

"Okay, well she'll need him to chain me up so we have to expect that she returns with him. Which means two against one, and she has a knife. He might too." Gwyn cricked her neck and winced. "And I'm no good at fighting. I might get one chance."

"A chance to do what? Gwyn, why is she doing this?"

"It doesn't matter why!" Gwyn was beginning to get annoyed with the whine in Alina's tone. She didn't consider how injured and frightened the other woman was, and how her own pain was making her short-tempered. "She's nuts or perverted or—" She stopped.

She looked at Alina, then got up stiffly and grabbed a torch out of the bracket. Bringing the light closer she peered at Alina's injuries.

"Where did she hurt you?" she asked. "Did she say anything while she was doing it? Did she... did she touch you in any way?"

"In a sinful way? No. She just laughed and... and made little slices on my face and arms. Said I'd never be pretty again, that she'd take all my beauty and keep it for herself." Alina's lip trembled, and Gwyn sighed. She couldn't be bothered arguing the sinful comment, even though she wanted to say that the sin or crime came when it was unwanted, not from two women touching.

Realisation hit her hard and she stiffened, groaning.

"What? What is it?" Alina wanted to know.

Gwyn swallowed hard. "I'm sorry I got you into this. I should have let you go. I thought I wanted to save you from Vlad, but really I wanted you for myself." She choked on the last word. *I'm just as bad as Vlad, taking what I want with no respect for others.* Shamed to her core, she turned away, looking at the door of the dungeon. She took a deep breath. Time enough for self-recrimination later.

The door was solid wood, and no amount of kicking or pushing at it would make it budge. It was the only entrance and exit, but the rest of the dungeon wasn't bare. Aside from the fancy chair and table, chains and manacles decorated the rear wall where Alina was, with loose stones and chunks of old wood scattered on the floor. Gwyn almost rolled her ankle on one such piece of detritus and it gave her an idea.

"What are you doing?" Alina wanted to know. She was sitting with her knees pulled up to her chest. Gwyn took off her cloak and draped it around Alina's shoulders. Forcing herself to ignore the pain from her shoulder, she shifted some of the rubbish to in front of the door. She dragged the table to the side of the door, swearing under her breath. The pain made her sweat despite the cold, but she welcomed the heat despite the nausea that accompanied it.

"I'm trying to give us an advantage," she growled. She was thinking hard, about the dying torches and whether light or dark would give them the most advantage. How long had they been in here? An hour? Several hours? When would the Countess return?

"Did the man who chained you up stay when she started to torture you?" she asked, searching the edges of the dungeon for anything else that might give her an edge. She found an earring, twisted gold that shone beneath the dirt that coated it. She dropped it hastily. Scouting the walls, she discovered one length of chain that shifted when she tugged it. Gwyn retrieved the goblet from the table and used the metal base to scratch out some of the mortar around the bolt affixing the chain to the wall.

"Stay? No, why?" Alina was watching her with interest now, and she had stopped crying. She'd had a big shock, and Gwyn thought grudgingly that it was no wonder the woman had been hysterical. Plus the drugged wine... *Maybe that's why I was skittish around Meric?* She felt ashamed, then told herself that given all the other experiences she'd had with men in this time and others, it was no wonder she'd felt threatened. *Meric never gave you cause to feel that, though—you should have trusted him.*

"Why, Gwyn?" Alina repeated.

"Um, because I'm guessing she won't come back until the morning then." *Scrape, scrape.* "Or even night time." That thought she didn't like to consider. How cold and stiff would they be by then? The Countess had to sleep some time—there was no way she could stay awake that long. She sighed, then renewed her efforts on the chain. The bolt was sunk deep, and no amount of yanking or bashing would release the chain from the wall.

"Shit." Arms aching, she gave up and extinguished some of the torches.

"What are you doing?" Panic returned to Alina's voice. "Don't leave us in the dark!"

"I won't." Gwyn ground the end of a torch out. "I want to save most of them. I'll relight them as the others die. If she doesn't come back till nightfall we'll be in dark long before then, and I'm guessing that's meant to frighten us all the more. We can't give in to fear. Let's be angry instead."

She finished her meagre efforts to turn rubbish into weapons. *Pitiful.* But she *was* angry. Pissed off at herself for staying in a time where she didn't belong, long after she'd completed her mission. Pissed off at Vlad for being such a bastard and making Gwyn pity Alina in the first place. How much of her love was driven by a desire to rescue Alina? She didn't know. And finally, she was pissed off at Countess Báthory for turning out to be a sadistic torturer and not having the decency to provide a dungeon with useful things lying about so they could escape.

"Right," she said, huddling next to Alina. "Now we wait. Do you want to sleep? We'll have to take it in turns."

"Sleep? She could come back at any moment."

Gwyn yawned and countered, "But she probably won't. What time was it when you went to the chapel?"

Alina thought a moment. "I don't know. Maybe the ninth hour of the evening. Not late."

"Can I have some of my cloak back? We'll warm up more if we share." It was an ironic turn of events. Gwyn edged under the cloak and hugged Alina carefully, not wanting to put pressure on the lady's bruises and not wanting to jar her aching shoulder. "We need to rest while we can and be ready."

"Be ready? For what?"

But despite her pain and the cold, Gwyn had fallen asleep.

THIRTY-SEVEN

2623 AD

"And you can study whatever you want?" Excited teens flanked Michelle even as she tried to eat her meal. It was annoying, for all that they weren't actually knocking her elbows. *But I don't have the authority to send them away, and even if I did, I'd feel like I was kicking a puppy.* The thought made her feel even more disgruntled.

"Yes." She chewed slowly, hoping that would satisfy them. Once it became obvious that it wouldn't, she gave up and swallowed. "You are tested and encouraged for certain vocations, but if you have your heart set on something, you are permitted to study it. Education is free, after all, as it should be."

"Someone has to pay for it," one boy pointed out. "Your planet is rich enough to support a supposedly 'free' education system."

"So is Earth," she countered, taking a sip from her juice. *Shut up, Michelle, you are just encouraging them!*

'The northern hemisphere is,' the boy replied. 'Even the South American Province. But the Pacific was hit hard by climate change, and these islands were never heavily populated. We have to be self-sufficient if we want to sustain our way of life."

"Teo's right," another girl piped up. "Aotearoa supports an extremely well-adjusted society. But the sacrifice we make for that is training us young for certain vocations, sending us off-world for education and experience, then returning to repay the society that supported us and seeing that it continues. It is a very good system though, with the right balance between individualism and community."

Michelle rankled. "Vivaldans are extremely well-adjusted!'

How dare this little punk lecture her about social well-being? Vivaldis was the most cosmopolitan human planet, with multi-cultural schools, universities and businesses. There were provisions for every Citizen—wasn't she an example of that? No family, no connections, yet had been cared for by the state and educated well, going into a successful, cutting-edge career.

Not very successful at the moment... She pushed that thought away.

"You do have issues on your planet, with respect." Teo clasped his hands together in a conciliatory gesture. "As does Earth, of course. Social hierarchies, economic rankings, the disenfranchised. That is unsurprising with billions of people. It is only in small societies like ours that you can ensure no one slips through the cracks."

"All Citizens have the same rights," she ground out between clenched teeth. Her irritation had her at breaking point, and it was taking all her years of practised self-control not to get up and walk away. What was wrong with her? She'd listened to a ridiculous amount of opinionated twats spouting all sorts of bigotry and prejudices in innumerable missions. How was this any different?

Because this is now. You can ignore what people have said in the past, because you know better. You haven't interacted much with humans outside of work for a while now. There had been so many missions, and she was usually exhausted from the constant time-jumping with the old chronokinetors, so she would spend her time in recovery mode. The new timepiece, the one that Gwyn had, was supposed to have helped with that, letting her do single big jumps. *But look how well that worked out,* she thought bitterly.

Out of the corner of her eye, she saw Harret raise a small hand. "That's enough," she said quietly. "We can debate social issues another time. Michelle is still very tired—I don't want anyone bothering her for the rest of the meal. Teo, tell me how your project is going?'

To Michelle's surprise, the teenagers all complied, despite looking disappointed. They all had so many questions about off-world travel and life. A tall boy with a long ponytail and a series of pretty earrings got up and poured a mug of tea from the drinks dispensary, coming back to the table to offer it to Michelle.

"Thanks," she accepted it, relieved to no longer be the subject of interrogation, but distracted as she tried to identify what was upsetting her. She barely saw the spectacular sunset over the ocean as viewed from the dining cave.

These kids are young and they live in a geographically isolated spot, but they're not ignorant. She listened to the conversations that ranged around her in the dining cave, as she had every meal since she'd arrived two days ago. Adults and teens alike filled the room, with younger children over to one side. Some discussions were fast-paced and intellectual, others were genial and more relaxed in tone, but all were thoughtful, respectful and balanced. Intervention like Harret's was hardly needed, as most groups self-moderated, and there seemed a genuinely cheerful atmosphere. It made her feel out of place, which had never bothered her before, and she couldn't work out why it did now.

Brrrys was in a natural sleep when she visited him after the meal.

"You'd like the kids here," she whispered to him. "They are cheerful and inquisitive, just like you." Stroking his fur, guilt panged again at how close she had come to losing him.

"He's resting well," Dr Quinn came into the room. "When he wakes tomorrow, I may even let him get up briefly. Mayash heal incredibly quickly."

Michelle nodded with relief. "Thank you, for saving him."

The doctor smiled. "It's my job. Now off you go, get some rest yourself."

Shooed out, Michelle hesitated in the tunnel outside, unsure where to go. "I hate feeling directionless," she muttered, knowing in her heart that it was more than a literal issue.

"Would you like to see the stars?" Harret's voice startled her. She tensed then relaxed again in a second when she realised who it was.

"Sure, why not?" It would fill some time before bed. Following the girl they passed through several caves and tunnels, then caught a Bubble, as Harret called it, to a higher level, disembarking to walk further. They passed several minutes in silence before Harret said, "I wondered if you might get claustrophobic, since you aren't used to living in caves like we are, but you are, as you say, well adjusted, and I thought perhaps it was all the people that were getting to you."

Michelle kept up easily as they climbed stone stairs cut into the rock, the tunnel winding up in a steep spiral. She relished the exercise.

"I'm just tired." She realised as she said this that the verve with which she ascended the stairs gave lie to her words. "I mean, I'm just under stress at the moment, so I'm easily irritated. Worried about Brrrys. I hope my behaviour earlier wasn't too anti-social."

"We understand." The girl smiled and stopped by an opaque forcefield that sealed a portal. She pressed her palm against the pad to the side and the forcefield shimmered into nothingness. They walked out onto the edge of a cliff.

"This way." Harret's voice had gone left, and Michelle hastily followed her away from the cliff edge, following the glowstones that marked a safe path. They climbed one more set of stairs that curved up onto a small lookout platform directly above the portal, and the panorama was laid out all around.

As with the view of the night sky in Sydney, the stars were brilliant and unfettered by light pollution. Unlike Sydney, however, there were no town lights to be seen, just the tall cold shadow of mountains marching away north and south, and the dark mass of the ocean down below with barely a flicker of moonlight upon it. Perhaps it was the company, Harret's easy going demeanour versus Jaysen Fitz' arrogance, that made it a better experience.

They stood not at the peak of a mountain but on a high spur that fell down away from the summit to their east. The mountain loomed over them, but not in a menacing way.

"It protects us," Harret said as if she'd read Michelle's thoughts. "This is the most stable area in the whole South Island. Sure, we get little tremors now and then, but it's nowhere near as bad as it was several hundred years ago. The tectonic plate has shifted us away from the fault line. We have legends too, about the spirit of the mountain, and out of respect for our ancestors we tell those stories at official family gatherings. Family is very important here."

Funny, Jay talked about family too. "Maybe that's why I don't fit in here." Michelle gave a half-hearted laugh. "I've never had a family. Don't particularly want one. They sound like a lot of work."

"They are." Michelle thought she could hear the girl smile in the dark. "But a good family is there for you, too. And work that you love is fulfilling."

Their musings were swept away in the cool wind that rushed down off the mountain and into the sea below. Michelle was starting to get cold, though she didn't want to admit it. She relished the chance to be almost alone. It was almost like being on a mission. Just her against the world, making a plan, playing the game.

"It must be nice up here in the day, too," she said, thinking she could come here to meditate. Who knew how much longer she'd be stuck in this bolt-hole?

"It is! At dawn the sun rises over the peaks, shooting sunlight down into the valleys and onto the water, melting the shadows into the ocean. During the day you can see up and down the mountains; white snow here and there, green vegetation further down the slopes and the blue-grey-green of the sea. At sunset everything goes pink and gold—it's beautiful." Harret's poetry was heartfelt.

"Sounds colourful," Michelle couldn't help mocking but immediately regretted it. This was the girl's home. So what if she had never seen the rings of Saturn or the dramatic rising of Vivaldis' moons? She obviously loved this place, but in a genuine, humble way, not the proud boastful declaration of superiority that had characterised Jay's attitude towards Earth.

"Sorry," she said after Harret didn't reply. "I would love to see it. It sounds beautiful. Perhaps it'll help with my frustration to meditate here, if that would be okay?"

She sensed rather than saw the girl relax. "Of course. I hope you'll find some peace. We'd best turn in for the night then. It's getting cold and if you want to see the dawn you'll want to be ready early." Her words held half a challenge; Michelle guessed that Harret doubted whether Michelle meant what she said about wanting to see the view at all times of the day.

"Of course," Michelle replied, choosing not to rise to it. She was a guest here. She needed to behave herself. "Let's go."

They turned to leave, picking their way carefully down the glowstone-lit path and back into the portal. Just before Michelle entered, she glanced up one more time at the stars, then stopped.

One star was brighter and getting steadily larger than the others. It also was lower than its companions... much lower. As it descended,

Michelle could make out the quiet whirring of sub-space engines as the star began to distinguish itself as a ship with a multitude of lights flecking its hull.

"Harret," she said, pointing.

The girl frowned. "Inside, quickly. I don't know who that is or what they want, but if it's you they're after then they have to go through Uncle Henare."

They scooted in and the girl used her palm to raise the forcefield in the portal, obscuring outside sound and view alike. As they descended the spiral stone stair, Michelle could feel a buzz of excitement.

Danger or no, she hoped that ship was for her.

THIRTY-EIGHT

1461 AD

It was Masada again, except she was there in time to see the killings take place. Joshua ran Sarah through with a sword and then hacked Adi down. Gaius fought him but had no chance, falling to a thrust through the heart. Joshua smiled and became Vlad, advancing on Gwyn. She screamed and tripped on Meric's body, but was saved from falling by Alina's bloody hands.

"Alina!" Gwyn tried to turn, to protect her by pushing her away from Vlad but the lady's hands tightened their grip and her face smiled sickeningly, morphing into Countess Báthory's.

"No!" she shouted, jerking awake. Alina squeaked and moved too, but Gwyn couldn't see her. She opened her eyes, thinking she was still dreaming, but blackness prevailed.

All the torches have gone out. "Alina! Why didn't you wake me?" Gwyn demanded, fighting the fluttering in her chest. She waved her hand in front of her face, trying to see it. She hit something.

"Ow!" Alina cried out.

"Sorry," Gwyn said automatically, then became annoyed. "Where are you? Why didn't you wake me?" she demanded again.

"I'm right here!" Alina's voice was inches from Gwyn's ear. "I... I fell asleep. Oh no! I told you not to put the torches out!"

Gwyn patted and found Alina's face, then her hands. "They would have burned out at the same time anyway." She tried not to be angry but it was hard. Now they had no light.

"What are you going to do now?"

Gwyn sighed, her shoulder aching. Annoyance at Alina and at the whole situation—including her fear of the dark—was giving her a headache. She snorted at the ridiculousness of Alina's question. "I'm going to do the same damn thing I was going to earlier. Stand on the table and jump on them when they come in, hoping they trip on the shit I scattered here. But I'll be blind until they come in. I'll probably get stabbed again and that'll be the end of it," she said bitterly. "I should have gone home when I had the chance."

"Gone home? You told me your family was dead?"

Ughhh. Does Michelle get sick of telling these lies? I suppose she doesn't care.

"They aren't alive." That was true in this time anyway. "I could have gone home, I didn't need to stay. I…" *stayed for you,* she wanted to say, but saying it out loud would make it real, and she wasn't sure it was anymore. Plus, it felt melodramatic and stupid. "I wanted to stay," she said. She had wanted to stay. Even now a tiny part of her hoped that a dramatic romantic declaration would bring them together like it was supposed to, like it did in stories. Surely Alina would see?

"What do *you* want?" Gwyn asked.

Alina sounded bewildered. "I want to escape here, of course."

Well, duh. "Sorry," she was glad Alina couldn't see her rolling her eyes. "I mean, in life. Did you want to marry Vlad? Do you want to… stay married to him? If you had a choice?"

"No." Gwyn was surprised at the emphatic answer. She expected more prevaricating, more 'duty to one's husband'.

"No? Um, what would you prefer?" *Me! Pick me!*

Pathetic, Gwyn. Stop thinking about yourself for a minute!

While she didn't expect Alina to declare for her, the answer she gave instead blew Gwyn away.

"I want to join a convent and become a bride of Christ to spend my days in prayer and contemplation of the spirit."

"What?" The word burst out of Gwyn's mouth with a halo of laughter before she could stop it. She had no doubt she wore an expression of incredulity but in the pitch black it was impossible to read Alina's face in return. Still, she heard a note of disapproval when the other woman replied.

"As I said. I want to remove myself from the temporal as much as I can. I cannot fulfil my duty as a wife so I know I would be better suited to marry Christ instead, and spend my days in prayer."

"Oh." For some moments the only sound was their breathing. Gwyn struggled with her thoughts. "Do you think your brother will let you do that?"

A small, cynical laugh met her words. "I don't know. Even if I can convince him, I don't know if Vlad will go through the embarrassment of applying for an annulment. He is... often much more direct when he wants something."

You don't say. The implication was clear. Especially if the world thought Alina was dead already.

The lady's next words were even more dejected. "Not that any of that matters anymore. Death will take us in this black pit and no one will ever know." A small sob escaped and Gwyn re-gripped her hands.

"No. Don't say that. I'll get us out of here. We'll get out of here together."

Alina's soft hands twitched and Gwyn thought she was going to pull away. Then they reached up Gwyn's arms and she was drawn into a soft embrace. Gwyn winced, but the pressure on her shoulder didn't make her dizzy so she noted absently it mustn't be as bad as she'd first thought. Being held by Alina, even in this dank and horrible dungeon, somehow made the world a better place.

They must have dozed for hours, for when they woke Gwyn badly needed to pee but was reluctant to remove herself. Fortunately, Alina felt her move and voiced the same urgency herself.

Gwyn sighed. "Oh God, I don't know, um. Hang on."

Gwyn groped her way to the table, retrieving the goblet she'd placed there earlier. She knocked it off with a clang and had to scrabble around to find it.

"You'll have to go by feel, sorry," she apologised as she passed it over to the chained Alina. Gwyn crawled carefully to a corner to avail herself of the privacy afforded by the darkness.

She took the emptied goblet back from Alina and sighed. *My weapons are unlit torches and a piss-stained goblet.*

"Gwyn!" Alina hissed.

"What?" Gwyn tensed.

"Listen!"

They listened. A faint thudding teased the edges of their hearing. Gwyn gripped Alina's arm and breathed, "Look."

The blackness wasn't completely black anymore. The barest sliver of grey could be seen creeping under the door, which was now identifiable opposite them.

"Stay silent until they are fully inside," Gwyn breathed in Alina's ear. "Once I've made my move start screaming as loudly as you can, and don't stop." She squeezed the lady's hand and crawled carefully to the door, clambering onto the table and gripping an unlit torch hard in both hands. She pressed herself against the wall and lowered her eyelids to slits, slowing her breathing.

It was worse than the Roma raid on their camp in the woods. Worse than creeping through the tunnels of Masada searching for Adi. The waiting stretched on and on and Gwyn needed to pee all over again. *Come on.*

The steps drew closer and the light under the door grew. It crept across the floor to where Alina was, huddled and chained. Gwyn expected the bolt to scrape so she wasn't ready for its smooth slide back. The door opened to reveal a short, balding man holding a large iron ring of keys and the Countess carrying a brightly burning candle.

Their captors were inside the cell before Gwyn could speak or move, so when she did react it was the Countess she attacked, not the man. She kept her eyes almost closed against the light and swung the torch as hard as she could—like a baseball bat with Báthory's head as the ball, even stepping to get the correct follow through.

A sickening *crack* resounded through the chamber and Countess Báthory dropped like a stone. The candle in her hand tumbled down and went out instantly, leaving them in darkness.

Gwyn opened her eyes wide and leapt on the bald man's back as Alina began to scream. He might have recovered had it not been for the ankle-rolling obstacles that sent him crashing to the hard stone floor. He fought Gwyn hard, though, and she had to use every ounce of desperation and anger she had to try to subdue him. She could just make out her goal by the glimmer of light from the torch in the stairwell outside the cell.

Alina was still screaming, whether deliberately or because she was terrified, Gwyn couldn't tell. She reached for the length of chain she'd tried to loosen from its bolt earlier. The man bucked and the chain yanked free and she whipped it back into the man's face.

"Argh!" He screamed and she felt warm blood seep down over her arm that wrapped around his neck. Whipping again she was rewarded by another sick, wet noise and she thought she was going to vomit. Unable to bear it anymore, she released him and pushed up, snatching at the iron keyring as she did.

"Alina!" She fumbled with the keys, then swore. "Wait here!"

"Where are you going?" Alina wailed as Gwyn rushed out the dungeon door and halfway up the stairs, chasing the light. She saw a torch in its bracket. Retrieving it carefully, she clattered back down, terrified that the Countess would wake or the man would recover and attack her. He was moaning and clutching his bloody face. She kicked him in the guts, hoping that would convince him to stay down.

Gwyn used the torch to light several others and tried different keys in Alina's manacles. The fourth one worked and she hauled the lady to her feet and out the cell. She slammed the door behind them and slid the bolt home.

"Hurry," she urged, but both women were in poor shape—bruised and cold. They limped up the stairway, frightened each time they had to stop and rest. Eventually they emerged into the little room behind the castle chapel. Gwyn made Alina sit down and dragged a chest across the doorway.

She foraged in a cupboard and pulled out some sacramental wine. "Drink this."

"Gwyn!" Alina was shocked.

"Just drink it, ask forgiveness later!" Now that they'd escaped the dungeon, she was planning how best to get them out of the castle. If it was as Meric had said, they'd be hard pressed to leave, especially covered in blood and cuts and big, purpling bruises. Gwyn felt dizzy and wanted nothing more than to take some serious painkillers and sleep, but it wasn't an option.

She went to the door that led into the chapel and listened. *Shit.* She could hear men's voices but there was no other exit from the room. Were these men waiting for the Countess? Indecision plagued her.

She thought about what she had achieved with the pocket watch; making herself inconspicuous and non-descript. She and Alina hardly looked non-descript, with bruises and scrapes, so she hastened about the lady trying to straighten her clothes and using the wine to wipe off blood.

"Ssh!" she hushed when Alina looked about to cry out. "I know it stings but it'll clean it. I need you to do the same for me. Here's my plan."

Alina was dubious but keen to get away from the door to the dungeon as fast as possible.

"Just act normal and let me do the talking," Gwyn instructed. She straightened her shoulders and after a second Alina copied her. "Let's go."

Two male servants looked startled when the women pushed through the door into the chapel.

"Ah, the Countess was wondering where you were," Gwyn told them before they had a chance to speak. "She asked you to wait here because she wants to talk to you both. It's very important." She ladled confidence and authority into her tone. The men stared at her.

"As you were," Gwyn nodded and clutched Alina's elbow to steer her past. Open-mouthed, the men were frozen in bafflement and she smiled benignly as if all was well. They exited the chapel and turned down the corridor to make for the main hall.

"Did you cast a spell on them?" Alina whispered in Gwyn's ear.

"Sort of," she muttered back. "Hurry, it doesn't work on everyone."

"My legs hurt," Alina sighed but she increased her pace.

They moved along the passage, skirting the edges of the great hall, and down the steps that led to the stables. Moving briskly but not hastily, Gwyn met all puzzled looks with a bland smile and a disinterested gaze. She breathed through her nostrils, endeavouring to stay calm and not break into a run. Alina stumbled several times but made no further complaint. Perhaps she could taste freedom too.

"Dammit." She scanned the stable yard. Meric was nowhere in sight. *Shit. There are a hundred places he could be.*

"We'll have to leave him," Alina tugged Gwyn's sleeve, who frowned back at her.

"Boy," she called out to a skinny stable hand. He paused from his task of mucking out that corner of the yard and wiped his eyes as he looked up. "Have you seen the new guard? Tall man, dark hair. Always wears a neckerchief."

The boy shrugged and turned back to his chore.

"Here." Gwyn thanked the foresight that had led her to tuck her purse into her skirts the previous night. She held up a shiny copper between finger and thumb. The lad's attention was immediately transfixed. "Well?"

"Him's gone and left," the boy mumbled, leaning on his shovel. "Went s'morning."

"Left?" Gwyn was baffled. "Where did he go?"

The boy eyed the coin hungrily and she flipped it to him. He caught it neatly and it disappeared into his stained woollen vest. "Rode out on fine horse, lady's horse. S'gone."

"He took *my* horse!" Alina hissed indignantly.

"Never mind that now," Gwyn risked losing her composure. *He left us...* Had she driven him off when he'd tried to warn her? *Yes, but if he can get out, we can too.*

Nodding thanks at the lad she marched Alina out of the stable yard and aimed for the tunnel leading to the main gate. There was a commotion up ahead. She and Alina looked at each other.

"Should we...?"

"We have to try get out now," Gwyn was firm. "Maybe we can slip past. Keep acting calm and confident and stay close."

Alina nodded and gripped Gwyn's hand tightly. They left the stables and emerged into the small courtyard that housed the main gate. Gwyn was dismayed to see the portcullis was down. An argument was going on between the guards and men outside the gates, and all attention was on that.

"How are we going to get past that?" Alina whispered. "We should go back and find somewhere to hide!"

Then Gwyn heard a voice she recognised, and hysteria bubbled up inside her. She stepped forward into the courtyard. "Open the gates!" she roared in her best parade-ground voice. "That's an order!"

Stung into action, the guard manning the portcullis turned the wheel.

Men on horseback trotted into the yard, bristling with weaponry and ready to cut down anyone hapless enough to get in their way. On Alina's fine mare, rode Meric, second only to the formidable figure leading the armed party.

Alina fainted and Gwyn staggered as the lady's weight fell against her. She managed to stay upright, though, and looked the lead rider right in the eye.

It was Vlad.

THIRTY-NINE

1461 AD

Prince Vlad took possession of Csejthe Castle without a fight. The guards were in disarray, believing the Countess had given the order to open the gate. Once they realised she hadn't they were not in a position to resist. Vlad's men were inside.

Elizabeth Báthory was retrieved from the dungeon, alive but unconscious. While they waited for her to awaken, Vlad heard the tale of torture from Alina and Gwyn—and the confession from the manservant, Thorko. Clutching his bloody face, Thorko admitted to luring hundreds of young girls to be murdered by the Countess. "She needed their blood!" he wailed.

Alina turned away in horror. Gwyn wanted to be sick. Even the battle-hardened men accompanying Vlad paled.

"Throw her from the walls!" Vlad roared.

"Please, my lord," Alina was pale and bloodied still. "Let King Matthias deal out justice to her. She is one of his nobles."

Gwyn was astonished that, even after her treatment, Alina was disposed to forgive.

"The Báthorys are a powerful family," Alina whispered to Gwyn. "My lord needs the Hungarian support. And I don't want her death on my soul."

They watched as Vlad ground his teeth. "Wall her up in her rooms," he finally spat. "Let Corvinus send someone to deal with her. I'll be seeing him soon anyway but I've lost a day coming here."

They stayed one night, hearing the screams from the Countess when she woke to her prison. They left the next day, riding for Kronstadt.

They cantered out the gate and kept to a swift pace, Vlad's party resuming their road from Moldavia.

Gwyn was simply glad to leave the castle of death and disillusionment.

* * *

"So you decided not to kill him, then." It was a statement, not a question.

Meric looked rueful. "My own life would have been forfeit had I even tried; besides, I knew it was more important to help you and this was the one person who could do it. It was a miracle I met his party on the road." He spoke so quietly that even riding right beside him Gwyn had to lean closer to hear.

She, too, kept her voice low. She had been so relieved to see the janissary, who had hustled her off to the side after Vlad reunited with his wife. He had looked after her stabbed shoulder, following her instruction to clean it with honey and wine, then binding it firmly.

"I thought... I thought you'd left us, actually," she said. "I wouldn't have blamed you. You've tried to protect me all this time and I still didn't trust you."

"I understand. You've been hurt before." He glanced ahead to the front of the line, where Vlad rode with Alina.

Gwyn raised her eyebrows in question, and Meric nodded with a dark look in his eyes.

"Don't wait for him to get you alone again," he warned.

"I know." The gates of Kronstadt loomed ahead and Vlad's party rode through, hooves clattering on the cobbles.

"The king of Hungary arrived a sennight ago, my Prince," Gwyn heard one man announce. She saw Vlad nod and they followed their guide to their lodgings. Whichever burgher had given up his residence (voluntarily or otherwise) was not present to welcome them, and even Gwyn noticed the slight.

"Send a message to Corvinus that I've arrived and tell him I'm eager to meet," Vlad ordered. "Say nothing of my wife."

"Yes, my lord." The man scuttled off.

"My dear, if you will join me a moment?" Vlad turned to Alina, then crooked a finger at Gwyn and Meric. "And you, and you."

Her stomach churned. But what harm could come to her in front of Alina? Still, it took all of her courage to dismount and follow the others into the brightly painted house.

The door shut behind them. Vlad indicated Alina should sit—Gwyn and Meric stood behind her, wondering what this was going to be about.

The Prince considered them all for a second, steepling his fingers and raising them to his lips. "I have a problem," he announced.

You have a lot of problems, buddy. Gwyn bit the inside of her lip, subduing the giggle that threatened to bubble up.

Alina tilted her chin up and asked softly, "What problem, my lord?"

Hands still clasped but forefingers extended, he pointed at her. "You, my dear. You are dead and the world knows it. As such I am brokering an alliance with the king of Hungary, based on marriage to his sister." The calm, reasonable Vlad was back—the homicidal maniac hidden for now—and he spoke as if this was a minor irritation.

"And you," he pointed at Meric now, "I know who you are, I remember that ear." Gwyn felt Meric stiffen. "Have you been sent by Mehmed to assassinate me?"

"No, my lord." Gwyn wondered what it must have cost for Meric to say these next words. "You are not the only one who longed to return to his homeland and be a prisoner no more. I waited for years for my chance."

"Hmm." Vlad gave no indication whether he believed Meric or not. Gwyn willed him to but felt no answering warmth from the pocket watch. *Probably only works for me.* She waited for him to address her next. He didn't.

"So what am I to do, dearest?" His attention returned to Alina. "Bigamy is a sin, but I need this alliance. Wallachia is in possession of my *brother*," the word dripped with scorn, "and those traitorous boyars must be punished."

Is he telling us he's going to kill her? And us too, for being witnesses? Fear made Gwyn angry. *This is bullshit, that he should play with our lives like this.*

"What about a convent?" Gwyn spoke up, placing a hand on Alina's shoulder and squeezed softly.

"What?" Vlad's eyes swung to Gwyn, noting the familiar touch. Everyone was silent for a moment.

"A convent, my lord," Alina spoke up, her melodic voice calm. "I will take orders, renounce this marriage and become a bride of Christ. If... if you ever had any affection for me, you will give me permission to take this path. I will leave behind my name, my title. No one will ever know who I was."

Gwyn watched Vlad struggle with the thought of giving up his wife.

"You are mine," he ground out.

"We all belong to the Lord," the lady replied, and Gwyn understood that what Alina had said about becoming a nun was true. Her heart saddened but she had no greater claim to Alina than Vlad.

Let her go. She glanced at Meric, who stood taut and silent. *And him too.* She couldn't interfere in their lives forever.

"I'm sure Prince Stephen could be convinced of the wisdom of this plan, my lord," Gwyn said. "If it is what my lady truly wants, she will tell him of your graciousness and thus your alliance with Moldavia will also be maintained. For the sake of his sister's life, surely he will keep the secret?" Calm, measured words lined up and marched obediently out of her mouth, all the while she raised her eyes to meet his and concentrated.

The connection with the pocket watch almost jolted her out of her carefully considered pose. Her brain felt alive again, and the warmth from her hand spread up her left arm and filled her whole body. She glanced down in astonishment and saw the spiral once again turned in the right direction, and she knew she could make a jump if she wished.

Baffled why it should choose to work now, of all times, but not questioning her good fortune, she added, "Send my lady to Moldavia, to a convent there, with Meric here to escort her. You need never see either of them again."

She added an air of finality to her words, then waited. She knew she'd gone and done the exact thing she'd dreaded—attract Vlad's attention—but knew also that it was the right thing to do.

Vlad said nothing at first. He clasped his hands behind his back and flicked green eyes between Alina, Meric, and Gwyn—lingering on Gwyn.

"Very well," he barked. "Prepare yourself to leave immediately. The janissary shall go with you," he ordered Alina and Meric. He stood to the side, indicating they should exit.

Not needing to be told twice, Alina hastened from her chair and made for the door, shooting a grateful look towards Gwyn before bobbing a curtsy of thanks to her husband. He waved her off, obviously wanting her out of his sight now that she didn't belong to him anymore.

Meric followed more slowly. Gwyn went after him but stopped when Vlad put a hand on her arm. Meric shot her a warning glance, but she smiled tightly and nodded that he should go on without her.

He didn't look happy, but obeyed all the same, recognising the opportunity to escape.

"Don't come back," was all Gwyn said.

* * *

The door closed and the room was quiet. Little motes of dust floated in the air, visible in the stream of sunlight that let itself in through the narrow glass windows. The colourful exterior of the burgher house was matched by the rich and ornate furniture and paintings that adorned the room. Saxon trade flourished here; the wealth in this room was evidence of the fact.

Vlad and Gwyn both stood still, his hand wrapped around her upper arm. A possessive hold, one from which she wouldn't have a chance of breaking free, unless he wanted her to. She waited for him to speak but he just gazed at her.

"Are you a spy?" he said abruptly.

She couldn't help but laugh for a second. "No." She shook her head.

"But not a servant girl." It was a statement.

She breathed out through her nose and shrugged. "No, not that either."

"Then what?" he demanded, eyes fierce.

She shrugged again. "It doesn't matter. I'll be gone soon."

He frowned at this and gripped her other arm. "You'll go when I say you can go."

She looked into his eyes. A handsome man, commanding and

powerful, but a monster nonetheless. Whatever magnetism had drawn her to him was still there—he both fascinated and repelled her, but she wouldn't let him dominate her. She leant towards him and tilted her mouth to his.

He responded to her kiss, melding his body to hers. She could feel his want for her as the kiss became fierce and urgent, and she was almost swept away by the thrill of being so desired. But enough of her brain was detached, watching cynically and wondering if the distraction was really necessary.

The door behind Vlad burst open. Gwyn shot a startled look towards it, expecting to see Meric and damming him already for such a rash move.

It wasn't Meric. Six knights filed into the room and fanned out, hands on the hilts of their swords. "Prince Vlad Dracula?" one of them asked.

"Can't you see I'm busy?" snapped Vlad.

The knight ignored him. He wore plate armour on his upper body over a tunic, with shiny black boots and red breeches. The others were similarly dressed, but it was the hardness of their faces that struck her the most.

"You are under arrest for treachery with the Turk. We have a letter signed by your own hand, betraying your alliance with King Matthias." He brandished a document, the heavy signature DRAKULYA clear at the bottom.

Vlad's head snapped around, furiously denying that he had ever signed such a document. Gwyn knew this was her moment. She closed her eyes calmly, reaching with her mind. She barely heard the shout of fury and indignation as the Hungarian knights grabbed Vlad and started dragging him from the room. One of them went to grab her too but his glove passed through blue mist.

Flick!

FORTY

2623 AD

Michelle returned to the dormitory and gathered her things, then insisted on joining Brrrys in the infirmary. "If there is some danger I need to be there to protect him. I got him into this mess."

Harret didn't bother to argue, merely nodded and escorted Michelle to the correct level. It galled Michelle—she didn't need to be babysat—but accepted it as the quickest way to get rid of Harret. The girl told Michelle to keep out of sight and left to find Henare.

"What's going on?" Brrrys was awake and Dr Quinn wasn't present. She must have deemed him stable enough to leave the room, trusting to the monitors around the bed to alert her if anything drastic changed.

"Not sure," Michelle replied, sitting on the edge of the bed and taking his hand. He was lying on his side and he curled around her sitting form in affection. "I was topside with the girl Harret, and a ship was coming in to land. Don't know if it's friendly yet so she hustled me inside and has gone to find out. She's very mature for one so young." She said the last begrudgingly, telling herself she was objective enough to recognise the truth.

"Citizen Harret," Brrrys corrected. Michelle was embarrassed, but sensible enough not to try to defend her rudeness.

"Yes. Citizen Harret," she said shortly.

His tail flicked up and over and patted her on the shoulder. "Your species aren't your enemy, and they aren't stupid."

"Some are," she pointed out.

"And so are some Mayash," he shrugged. "Shaggy-furred, we call them, those that want 'the good old days.' I've heard young Nolii joke that some of their ancestors have turned into rocks for lack of moving, and I'm sure calling a Rilan a puddle-muddler means they spend too much time in the swamp, figuratively speaking."

She couldn't help but laugh at that last one. "I suppose. I don't see any of them actively trying to upend the Allied Planets, though. They might grumble but they don't plot."

"That you know of." Again, he shrugged. "We only found out about this mob by chance. You forced their hand when you let Hera capture you and brought Citizen Gwyn to our time. Perhaps we have been lucky they have moved against the government now and not later."

"Hardly!" Her hands flew up in exasperation. "We are losing precious time every day that passes and we don't fix errant timelines!"

He caught her wrist with his tail and brought it down to her lap, grabbing her other hand with his. He closed his eyes briefly.

"I'm sorry, you're still not well," she lowered her voice, hoping not to bring the doctor's wrath down upon her for disturbing the patient. "I just want to be out *doing* something, not hiding in this hole."

"I don't like it any more than you," he sighed. "But we're stuck, and we have to hope our betters know what they are doing and that the information we obtained is proving to be of some use."

She had her doubts. Rolling her eyes, she said, "It's hard to have faith in the Shanista this far from Vivaldis, stuck in a cave on the wrong side of a backward planet."

"Perhaps you mistake the time you are in, Agent Michelle, as humans would never have been invited to join the Allied Planets had Earth been considered backward. Your species is young, but it has great potential."

The voice was quiet and held no hint of reproach, but Michelle leapt to her feet as if she'd been stung. Her back had been to the door, which was unlike her, but the newest arrival in the infirmary would have surprised her anyway, though it was polite enough not to click its amusement at her shock.

"Citizen Colsa!" Shame flooded her, but she knew better than to try defend herself. "You heard me voicing my frustration and doubt, I am sorry to say. I fear I am failing in this mission.'

The Shanista cocked its insectile head, large faceted eyes glittering like polished obsidian. "I think not. It was never a formal mission, but regardless, it is not over. As usual, your methods are ethically questionable but have yielded results. It is difficult to reconcile when the fate of billions is at hand. The Shift is coming."

"What is the Shift?" Doctor Quinn had followed her visitor in, obviously nervous yet excited to be in the presence of such an esteemed scientist. Michelle kept her face impassive. She knew not to discuss such things in public and she'd be surprised if Colsa was going to talk to the doctor about it.

Colsa went ahead and surprised her. "It is a force that will prevent us from going back into history and correcting timelines that are straying from their course. More explanation than that would require a great deal of scientific detail, and while I have no doubt of your ability to understand the principles, I'm afraid I don't have the time to go through it with you, Citizen Doctor." Colsa was succinct and matter of fact, and while Quinn looked poised to argue, the Shanista simply kept talking. "Guardsperson Brrrys, do you feel well enough to come with us?" Colsa used the Mayash' formal title to remind him of his duty to the Agency, Michelle was sure. It needn't have bothered.

"Of course," Brrrys looked at Doctor Quinn. "Do I have your permission to go, doctor? I'll be going regardless, but I'd prefer to be given the all clear."

Despite being overwhelmed by all that was going on, Quinn shook off her bafflement and moved to give her patient a final examination.

"You are healing remarkably quickly," she said. "But you must avoid quick movements and I don't recommend sudden acceleration." She looked pointedly at Colsa. "Does your ship have appropriate patient transport facilities?"

"It does." Colsa showed no offence, though it was well known that Shanista technology was at the forefront in practically everything, and certainly in space and atmospheric travel. "Do you wish to inspect the facilities?" It knew that Quinn was simply adhering to correct medical procedure. "I will take over as attending physician; you may check my credentials."

Michelle was surprised. She didn't know Colsa was a medical doctor too but the Shanista tended to have multiple degrees.

"I will." Quinn accepted a data crystal and scanned it into a wall computer, eyes flicking back and forth as the details came up. "Very well. Brrrys if you are ready, we can go. I presume you want to leave immediately?" She directed this question at Colsa and Michelle.

"We do."

Well, my wish was granted faster than I expected, that's for sure! Michelle helped Brrrys up and found a brush in his bag to help him tidy his fur, stepping into the hygiene facilities to do so.

"You don't have to come," she murmured. "Not if you don't feel up to it. I'd rather you just get well."

"I'll be fine." His tail curled around her arm, for steadiness or affection, she wasn't sure. "Someone's got to keep an eye on you." He grinned and it made him seem more like his normal self, instead of the worn-out bloodied wreck she'd carted over here.

Doctor Quinn was swift but not cursory in her inspection of Colsa's ship. A Nolii pilot stood talking to Henare, and Harret was unsuccessfully trying to contain her extreme excitement from being so close to such a variety of non-humans.

"They're just people like you and me," Michelle slipped up behind Harret, causing the human girl to jump. She had stowed Brrrys inside the ship and come back out to thank their hosts as they waited in the dock. The Shanista vessel was shaped like an elongated egg, snub-nosed and tapering outwards into a rounded stern. Wings that had nothing to do with lift in the traditional sense—but assisted in the aerodynamics of atmospheric flight—were currently folded in and up against the hull. Their honeycombed texture and pattern stood out in light gold against the darker bronze of the ship.

"I know," Harret blushed. Michelle felt bad that she had been so abrupt to the young people here. Seeing Harret's expression she realised how truly exciting it must be for these kids to meet off-world travellers since they had yet to go anywhere themselves. Wouldn't she have been curious too?

"I know you said you don't go off-world, but if for some reason you do end up on Vivaldis, or if any of your peers do, you can drop me a line." She indicated Harret's wrist com and asked, "May I?"

"Please." Michelle was rewarded with a genuine smile, and she tried not to squirm. As she tapped in her public com address, she warned,

"I'm away a lot for work so I won't always be reachable. But if I'm about and not busy, I"d be happy to show anyone around the university." *You'll probably never have to,* she whispered reassuringly to herself.

"Thanks, Michelle, that would be fantastic!" Harret gushed. "I'll make sure everyone has your address, but to keep in mind that you are a busy person. We tend to get scattered across a variety of schools and facilities so we don't usually know anyone."

"Yes, well, good luck and all that," Michelle bowed to both Harret and Henare. "Thank you for taking us in and protecting us. I hope there is no trouble because of it."

"Just doing our duty," Henare bowed back.

There was little conversation as the ship took off and soared quietly through the night. Brrrys was asleep and Michelle wanted to do the same but she wanted to know where they were going first.

"The Agency's facility here on Earth," Colsa replied, not giving anything more away.

Back to Berlin. "And has the restriction on Agents time travelling been lifted? I presume you have missions for me?' She tried to keep the eagerness out of her voice.

"No."

No? "Then what?'"

"Rest now, Agent." The delicate arm pointed one of six equally delicate digits to a sleep pod. She obeyed, climbing into a pod, but felt disgruntled until the calm wash of sleep crept over her and brought her racing thoughts to a halt.

They must have lingered in the atmosphere some time, travelling much slower than was necessary, for it was just before dawn when they landed. Somehow Michelle slept through the landing, which meant the Nolii pilot was one of the best, bringing down the ship with the sort of precision that was reminiscent of the original lunar landings, albeit under much greater gravity.

Michelle awoke and was dismayed to see it was mid-morning by the ship's clock. Everyone else was gone, even Brrrys. She stepped out cautiously into the small hanger that graced the rooftop of the Agency building. It was an open-topped cylinder with a forcefield that protected ships and people alike from the elements—except for during take-offs and landings. The forcefield was currently opaque like the ones in the caves of Aotearoa, so she couldn't tell if the sun was shining or not.

No one was around, which she found extremely odd. In the past when she'd travelled here, she'd gone via normal transport and landed at the main spaceport of Berlin. There was usually a gap of at least several weeks between missions, so she'd always gone home to Vivaldis and done more training and study at the Agency headquarters there. Even the rescue missions of other Agents—or recovery missions, twice—had not been something for which she'd been rushed to Earth. Better to prepare and then time it correctly.

Surely someone should be in attendance on the dock, though? She poked around, familiarising herself with the layout. *Not even a robot to operate the forcefield?* Even the small control room was empty but not locked.

Michelle started doing mental calculations. Her training covered a variety of skills, but piloting a ship wasn't one of them. Even if she could somehow lift off, there were security protocols for both ship and forcefield to bypass. And then she'd have to fly illegally through European airspace to the Carpathians and land... She dismissed the idea. If going rogue was what the Shanista wanted her to do, they were going to have to make it a bit more obvious. She didn't think they'd stoop to that, though Colsa's acceptance of what she'd done to Jay Fitz struck her as out of character for such an ethical person.

The Shift is coming... They are getting desperate. The thought rose unbidden in her mind. She squared her shoulders and made for the lift that would take her down to the main levels.

"I'm sick of being in the dark," she said. "Time to find out what's going on."

FORTY-ONE

PRESENT DAY

Gwyn stumbled out of the museum, apologising to patrons and collecting strange looks as she emerged onto Piața Sfatului. She hoped Meric and Alina had got out in time, and were riding hell for leather to Moldavia. Or had ridden... The jolt that once again she hadn't said goodbye to the people she cared about hit her hard, and tears mixed with rain as she hurried across the square to the Black Church.

She sniffed and wiped her nose with her sleeve, realising the ridiculousness of her outfit. All she wore from this time were her boots—the rest was all fifteenth-century dress, complete with petticoats and cloak.

It's a good cloak, at least. It shed the light drizzle without drama and was warm as she wrapped it around herself against the breeze that gusted into the doorway of the church. She lingered a moment, wondering how to explain her clothes.

"Gwyn!" Her mother appeared from the depths of the church and looked astonished. "I've been looking for you everywhere for the last half an hour! Where have you been? And... what on earth are you wearing?"

"Mum." Gwyn fought to hold back the tears that she'd only just managed to halt. "Can we go back to the hostel? I've had enough of history for today."

Danielle Turner looked astonished. "You? Had enough of history? Are you not feeling well?" she joked, but her smile faded when she looked at her daughter's face, taking in the bruises and cuts Gwyn knew where there. "Honey?"

"It's alright, mum, can we just go? I'm cold and I want a shower and something to eat."

"Darling, what's wrong? Are you hurt?" Danielle shrugged into her own rain jacket and followed Gwyn out onto the wet street. They walked quickly, huddled against the weather and Gwyn replied,

"I'll tell you when I'm cleaned up, I promise."

She made it to their room without anyone else in the family seeing her, Stephen Turner having corralled the twins into assisting with dinner. Gwyn revelled in her shower and sighed almost indecently at the feel of soft, clean clothes on her body. She shaved her legs and washed her hair three times—it fluffed out like a mane when she dried it with her mother's little travel hairdryer—and then brushed it.

After dinner, she mentioned to her dad she wanted to talk to her mum and Naomi alone. "Girl stuff," she explained.

"Come on, Justin! Let's see if you can beat your old man at table tennis." Stephen ushered his son out of the dorm room.

"Is this about why you've been acting so weird?" Naomi was almost bouncing with excitement.

"Yes," said Gwyn. Her shoulder ached and she touched it unconsciously. "It's going to sound crazy, but I need you to listen."

And she told them.

FORTY-TWO

1474 AD

Vlad watched the rat squirm as he skewered it with a sharp knife. It was his sole entertainment these days, so he didn't look up when one of his guards entered the room.

"Letters for you, my lord." The parchment was placed on the table and the guard left the room.

Vlad left the rat to die and cracked open the seals. The first letter was from the Hungarian kind, confirming Vlad's marriage to Corvinus' sister was finally to go ahead, over a decade after it was first brokered. Vlad smirked. *He can't stomach Radu anymore, can he? That's why he's kept me alive all these years, because I'm the best weapon he has against Mehmed.* The smirk turned bitter and he itched to get his vengeance for the forged letter that had brought about his downfall.

The second letter was from his cousin Stephen, now called "the Great" of Moldavia. *The title should have been mine. I'm twice the ruler he is!* He ignored the fact that Stephen had managed to balance the power of his nobles without the widespread executions Vlad had inflicted, but even if he had considered it, he would have thought it a sign of weakness.

Still, Stephen had been campaigning for Vlad's release for some years now, and Vlad knew he owed his cousin gratitude for that. Plans for a new campaign into Wallachia to drive out the pro-Ottoman boyars filled the letter, but a few lines caught his attention.

I must pass on the sad news of the death of one Sister Mary, at the Convent of St Philothea. She died after a wasting sickness, and I have ordered prayers to be said for her soul. Congratulations on your new marriage.

Vlad put the letter down and walked to the window. His rooms looked out over the Danube, and he could see the city of Pest across the river.

So she is dead. I am finally free to remarry and gain my release. I will burn into Wallachia and kill my wastrel of a brother, and drive those Turks back into the sea.

He felt a surge of anger that this had not happened sooner. That he had wasted twelve years of his life trapped in a gilded cage when he should have been fighting and ruling and rising to greatness.

It's all because of that girl.

Read on for a sneak peek at Gwyn's next time-travel adventure:

To Kill An Emperor.

ONE

PRESENT DAY

Betrayed. Gwyn felt betrayed.

Why had she thought it was a good idea to tell her mother and sister about her time travel? She had arrived back from Transylvania battered, heartsick and injured and the pressure had been too much. Now they were treating her like she was crazy. She could hear the whispers between her parents as they hastily discussed potential psychologists here in Rome.

"What about Dr Rose Tran? Wasn't she having a sabbatical in the south of France? We could detour on our way to Spain." *Typical dad, trying not to upset the family holiday too much.*

"Stephen, she needs to see someone *now*. I don't know if she actually believes all this or if it's just a cry for attention, but it's serious. She's been starving herself, I'm sure, and engaging in self-harm."

Gwyn clenched her jaw but remained quiet as she listened at the door. She had lost weight but her body had toughened into muscle. Horse riding and walking every day—not to mention a far more restricted diet—would do that to a girl. But the self-harm comment upset her—her cuts, bruises, scrapes and wounds were proof of what she'd endured. Or so she had thought.

* * *

The cloudless blue sky offered a spectacular backdrop to the Spanish Steps and the Trevi Fountain, but by mid-afternoon the sun beat down and her parents called for a gelato break. Her brother and sister fanned themselves gratefully with paper serviettes. Gwyn slid into a hard plastic chair simply because it was in the shade. She could have kept walking, following the cheerful tour guide up and down the crowded streets of the Italian capital, losing herself in tales of history.

The gelato *was* good, if ridiculously overpriced. She shouted her family, wanting to make sure they hung around for the next tour. She didn't want to go back to the cheap hotel near Termini and she knew they wouldn't let her stay out by herself. *Huh. I've faced far worse than a bit of street harassment and risk of pickpocketing.* Her parents had been treating her like glass ever since they had left Romania a week ago.

"Well," her father said brightly, "isn't all this history interesting, Gwyn? Justin, Naomi—thank your sister for the ice cream."

The twins mumbled thanks through lemon sorbet and double chocolate and Gwyn's anger threatened to bubble out. Her parents were scientists, sceptical of wild tales, and rightly so. But the evidence she'd shown them—the stab wound in her shoulder, still healing, and the pocket-watch itself fused into her hand—should have been enough to make them believe her. *This stupid pocket-watch only works when it wants to!* She ground her teeth. She'd broken her word to the Time-Agent Michelle, telling her family about her time travel, and this was her reward.

Gwyn found her anger directed at Michelle. *Interfering, arrogant cow! And where is she when I need her?* Gwyn had brought herself back to her own time without the help of the Time-Space Agent but she expected the woman to show up and… fix things?

Instead she was trying to act normal when her family thought she was nuts. This was supposed to be a holiday to escape her boring life back home. She needed time alone to think, to sort through everything that had happened to her, to exorcise the demons of her nightmares: Joshua and Vlad.

"The Turner family?"

They all looked up. A fashionably-dressed Italian woman with a lanyard and name tag proclaiming her to be Maria Sinardi, Official Tour Guide, smiled at the Australians. Gwyn snorted as her father inhaled the last of his gelato and, coughing slightly, held out a sweaty hand to shake.

"That's us! You're taking the Colosseum and Palace Hill tour?" he asked.

Gwyn rolled her eyes, "Palatine Hill, Dad."

"Yes, I am." Maria smiled, her makeup immaculate despite the heat and her Gucci sunglasses balanced on her elegant curls. For a second Gwyn was reminded of Alina but Maria was taller and slimmer. Gwyn scooped the last of her gelato into her mouth to suppress the dart of pain that struck her chest then fussed with her bag.

"Let's go, kids." Gwyn's mother encouraged them out of the café and the tour began.

* * *

"Actually known as the Flavian Amphitheatre, this arena was a grand attempt by Vespasian and his sons to ensure their popularity in Roma." Maria spoke smoothly, her Italian accent not marring her clarity. "The Flavian Emperors were a new dynasty that established themselves after the chaos of the Year of the Four Emperors. They knew that keeping the people of Roma entertained with gladiator fights and races in the Circus Maximus meant fewer plots to overthrow the Emperor."

"Where did the gladiators come out?" Justin had been bored on the earlier tour, but the prospect of blood and death caught his interest.

"And the lions?" Naomi seemed to be competing with her twin for morbidity. "What did they do with all the bodies—feed them to the lions?"

Their guide fielded their questions with an indulgent look, seemingly unsurprised by the typical tourist area of interest. Gwyn wandered down steps and closed her eyes, imagining how it must have looked in its heyday: sparkling marble, large shade-sails over the seats rising up behind her, crowds bustling and the shouts of gladiators and other entertainers in the arena below.

A bump from a careless American tourist jolted Gwyn out of her daydream. She shot a furious glare at the American's oblivious back and thumped her fist on the railing, then saw her mother watching her worriedly. Gwyn scowled in the other direction.

"If you'd like to follow me?" Maria herded her charges through the crowded Colosseum, giving interesting facts and tidbits of information, before leading them out past the costumed centurions towards the Arch of Constantine. The twins sniggered at the centurions heckling other tourists but Gwyn just glared at any who dared cross her path. One persisted and told Gwyn to smile.

"Fuck off," she snarled. *I'm not here to light up your day, buddy—smiling is not a bloody obligation.*

"Gwyn!"

"Sorry, Mum." She didn't sound sorry but she didn't care. Accelerating past the last of the impersonators, she reached the Arch of Constantine first.

"We're doing all these tours to keep you happy, you know." Naomi was hard on her heels. "You don't have to be such a bitch to everyone."

Gwyn's response was fortunately cut off by Maria joining them. The rest of the Turners trailed her and the tour on the Palatine began.

"While an imperial house was built here by Tiberius, it is best known for being Domitian's palace. He was the third Flavian Emperor, and was assassinated by his servants and his wife. He was so paranoid he had the walls polished so he could see the reflections, so nobody could sneak up on him. He was also infamous for stabbing flies with his writing pen."

"Like a nasty little boy who never grew up," Gwyn's mum commented.

"He was not a nice person," Maria agreed. "He took his niece, Julia, for a mistress, but when she became pregnant he forced her to have an abortion and she died. He was heartbroken—Julia was his true love and after he was assassinated his old nurse mixed his ashes with that of his niece so they could be together forever." Maria gestured for them to follow her and pointed out features of the palace, like the gardens and the banquet hall.

Gwyn reflected that this is why people took tours on these ancient sites; crumbled stone walls and grassy steps hid the significance of the site. *Maybe I'll go on to study archaeology so I can actually interpret sites like these.*

At least there was a breeze up here. "The Ancient Romans were quite sophisticated when it came to heating and air conditioning their palaces," Maria told them as they walked on. "Tunnels under the floors carried cool breezes through in summer, and in winter fires were banked at the entrances of those tunnels and slaves fanned the warm air along."

"Clever." Gwyn's dad was impressed. Gwyn herself wasn't feeling so well. The breeze wasn't doing enough to cool her and her stomach turned over. A noise like waves on a beach filled her ears but they were nowhere near the sea. Her eyes blurred and a spine-tingling sensation washed through her. When her vision cleared she saw her mother peering in concern.

"What's wrong? Are you about to faint?"

Gwyn waved feebly and sat down hard, feeling sick. Orange blossoms peeked out from the grass edging the ruins. She focussed on the petals until her breathing slowed.

"Is she alright?" A bearded man crouched beside Gwyn. "You might need some water," he offered.

Gwyn stared at him. She knew she'd never seen him before but his name tag pronounced him to be Mario Sinardi, Official Tour Guide.

"What happened to Maria?" she exclaimed.

Her parents exchanged puzzled glances with the guide. "Who's Maria?" her father asked.

Nausea retreated and Gwyn hauled herself to her feet. "I... I just felt a bit sick for a second. Sorry." She tried not to freak out at the fact that her father's hair was much shorter than it normally was—had he had it cut and she hadn't noticed? No, other things were different. Her mother wore a blue shirt, not the floral blouse she'd had on earlier. The twins were dressed differently too and when she gazed back down the hill to the Colosseum she gasped to see a massive tower on the far side which had not existed when they had walked around the ruin not half an hour past.

Don't panic. Something has changed. You just need to work out what. Her mind leapt to that awful, impossible, obvious conclusion. Only she had felt that sensation, and only she noticed a difference in the world.

History had changed.

AUTHOR'S NOTE

When I was eighteen I lived in Bucharest, Romania, for five months teaching English in a kindergarten. It was a fantastic experience, and very different to my previous four months teaching English in China. There were quite a few weekends spent visiting other towns such as Sinaia, Braşov, Sighişoara, Sibiu and Constanţa. I went to Braşov a number of times—it is the gateway to Transylvania and a fascinating town in its own right. The countryside, the churches, the historical houses and castles were terrific for a history nerd like me, and provided a great base of personal experience for me to draw upon for Gwyn's present day travels. The incident on the train did actually happen, albeit slightly less dramatically—I was thrown towards the open door but not out of it, catching myself in time.

As for the title character; Vlad Dracula has been portrayed in non-fiction and fiction as both a national hero and a diabolical madman. There is no doubt Vlad's harsh upbringing shaped his behaviour and the political landscape in which he existed was treacherous and convoluted (his father and older brother were murdered by their own nobles). Many tales demonstrate him to be a fierce upholder of the law (for example the Golden Cup in the Fountain tale) but there is no doubt he ruled through fear, and his methods of punishment were considered extreme even in such a brutal and violent age. My bibliography contains some excellent texts about Vlad, and in writing *Transylvanian Knight* he grew from being a background character to a force in his own right.

With regards to Vlad's first wife (real name unknown), most historical texts document that not much is known about her. At first this dismayed me, but then I realised it was a marvellous opportunity to create my own character and insert her into the story. To balance that,

I've endeavoured to interweave as much colour from my research into other areas of the book, including details from real events such as the Night Attack, the body count of those found impaled outside Târgovişte and reaction of the Sultan just after the battle.

I took greater licence with Countess Elizabeth Báthory, known as the Blood Countess, who was alive at the same time as Vlad, but just a girl. Castle Cşethje is in northwest Hungary, not Transylvania, but the Báthorys were one of the ruling families of Transylvania at the time. I brought her crimes forward several decades and relocated her because the horror of her hideous deeds was too good to miss, and I thank Team Awesome Mums for inspiring me to include both Báthory and the Roma.

I hope you enjoyed the tale! Please leave a review on Goodreads or Amazon, or you can get in touch with me via my website: www.jodielane.com

ABOUT THE AUTHOR

Jodie Lane is an avid amateur historian, combining her love of travel and adventure with fascinating stories from the past. Brisbane based, she studied a variety of modern history at the University of Queensland, and loves to read a wide range of historical and science fiction.

Her travels have taken her all over the world: she has lived and taught English in China and Romania, backpacked through Europe and South America, and holidayed in the Middle East, Central and North America, South East Asia, New Zealand and South Africa. She speaks basic Spanish as a second language and her sport of choice is wing chun (kung fu).

Transylvanian Knight is the sequel to *The Siege of Masada* in "Turning Points"—a time travel adventures series visiting pivotal historical events and exploring an exciting new future for humanity. You can find out more via www.jodielane.com

BIBLIOGRAPHY

Fraser, Angus. The Gypsies. Cambridge, Massachusetts: Blackwell Publishers Inc. 1992

McNally, Raymond T and Florescu, Radu. In Search of Dracula: a true history of Dracula and vampire legends. Greenwich, Connecticut: New York Graphic Society Ltd. 1972.

Panaite, Viorel. The Ottoman Law of War and Peace: The Ottoman Empire and Tribute Payers. New York, Columbia University Press, 2000.

Pascu, Ştefan. A History of Transylvania. Translated by D. Robert Ladd. Detriot: Wayne State University Press. 1982.

Romania National Tourist Office. Braşov.
www.romaniatourism.com/brasov

Stoicescu, Nicolae. Vlad Ţepeş: Prince of Walachia. Translated from the Romanian by Cristina Krikorian. Bucharest, Romania: Editura Academia Republicii Socialiste România. 1978.

Sugar, Peter F. Southeastern Europe under Ottoman Rule 1354-1804. Seattle: University of Washington Press. 1977.

Vlad the Impaler. www.vladtheimpaler.info

Yaron, Matras. The Romani Gypsies. Cambridge, Massachusetts: The Belknap Press of Harvard University Press. 2015.